ABOUT THE AUTHOR

Roland Perry OAM started his writing career as a journalist on *The Age* from 1969 to 1973, after which he moved to the UK where he spent five years making documentary films. In 1979 while still in London, he wrote his first book, a novel and international bestseller, *Program for a Puppet*. He is now one of Australia's most prolific writers with 30 books to his name in a range of genres from biography, politics, espionage, history, to sport and fiction, many of which are bestsellers. His 30th book and fifth work of fiction, *The Assassin on the Bangkok Express* is a sequel to *The Honourable Assassin* which was published in 2015. His non-fiction books include *The Australian Light Horse*; *Monash: The Outsider Who Won a War*; *Bill the Bastard*, voted one of the 50 top reads in 2013 in the national *Get Reading!* program; *Changi Brownlow*, which was short-listed for the Australian Booksellers Industry Award for non-fiction in 2010; *Celeste*; *The Queen, Her Lover and the Most Notorious Spy in History*; *The Fifth Man*; and many more.

In 2011, Perry was awarded the Medal of the Order of Australia '*for service to literature as an author*', and in 2012 he was appointed adjunct professor at Monash University and 'Writer-in-Residence' in the University's Arts Faculty.

Roland Perry divides his time between Melbourne and Chiang Mai.

ALSO BY ROLAND PERRY

Fiction
Program for a Puppet
Blood is a Stranger
Faces in the Rain
The Honourable Assassin

Non-fiction
Celeste
The Queen, Her Lover and the Most Notorious Spy in History
Horrie: The War Dog
Bill the Bastard
The Fight for Australia
The Changi Brownlow
The Australian Light Horse
Last of the Cold War Spies
The Fifth Man
Monash: The Outside Who Won a War
The Programming of a President
The Exile: Reporter of Conflict
Mel Gibson, Actor, Director, Producer
Lethal Hero
Sailing to the Moon
Elections Sur Ordinateur
Bradman's Invincibles
The Ashes
Miller's Luck: the Life and Loves of Keith Miller, Australia's
Greatest All-Rounder
Bradman's Best
Bradman's Best Ashes Teams
Don Bradman
Captain Australia: A History of the Celebrated Captains of
Australian Test Cricket
Bold Warnie
Waugh's Way
Shane Warne, Master Spinner

THE ASSASSIN
ON THE
BANGKOK EXPRESS

ROLAND
PERRY

WILD
DINGO
PRESS

Published by Wild Dingo Press
Melbourne Australia
books@wilddingopress.com.au
www.wilddingopress.com.au

First published by Wild Dingo Press in 2017

National Library of Australia
Cataloguing-in-Publication Data

Perry, Roland, 1946– author.

The assassin on the Bangkok Express / Roland Perry.

ISBN: 9780648066347 (ePDF)

Drug dealers—Fiction.
Murder—Investigation—Fiction.
Suspense fiction.

Cover design: Katarina Ozegovic & Emma Statham
Editing: Jackey Coyle
Typesetting: Midland Typesetters

To Jo Butler

Preview

In the previous book, *The Honourable Assassin*, we meet Victor Cavalier as a young man trying to make the grade for admission to the elite Special Air Services Regiment (SAS). He wins every examination, physical and intellectual, but fails because of a weak Achilles tendon that may have let him down in an assignment.

After this disappointment, he joins a newspaper. But the capacities and skills in the SAS trials are so outstanding that the Australian secret services and the Australian Federal Police want to employ him for certain clandestine activities that need an untraceable lone wolf. The major difference between Cavalier and other such shadowy figures is that he suggests his own assignments, and will only take commissions that he feels are morally acceptable to him. They must be for what he judges as 'the greater good'.

His job as an investigative journalist becomes a near-perfect cover for his secret work.

*

Thirty-five years after he joins the newspaper, his life appears a bit of a wreck. His girlfriend has just walked out on him and his editor is under pressure to fire him for his reporting on Melbourne gang wars, which brings death threats to the paper's chairman. Cavalier's drinking habit is also winning the war with his better angels. On top of this, his editor wants a story about a Mexican drug cartel operative, Virgillo Labasta, who has been murdered by a sniper in a Carlton laneway.

It is midnight. Cavalier is watching a replay of his football team's defeat that night when the editor calls and demands he cover the killing. Cavalier is most reluctant, for reasons not entirely apparent at that moment. But he is intrigued to meet a stunning Thai special investigator at the scene of the crime, Jacinta Cin Lai. She is looking into the Mexican's links to illegal drug operations in her country.

His editor now wants a story on Jacinta, a colour piece on the life and work of this mysterious beauty. Cavalier refuses the offer, just as he is finally fired from his job. But then he receives a video from an unknown source that appears to depict his daughter being guillotined by Virgillo Labasta's boss, the Mexican drug lord Leonardo Mendez.

Cavalier is shattered. The video seems to confirm his worst fears that his daughter, who had been travelling through Mexico seven years earlier, has been murdered. This galvanises him to investigate the drug cartel in Thailand. He then takes up the offer as a freelance journalist to do a feature article on Jacinta, which means contacting her in Bangkok.

His arrival there is complicated by a sudden Thai military coup, when a junta takes over the country. This adds an element of danger. His assignment uncovers corruption in high places in the Thai elite. But the coup and its disruption also opens up leads and opportunities for the resourceful Cavalier.

*

Unbeknown to his paper, he has been gathering information on the Mexican drug lords and their cartels ever since his daughter went missing. He has shared this intel with his contacts at the Australian Federal Police. Now he has a loose alliance with the inscrutable, stunning Jacinta, who he discovers is not all she purports to be. For one thing, she is Thailand's most feared Muay Thai boxer, who retired from this 'trade' years earlier to join the Thai secret police. She still performs in annual exhibition bouts. Jacinta is also known to be a crack shot, the best among the Thai police, where she is from time to time employed as a professional assassin. For another thing, she is a transsexual.

As the relationship builds, Cavalier learns that Jacinta has a similar debt to settle. Her two closest friends have also been beheaded by Leonardo Mendez. Jacinta and Cavalier both have the highest incentive to kill him. Evidence emerges from the Australian Federal Police that Jacinta may have shot Virgillo Labasta in Melbourne. But did she?

Cavalier travels to remote parts of Thailand to gather telling data on Leonardo Mendez, who has temporarily set up his organization in Bangkok and Chiang Mai to reap profits from illegal drug deals throughout South East Asia.

Jacinta aids Cavalier with information from inside the Thai Police, yet she is disdainful of what a newspaper exposé in Australia or on the Internet will achieve. She says that nothing short of getting rid of Mendez will gain them a measure of retribution for their loss of loved ones. But Jacinta is controlled by the corrupt Thai Chief of Police, Aind Azelaporn, who is assigned to protect Mendez. Her chances of carrying out his elimination are limited. Cavalier realises that any action against the Mexican is up to him. Despite her assurances that Cavalier is not being monitored by the Thai police, he cannot be sure that she will not apprehend him.

*

In the middle of the coup, a rival Thai general to the junta is shot by a sniper when making a speech to a rally of supporters in Bangkok. Chaos ensues.

Cavalier seizes the moment.

He has studied his potential quarry like an etymologist dissecting an insect. He knows Mendez's strengths and weaknesses, right down to his pathological attraction to beheadings, and his sexual proclivities. The latter gives Cavalier the thinnest of opportunities. Mendez frequents Bangkok's most notorious brothel centre, Nana Plaza, surrounded by his twenty cut-throat bodyguards.

Disguised as a Swedish tourist, Cavalier books a room in a hotel looking into the Plaza. During a blackout, which at first seems to stymie his minutely planned effort, Cavalier delivers the mortal blow to the psychopath who had indiscriminately slaughtered hundreds of people.

A manhunt follows. Cavalier is forced to escape Thailand via Cambodia. He seems trapped when a three-man squad from the cartel, led by its top hit man, Jose Cortez, and Jacinta chase him by boat at night from Phnom Penh down the Mekong to Vietnam. Jacinta, in a daring plan, appears to want to protect Cavalier, although she cannot expose herself as his accomplice.

Cavalier manages to evade his pursuers by bluff and expert marksmanship.

*

Questions remain. He suspects that Jacinta sent him the video of his daughter's guillotining, which she does not deny. It pulled him into the investigation and the eventual destruction of Leonardo Mendez. Jacinta suspects that apart from Mendez, Cavalier eliminated the Mexican drug lord's number two, Virgillo Labasta, which he too, does not deny ...

Jose Cortez, who has 80 'kills' to his credit in the USA and elsewhere, puts a high-priced contract out on Cavalier, who has escaped to Australia. The Federal Police advise him to 'disappear' for six months, the time they hope the US intelligence services will take to track and liquidate Cortez and his squad.

In the meantime, Cavalier must decide where he can hide out without detection when Cortez sets out to avenge the assassination of Mendez. Cavalier the hunter, has become thehunted.

PART ONE
30 YEARS AGO

1

RE-ACQUAINTANCE
BY ACCIDENT

A woman on a motorcycle sped over the Meng Rai Bridge on the Ping River. The traffic light was green, but in Thailand's Chiang Mai this was often merely an invitation to negotiate with drivers running red lights. A Toyota sedan clipped the bike, spinning it and throwing the rider several metres. Victor Cavalier, on his early-morning jog, was about to cross the bridge. At the squeal of brakes, he turned to see the woman hit the ground. He smelled the burning rubber from hard-braking vehicles as he dodged the traffic and reached her.

The woman lay motionless and crumpled in the middle of the road. He eased off her helmet, and felt her pulses at neck and wrist. He called in Thai for someone to phone for an ambulance. Then Cavalier noticed a tattoo, poking through the torn back of her dress. It was a phoenix, and seemed familiar. He mentally pushed it aside and concentrated on the stricken woman's condition.

'The hospital is on the Chang Klan Road,' he said, pointing, in Thai to the young male driver of the offending vehicle. His voice was calm and authoritative. 'Move fast!'

The driver stood frozen, either dumbfounded or in two minds about doing a runner. Seeing his hesitation, a female on a motorcycle volunteered to fetch an ambulance. In the fifteen minutes it took to arrive, the young victim stirred, opened her eyes and tried to sit up.

'Serena …' she mumbled, 'Serena … is she okay?'

Cavalier looked around. A doll was lying on the ground a few metres away, its legs crushed. Mud was smeared on its face and head.

'She'll survive,' he said softly. The woman looked dazed. He wiped blood from her nose. Then he recognised her.

'Pin!' he said in surprise, 'it's you!'

'Victor!' she cried, scrutinising him.

They had first met four years earlier when she was a medical student in Chiang Mai. She was funding her studies by working for a tour company, and she had driven him to the notorious Golden Triangle, in Thailand's north-eastern corner.

'I can't believe it's you,' Pin said. Still confused, she looked about and asked, 'What happened?' She grimaced and flexed her shoulder.

The ambulance took her the few kilometres to the hospital, where a wheelchair was waiting. Paramedics placed her in it. Cavalier pushed her into an emergency room.

'This is crazy!' she said. 'This is my hospital. I work here.'

'Not today,' Cavalier said gently.

'I have patients to see.' Pin looked up at him, aggrieved.

'You were unconscious when I reached you,' he said. 'Better let a colleague examine you.'

'Never! They are all quacks!'

Cavalier couldn't help smiling, unsure if she was joking or not.

'My bike!' she cried.

'I'll get it,' he said.

'My baby!'

Cavalier was startled. Had a child been thrown clear? he wondered for a second.

'My Serena!' she said. 'My doll!'

He was driven by tuktuk back to the bike on the side of the road, where it had ended up after the hit. The rear fender was dented. The key was still in the ignition. He started it, all the while looking for the doll. He spotted it off the road and retrieved it. Satisfied the bike was rideable, he drove it to the hospital, gave the doll to a nurse and waited an hour for Pin to be examined.

She came to him with a bandage across her nose and face. Her left shoulder was also strapped. She clutched her doll, its crushed legs dangling by threads.

'They think I have mild concussion,' she said, with a roll of the eyes. 'My shoulder has a bit of bruising, but I'm fine. I'll take the day off. Back here at work tomorrow.'

'I'll book you a taxi.'

'Thanks for saving Serena,' she said, hugging the doll. 'Sorry you have to see us like this.'

'You're still easily the most beautiful woman in Thailand.'

'What about my Serena?'

'She … she has some interesting features,' he said, glancing at the big-eyed doll, with its scrawny hair and a lifelike look that he found eerie.

'*Interesting*? She is very beautiful and special.'

Cavalier scrutinised Pin and wondered if she was serious.

'A doll is a doll,' he shrugged.

'Not dolls like Serena. They are important in the Thai culture.'

'Important in what way?'

'They have been blessed with special powers.'

'Blessed?'

'By certain monks.'

Cavalier remembered, vaguely, reading a feature article about this strange, centuries-old belief, which he considered was superstition. He decided not to pursue the discussion.

'You haven't changed,' she said.

'Nor have you, *Miss Thailand University*.'

'Sweet mouth!'

'You *have* changed in some way ...' he said, looking closely at her features.

'I have to appear professional.' She chuckled. 'I even have to advise young couples on their sex lives. My hair was blonde. I've gone back to my natural colour, and it's shorter.'

'You still have that tattoo ...'

'Oh, you noticed ...' She paused. 'I must hide it under my clothes as much as possible. It's a bit risqué for my patients, not to mention my rather stiff fellow medicos.'

She touched his nose.

'You are even better looking than before. Fuller in the face. But what happened to your nose? It was like a Thai's with a bump in it.'

'I've broken it a few times.'

'Not that stupid game you love so much?'

'Once from that, yes,' he said. After hesitating, he asked, 'Would you have dinner with me?'

'Too busy at the moment, sorry.'

Cavalier tilted his head, wanting an explanation.

'Look,' she said, observing his reaction, 'I've had some issues recently. I'm working through them. I had a bad relationship with my very bad ex-husband.'

'Do you want to tell me about it?'

'No. Maybe later.'

Cavalier shook hands with her.

'I'll call you,' he said, patting the doll on the head.

2

PIN'S PASSION

Cavalier could not push Pin from his mind. He was confounded by their chance meeting. He believed he loved her on their first encounters four years earlier. She was unattainable then. If anything, she had even more appeal now. Cavalier had not come across anyone with anywhere near Pin's attraction. Apart from her outstanding looks and forceful personality, he recalled the good conversations they had had, punctuated with sharp humour—well beyond the monosyllabic discourse he'd experienced with other Thai women.

His Thai was fair; her English was good. Pin had been educated in Australia and was exceptionally bright, having been equal dux of her school. Yet her preoccupation with a doll seemed weird and out of character for such a worldly young woman. At first, he thought she may have joking, but her solemn comments about Serena suggested otherwise.

After a few polite letters and some difficult phone calls, they had lost contact, as was often the way with long-distance relationships of that era. Now, seeing Pin again, his passion was reignited.

He rang the hospital several times before she would speak to him, and he asked her out again. Her responses were brusque. She finally agreed to see him briefly, saying she would squeeze him into a half-hour dinner break from work. A week later they ate at a street stall on the Lamphun Road in Chiang Mai's south-east, on the Ping River not far from her hospital. It was 10 p.m., and her long night shift would finish about 8 a.m. The traffic had subsided to a trickle of motorcycles. The street of stalls was shutting for the night, taking with it the myriad enticing food smells and allowing the odd stench of drains to surface.

'What brings you here?' she asked. 'Last time it was something to do with a bank …'

'A rather odious bank,' he said with a rueful grin.

'Something to do with a body part,' she commented with a frown.

'Your memory has not been affected by the accident,' he observed. 'It was the Handy Nugget Bank.'

'Ah, yes. It had a base here and you were investigating it for your newspaper. Laundered money from drug deals in the Golden Triangle, yes?'

He nodded, not wanting to expand.

'And now?'

'I'm acting as my paper's foreign correspondent in the region. I'll be covering Northern Thailand, Burma, Cambodia and even Vietnam. Maybe Hong Kong and mainland China too.'

'That's all?' she asked with a smile as she sipped a soft drink.

Cavalier looked defensive. 'What do you mean?'

'I was being cynical, the way you Australians love.'

'Oh, I see. There is an old pro journo based in Bangkok. We'll cover the region. I expect he'll do the big stories; I'll be left the table scraps.'

'Doesn't sound like you,' she remarked with a sceptical grin.

'I'm lucky to have the job. Had to push the paper for it. Paid for my own plane ticket and accommodation to seal the appointment.'

Cavalier sipped his drink. After a pause, he asked, 'Are you still with that young doctor?'

'He never qualified, but we married, unfortunately. I left him. We are divorced.'

'Last letter I had said you were pregnant to him.'

'We have a baby. Her name is Far. She's four years old.'

'What went wrong?'

Pin seemed reluctant to answer.

'If it's private ....' he said, touching her hand.

She stared for a moment. 'He was into drugs. I said I'd support him. My first job after graduating was in a hospital in Mae Sot.'

'I know of it: a town on the Burma border. Known for all sorts of intrigue.'

Pin was silent. She picked at her food before saying:

'He—Kun—is now a big mafia figure there.'

'Hmm. Then you are best rid of him.'

'He has my baby, Far.'

'Oh!'

'When we split, he took Far and would not let me see her. He … he … beat me up. He beat my mother up when she tried to intervene.' Pin began to cry. 'I had to escape from him. I left my work in Mae Sot and took a job here. I've seen Far three times in the last two years. I worry about her every day.'

'What about the police?'

'Huh! They do nothing. He controls them.'

Pin pulled back her hair to show him a thin scar running across the top of her forehead.

'Not a beauty queen any more,' she whispered. She was distressed for several moments before saying: 'I have thought of you often. I made a mistake in not dumping him for you. But our families wanted the marriage. We were both doing medicine. You were the first farang I ever really knew.'

'You studied medicine for a couple of years in Sydney …'

'Yes, and I was educated at a Catholic girls' school there for two years before that. But I always knew Asian boys. Not Australians.'

Pin looked at her watch. 'Must return to work,' she said.

'I want to see you again,' he said.

'Why?'

'I enjoy our conversation,' he said, opening his hands.

'I'm really not ready for a relationship at the moment. The other stuff is still …'

'Raw?'

'Yes.'

'I just want you as a friend.'

Pin scrutinised his expression for several seconds, and said finally: 'All right, friends.'

*

The next day Cavalier flew to Rangoon, to interview a young and beautiful Burmese political activist, Aung San Suu Kyi, whom he had first met in London a few years earlier. Her main aim in life, she told him, was to bring democracy to her country. His paper was at first reluctant to take the story because the woman was not well known, but the editor liked the accompanying photographs. It was accepted and buried in the paper's weekend magazine.

On his return, Cavalier made contact with Pin and invited her to his humble hovel off the Chiang Mai Land Road. His apartment was narrow like a tramcar, with a small lounge, a bathroom and bedroom. He prepared an evening meal of chicken and mixed vegetables on her Monday night off work. They sat at table in a tiny courtyard off the bedroom.

'More like a court-*inch*,' she said glancing around at the close walls.

As they drank a French Chablis, the first rain in three weeks rapped on the canvas awning covering half the small patio. He refilled her glass.

'You can't ride your bike home in this,' he said.

'It will pass.'

He leant across and kissed her on the cheek. She ignored the gesture.

'How long are you here this time?' she asked.

'A few months. Then the paper will review my position.'

'Have you a wife, or girlfriend?'

Cavalier shook his head.

'Why not? You must be nearly thirty …'

'Commitment is not easy for me.'

Pin looked at him sceptically. 'C'mon,' she said, 'you've been having too good a time, no?'

'My work has prevented me settling anywhere. I am always off on an assignment.'

'You are a proactive type. If you want a wife and family, I am sure you would pursue it.'

'I do want a family.'

'Then what stops you?'

'You.'

Cavalier held his glass up to her.

'What?' she asked.

'After we first met on that trip to the Golden Triangle, I …' He stopped speaking, waving a hand as if she couldn't be interested.

'Tell me.'

'I knew you were engaged. I knew I had no chance. You were a gold standard. If I couldn't have you, I wanted someone like you in my life. I've not met anyone like you.'

Pin half smiled, half winced. 'A fantasy!' she said. 'I am driven; very selfish!'

'Yes, true, you are a fantasy.' He leaned towards her again and kissed her briefly on the lips. She looked at him, more interested in his words than his advance.

'You would have proposed?' she challenged him.

'Well, I …'

'You see! All sweet talk!'

'Stay and I'll show you.'

'Oh, please! Sex is not love.'

'It can be a good part of it.'

'I need to be home.'

'It's still raining.'

'I have a headache.'

'The wine?'

'No, it's good.'

'In Australia, if a woman says she has a headache, it means she wants to make love.'

She frowned. 'I thought ...' she began, and noticed his slight smile. 'Ah,' she said, 'you are joking, right?'

'No. You should try it.'

They moved into the bedroom.

'Seriously, have you something for a headache?'

Cavalier searched for an aspirin in the bathroom, while Pin lay on the double bed.

'Please, try to sleep,' he said, returning with a tablet and glass of water. She swallowed it. He switched off the light, shed his clothes except underpants, and lay on his back beside her. He heard the steady tempo of her breathing, registering sleep. Cavalier studied her face. He did not think he'd ever encountered anyone with her appearance, which he considered more attractive and character-driven than classic beauty. The large, sweeping eyes, nose with a notch of imperfection and overgenerous full lips were enhanced in her repose, a sort of divine tranquillity, which belied the frenetic energy of her conscious state.

After a few minutes of contemplation, he too was dozing. A few hours later she rolled over and draped an arm over him. Cavalier turned to Pin and kissed her. She responded. He kissed her ear. Her reaction was strong and they were soon coupling with passion.

*

Cavalier allowed himself few blissful moments in life. This was one of them. Here was a stunning woman, who only a few years earlier he had fallen for but accepted as unattainable. Now she was available and making feverish love to him.

And that fervour had an added dimension. He had not had sex with such an aroused partner.

'Thank you,' she whispered in his ear.

Cavalier smiled. *She* was thanking *him* for the best love-making he'd ever experienced. No woman had ever said that to him after sex.

'Oh, and thank you,' he said.

'Did you come?'

'Twice,' he said. He did not say, but later told his diary he had been more intent on pleasing Pin than himself.

'I have multiple orgasms …' she said.

'I noticed.'

'I'm sorry …'

'Please don't apologise,' he smiled, kissing her on the cheek.

'Can you cope?' she asked, running a finger around his face and lingering on his nose.

'Have I?'

Pin kissed him. 'I'm demanding,' she said in a warning tone.

'I am not complaining. I enjoy it; every wet and sweet moment of it.'

Pin smiled. 'You should know that I am mad,' she said.

'Mad?'

'I may be bipolar.'

'Bi-what?'

'Not bisexual, bi-*polar*. It's a medical term more usually known as manic depression.'

'Oh.'

'I'm reading more and more studies about it. Some research says those with a bipolar condition have an abnormally high sex drive.'

'I see,' he said, smiling and sitting up on one elbow. 'So I should comb the nut-houses for the best lovers?'

Pin laughed.

'Perhaps,' she said, 'but in my case, I may be simply highly sexed.'

'So you can't live without lots of ...'

'No, that's not the case, at least with me. I have not had sex with a partner since the debacle with my ex. One must feel something strong. It's all in the "feeling". That triggers the desires and action.'

'Pleased to hear that. Have you a problem or not?'

'I've studied it. Feel like writing a dissertation. I do have the mood swings, which is a key determinate. But mostly I am fairly even-tempered.' She looked at him and smiled. 'Not quite as laid-back as you, but not hysterical either.'

'So it could be that you are just "hot" when turned on?'

'Something like that.'

'I didn't use a condom ...'

'I'm on the pill.'

'Not worried about disease, *Doctor*?'

'Are you carrying something?'

'No.'

'Then don't worry. I recall how you were when we first met.'

'How was I?'

'You didn't play around. You didn't do the bars down the road here. I never saw you with a bar girl, or any woman for that matter.' She paused to kiss him. 'I apologise. I should have asked for a condom.'

'I have one in my wallet. Have ever since I was fifteen.'

'Same one?'

Cavalier laughed.

'You were very serious about your work in those days,' she said.

'I had an assignment that needed all my concentration.'

'You never told me what it was about.'

'I can't discuss it.'

'Can't or won't?'

'Both.'

'Not sure I like hearing you have secrets. My ex now is a small-time crim. He had plenty of things he hid from me.'

'There are some matters I just can't discuss.'

'So, what I see is not what I get?'

Cavalier smiled, but did not reply. He kissed her tenderly.

'So?' she said.

'Right now,' he said seductively, 'what you see is what you get.'

3

THE PROBLEM

Cavalier volunteered to do a blood test at her hospital. It was clear. She rang to let him know the result.

'It suggests that you still don't play around,' she observed, 'although I worry about that lonely condom in your wallet.'

'Just precaution.'

'For what?'

Cavalier didn't answer.

'If you are going to date me,' she said, 'you won't need it.'

'Are we going to date?'

'That's up to you. I would like to. You are a beautiful lover. You care about my feelings. You have compassion. That, and your smile, is what I remember about you when we first met. Oh, and you have eyes like the actor Michael Caine.'

'I'm more than pleased you've changed your mind,' he said in a surprised tone.

'I was against any new involvement. But you've come along. It's timing. I have buried myself in my work for too long because of what happened.' She touched his face tenderly. 'You've made me feel good about myself again.'

*

Cavalier urged Pin to take days off rather than store them up for some future, unspecified leave that she wasn't sure she could take anyway. He hired a small plane and flew her over the mountains north to Chiang Rai for a weekend. Cavalier drove her to the Temple of the Golden Mountain—Wat Phra That Doi Kham—for a day's outing. They dined together twice a week and he took her to a jazz club and the movie *Body Heat*. Their emotional involvement grew. Pin disclosed more about the major issue over her ex and his hold over their daughter.

'He sounds very bad,' Cavalier said.

'I'd like to see him dead! I really would! I worry so much about my daughter. Some of his friends are deviant, drunken types. I fear for her.'

They sat in silence as the bar began to fill with patrons, mainly foreigners on holiday. The walls featured prints of Picasso's late 'erotic' period of sketches of people coupling. Staff dressed in colourful uniforms, the women in short skirts and high heels.

'I shouldn't say this,' Pin said, lowering her voice and glancing around to see if anyone was in earshot. 'My mother's best friend has some mafia connections, who think my ex has gone too far.'

'Meaning?'

'Meaning they have asked her if she wished to do something about it.'

'What?'

Pin looked nervous. 'I shouldn't have told you,' she said.

'You're hinting you want him dealt with using the Mae Sot mafia?'

Her lack of denial seemed to affirm his suspicion.

'I truly hate him,' she said.

'You said you wanted him dead ...'

'I mean it.'

Cavalier believed she was serious.

'He will murder someone in my family if we don't do something—my mother, me or my baby.' She began to cry again. He comforted her.

'If you instigate this,' he said softly, 'suspicion is sure to fall on you and your family.' Pin looked down. 'You said the police were in his pocket ...'

'The ones in No Man's Land between Burma and Thailand at Mae Sot are. It's where my family home is.'

'You couldn't go higher, to the province's chief?'

'You don't understand. No one would support me.'

'You're a respected doctor.'

'I am a woman! I am not a local. My ex is.'

Cavalier nodded understandingly. 'What about your Hippocratic Oath to save lives, not destroy them?'

Pin shook her head. 'You don't grasp how desperate I and my family are over this,' she said, her voice now a hoarse whisper.

'Your eliminating him can't be the solution.' Cavalier touched her arm and kissed her on the cheek. 'You would risk so much.' He gently lifted her chin so that she looked him in the eye. 'I will help you try to find a better way.'

*

The relationship continued for several months; Cavalier flew to Hong Kong, Vietnam and Cambodia for stories while Pin worked her long hours at the hospital. He was in Phnom Penh when he had a call from her.

'I'm pregnant,' she said.

'What?'

'I'm pregnant,' she repeated. 'I have been on the pill. Sometimes I forget to take it.' Cavalier was stunned and silent. 'I know, don't say it. I'm a very bad doctor.'

'I am not thinking that at all.'

'What are you thinking?'

'We must talk.'

'No time. I am going to Mae Sot in two days. Taking a couple of days off.'

'I'm coming with you.'

*

Cavalier rode his motorcycle to a rough airfield a kilometre from Chiang Mai airport. There was a shed for a hangar that housed four Cessna planes. Cavalier met the owner, a forty-five-year-old American Vietnam War veteran who ran the small business. Cavalier took a one-engine Cessna for a half-hour flight around Chiang Mai, then asked the owner if it could be delivered to the airfield at Mae Sot.

'When?' the owner asked. 'I have four planes on hire and they are in demand.'

'Can I give you notice?'

'Sure. I'll need twenty-four hours.'

*

The continuing bad weather coming down from China had sent January temperatures dipping to under ten degrees Celsius for the six-hour, 450-kilometre bus ride over the mountains due south of Chiang Mai and the town of Mae Sot on the river border with Burma.

Pin took her doll Serena, fully restored and cleaned up, out of a bag and placed it on the seat between them. It was dressed in expensive-looking clothes and had a special hairdo.

'What is this?'

'Not "what", "she". You remember Serena. You saved her. I take her on trips.'

'For your daughter?'

'No, for me.'

Cavalier was surprised.

'Serena has been blessed,' Pin said, noting his expression. 'She is special.'

'Not one of those ghost dolls, blessed by sorcerers or shamans? She has a scary look.'

'No, she is blessed by a monk. I think she is beautiful.'

'She is taking up a whole seat.'

'I paid for it.'

'You're kidding!'

'I have even taken her on a flight, and paid for the seat.'

Cavalier was perplexed.

'You know nothing of Thai culture, our beliefs.'

'You mean your superstitions.'

'You can't see how an educated woman like me can be so … so *primitive*.'

'I didn't say that.'

'But you were thinking it.'

Cavalier looked out the window for several minutes as the bus reached the road over the mountains.

'Is she a substitute for Far?' he asked.

'She keeps me company. She brings me comfort and good luck. She will on this trip, you'll see.' Pin added on reflection,

'She is also a way for me to control my anger. She is loving and warm and affectionate.'

Pin noticed Cavalier's concern as the bus skidded its way around a precarious mountain road, made worse by heavy rain and very low cloud that limited visibility. In the valleys below were smashed cars, buses, trucks and motorcycles, intermittent reminders of the dangers of speeding, or merely moving along this route.

'You okay?' she asked, squeezing his hand.

'I would be if I were driving,' he said.

Just before arriving at Mae Sot's bus terminal, Pin opened up about her plans. When Cavalier had tried to find out early on the ride, she had refused to talk. She said, 'I'm thinking about it, now. Do you want me to keep the child?'

'Yes,' he said without hesitation.

'That's fairly succinct,' she said. 'I want your thinking.'

'I love you. I would be happy to be the child's father.'

'What is love to you?'

'It's a passion, a desire to be with you. The strongest possible emotional feel a person can have for another.'

Pin smiled. 'Nice answer,' she said, softening her expression, 'but how would we work this? Your home is in Australia. I am going to be in Chiang Mai for a few years yet.'

'We can manage.'

'What about your work? You're always disappearing somewhere for one of your … your "assignments".'

'My position here may be permanent after this trial period.'

4

THE GUN

The bus rolled out of the mountains on the road into Mae Sot, which marked the end of the proposed new 'Silk Road' from China through Burma. It was a gateway and the perfect trading point between Thailand and the Burma town of Myawaddy. As such, it was a peak of illegal activity, including people trafficking and drugs. Smugglers, spies, stateless people, runaways and a variety of criminals haunted the No Man's Land between the two countries. Cavalier noted that a small airfield was only about two hundred metres from the bus terminal on the town's outskirts. They took a taxi, and ten minutes later were at a Thai border point. Security guards had a cursorily look at their backpacks.

Cavalier was introduced to Pin's family: a younger brother, half-sister and grandparents on her mother's side. They had all relocated there to be with her as the major breadwinner. Her salary at the local hospital had been ten times that collectively of the rest of the family, and in the time-honoured Thai way, most of her income supported these dependent relatives. Pin's father, a successful builder, had died by accidental poisoning when she was twelve. Pin had bought a modest, yet comfortable two-level home cheaply in this zone. When she moved back to Chiang Mai the rest of the family had stayed in Mae Sot, mainly to be close to Far.

Pin's mother, Farn, emerged after several minutes. She had two black eyes, a cut mouth and one arm in a sling. She and Pin embraced.

'What happened to you?' Pin asked. When her mother began crying, her daughter knew the reason.

'Your ex?' Cavalier asked softly.

Pin nodded and wiped her eyes. 'I really want him dead!' she hissed, with a menacing look. Her mother, even with the injuries, was an elegant, attractive woman in her late forties. She attempted to placate Pin. A meal was prepared and as the day faded, Pin said she was going 'shopping'.

'For what?' Cavalier asked.

She glared at him.

'What?' he insisted.

'A gun,' she whispered.

Cavalier shook his head. 'I told you that would be most unwise.'

'I just want it for self-defence.'

Cavalier considered her. He knew that fierce, even demonic look. 'I'll come with you,' he said.

'No. I must go to a village in No Man's Land. It is not good for farang. It's too dangerous.'

'I'm coming,' he said and followed her to a motorcycle sitting with a battered Toyota under a pergola. He climbed on behind. They drove along a dirt track in No Man's Land and had glimpses through high grass and scrub of shanty towns and lean-tos. Closer to the river, dirt-covered locals collected rubbish that had washed up on the riverbank. The weather was bleak and cold as they entered a village at nightfall. There were no bars, but a few tin hut brothels where Burmese girls, probably underage, sat looking forlorn rather than alluring. Many watched Cavalier and Pin as they walked to a market. Pin motioned for Cavalier, wearing a baseball cap, to push his black leather jacket's collar up and hood over his head.

'Better if you are not so recognisable as a farang,' she told him. 'Don't say anything. Let me do the talking.'

Pin spoke to a muscular tattooed man called Char, whose face was festooned with trinkets for ears, nose, forehead and lips. He had one heavily strapped arm and scars on his neck. They chatted rapidly in a dialect that Cavalier had trouble following. He picked up enough to know that Char recognised his former doctor, who had saved his life after a knife attack by her ex-husband, Kun.

'He tried to kill me again a few weeks ago,' Char said.

He seemed to be showing Pin respect, albeit begrudgingly. Char's narrow slit eyes flicked often to Cavalier, whom he asked about.

'He is my partner, also a doctor,' she said. Amid shifty looks, Char pulled out several handguns and placed them on a wooden counter.

Pin turned to Cavalier. 'Which one should I choose?'

'Why do you ask me?'

'I recall you told me you once did army training.'

'Air force.'

'You must have handled weapons.'

Cavalier hesitated, glanced at her and Char, and began to examine the guns.

'This one could kill only at close range, but would also frighten anyone,' he said, fondling what looked like a modified old snub-nosed Beretta pistol. He picked up a bigger, heavier gun. 'This one could blow a man's head off at five paces. It would put such a hole in a vital organ, the victim would die.' He made sure the chamber was empty and then aimed the gun, holding it with two hands. 'This is too heavy for you. I have strong forearms and I'd always steady it using both hands.' He put down the second gun. 'Take the smaller one.'

Cavalier spoke in a friendly fashion to Char, whose manner relaxed as Cavalier plied his rough but passable Thai discussing another of the guns on offer.

'It's a very new product,' Char said, 'a Glock 17. Made by an Austrian company. It has just been taken up by Austrian military and police.'

'It's plastic.'

'Polymer frame, yes.'

'I've never seen one. Can it be durable, reliable?'

'The Austrians are happy with it,' Char said with a shrug, 'but it did cause the police concern. It is invisible to metal detectors at airports.'

Cavalier nodded, as if disinterested.

Pin bought the smaller gun and a box of twenty bullets for the equivalent of nine dollars.

As they drove away from the village, she said: 'I didn't want you to engage with him. I am trusted; you are not. Besides he would think you were a rich farang, and therefore up the price by at least a couple of dollars.'

'I'm just a friendly guy,' he said with a shrug. 'Why did you say I was a doctor?'

'Not good to admit you're a journalist around here. Doctors are respected. Even crims like Char know they'll need one. Gang wars, killings and woundings occur almost daily. Just visit the emergency ward at the hospital.'

'Can you trust Char?'

She nodded. 'He hates the police, and hates Kun even more. They are in rival gangs trying to rule Mae Sot's underworld. Char was badly injured by Kun in a gang fight. Kun shot and knifed him. He told me of a more recent second attack by Kun. Char is lucky to be alive.'

*

Pin placed Cavalier in a guest room at the family home, explaining that she would lose face if she was seen to sleep in the same bed as him.

'If we were married it would be different,' she said, not looking at him.

Cavalier ignored the comment. He was not sure if this was a hint or not. The more he was with Pin, the more of a mystery she appeared. He wished to chat more about their relationship before he considered marriage.

The next morning, Pin drove her mother and Cavalier in the family car to the hospital where she once worked. Some staff recognised her and they were fast-tracked to an examination of Farn. One of her eye sockets had swollen and Pin wanted an X-ray done to see if it was broken.

'I was thinking about your husband,' Cavalier began.

'Ex,' she corrected, 'perhaps even soon to be extinguished.'

'Okay, your ex and your daughter. Why shouldn't we offer him money ...?'

'Never. He would bleed us dry.'

'I would offer enough to persuade him to hand over your daughter. He doesn't sound like the type who would be able to cope with a child's needs. Once you have her safely back in Chiang Mai, you could stop any further payments. He won't chase Far there. You could probably make a good case to the Chiang Mai police ...'

'No. As I've said, the police will not help a woman in such a case.'

'Okay. What do you propose?'

'Kidnap her.'

'What? How?'

'Go to her preschool and remove her; then take the bus back to Chiang Mai.'

'What about the teachers? Wouldn't they stop you?'

'They are female. It's one area where the sisters would stick together. They endorse my position. They know what a nasty bit of work Kun is. They have complained to my mother many times about his drunken, druggie behaviour. They see my darling Far being maltreated by him.'

'You'll be breaking the law,' he said. 'I'm not sure I want to have anything to do with it.'

'Then go back to Chiang Mai.'

'If this became public, my paper would fire me.'

'Damn your paper! This man has already murdered at least five people. He will kill me or my mother. He could murder my daughter.'

35

5

KIDNAP

Later that day, Cavalier went for a lone ride on the family motorcycle, familiarising himself with No Man's Land. He drove beyond the border point, pulled into a hotel and used a public phone to ring the American running the Chiang Mai plane-hire company.

'Could you leave a Cessna at Mae Sot airport?'

'Sure,' the American said. 'I'll prepare a flight plan for you and notify the Mae Sot manager; when will you pick it up?'

'Probably tomorrow night.'

'The keys will be left in the ignition.'

'Who do I see?'

'After ten p.m., no one. The airport, such as it is, closes down at that time. There is no rule about flying out in a small plane. It will most likely be the only one there.'

*

Early afternoon the next day, Pin drove the family Toyota to her daughter's school a few kilometres away, still in No Man's Land. Cavalier insisted on going with her. Farn sat in the back seat, her eyes still showing considerable bruising. She was most concerned about her daughter's actions, and agreed with Cavalier that this move was risky. Despite their protests, Pin, in an aggressive mood, was hell-bent on her mission. She had her bag packed and would go straight to the bus depot after taking her daughter.

Pin pointed out a lonely farmhouse, barely discernible among trees on a small hill about a hundred metres from the road.

'That is where my ex lives in squalor,' Pin said, 'with about half a dozen of his crim cronies. And my daughter.'

A kilometre further on, they arrived at the preschool. About thirty children were playing in a yard outside the brick schoolhouse. Two female teachers could be seen sitting outside, watching the children.

'You two stay in the car,' Pin ordered. She tapped the gun in a pocket of her windcheater jacket, jumped from the Toyota and hurried about fifty metres to the children. She grabbed Far, who looked pleased and surprised. Just as Pin hastened back to the car with Far, a tall, bearded Thai with long, thick, unkempt hair emerged from one of several cars on the verge of the yard. It was Kun. He was followed by two other men. The three of them rushed to cut off her run. Cavalier jumped from the Toyota.

'No, Kun,' Pin cried, 'no! I'm taking her!'

Pin stumbled. She and Far fell to the ground. Pin groped for her daughter but Kun and his companion were upon them. Cavalier reached them. Kun pulled out a handgun, forcing Cavalier to stop. Kun's companion hoisted the kicking, screaming child onto his hip, as a third Thai came running to support Kun. Cavalier pulled Pin away. When

Kun and his companions reached their car, she pulled out her pistol. Cavalier took it from her.

'No!' he said. 'They have weapons!'

Kun's car sped past. He was in the back seat. He aimed his gun, causing Cavalier to pull Pin to the ground a split second before three bullets ripped into the Toyota, just missing a crouching Farn in the back seat.

*

Cavalier and her mother were adamant—Pin had to leave Mae Sot. She admitted that she had to be back at work by the next day.

'He will come after you,' Farn insisted. 'You must leave.'

'You jump on that bus as planned,' Cavalier said. 'I'll stay until later today.'

Pin, emotionally broken by the kidnap attempt, was in no state to argue. Her mother and Cavalier drove her to the bus. Gone was the brave person ready to fight for her daughter. The strain had been too much.

'That's a problem with bipolars,' she whispered tearfully, 'we can take on the world when we're on a high. But when the lows hit ...'

'I think you should seek medication.'

Pin kissed him.

'I mean it,' Cavalier insisted. 'You were very brave today. Braver than me.'

'You've been supportive. That's what matters.'

Cavalier didn't respond.

'Promise me you won't approach Kun with money,' Pin insisted.

'Almost all people have a price. I think I understand Kun's price.'

'Vic, you mustn't see him!'

'I'll stay until midnight, and take the last bus.'

After a tearful farewell, Pin, with Serena the doll underarm, left on the bus.

Farn drove Cavalier back to her house. She cooked a meal for him and they watched local TV with the rest of the family, hoping that the incident they'd been part of did not make the news.

Two policemen arrived after dark. Farn pushed Cavalier out of sight into a bathroom. They interrogated her, unaware she had been present at the schoolyard. Farn told them Pin had returned to Chiang Mai. She innocently asked what it was about. The police ignored her.

'If there has been any trouble over my granddaughter,' she said bravely, 'I hope you are going to question her pig of a father!'

The policemen glanced at each other.

'We have spoken to him,' one said.

'He is a bad man; a murderer!' Farn said. 'You should speak to him again, and ask him about how he beat me up! How he and his criminal friends abuse my granddaughter. She is only four years old!'

'All right, calm down,' one of them replied to appease her. 'We shall question Kun about that.'

The policemen departed, with Farn shouting about Kun.

Cavalier prepared his backpack.

'I may not return,' he said. 'It's too dangerous for me. I can't afford to be interrogated by the police.'

Farn agreed.

'With police asking questions, even he won't try anything here,' she said. 'He's cunning. He'll wait a week.'

Cavalier smiled and held her.

'I want you to pick up your granddaughter from school tomorrow,' he said, 'and then bring her to Chiang Mai.'

She frowned and shook her head.

'Kun will kill me!'

'No, I think he'll be with the police,' Cavalier said.

'He'll kill me!' she repeated.

'Farn, listen to me please,' Cavalier said, looking her intently. 'Just in case Kun is not there, someone has to pick up Far.'

Farn seemed confused. She nodded agreement.

Cavalier asked if he could drive the motorcycle to the bus terminal. Farn said she would have her son pick it up the next day.

'Everything is going to work out all right,' Cavalier said, holding Farn. Then he repeated, 'Just see your granddaughter tomorrow.'

6

THE SHOOTING PARTY

Cavalier, wearing his hooded jacket, tracksuit trousers and running shoes, slipped his backpack on. He jumped on the motorcycle and drove to the village where Pin had bought her handgun and found the stall owner. Char was alone and closing down for the night.

'Doctor,' he said, 'what do you want?'

'Could I see that plastic semi-automatic?'

'Sure.'

Char retrieved the Glock 17.

Cavalier examined it.

'Accuracy?' he asked Char.

'Surprisingly good for a polymer structure.'

'Have you practised with it?'

'I try out all the guns I sell. It's as accurate as any one of them.'

'From how far?'

'Twenty or thirty metres. If you are good shot, that will do it.' Char paused before asking: 'Are you a good shot, Doctor?'

Cavalier didn't reply.

'I hope you are discreet, Salesman,' he said, staring into Char's eyes.

'These guns are illegal and not registered,' Char said. 'I don't want the police closing me down.'

'Would you have a silencer for this, by any chance?'

'No. What do you need the gun for?'

'Self-defence.'

'With a silencer?'

Cavalier ignored the question and made an offer for the gun. After some bargaining, he had it and twenty bullets for thirty dollars.

He rode off and at first had trouble locating Kun's home in the dark. After about twenty minutes searching, Cavalier traced it as the only place in the area that was lit up. He parked his bike off a track leading to the house. He removed his backpack and took the gun from it, pushing it into his inside jacket pocket. He then camouflaged the bike with shrubs and tree branches.

Cavalier crept along the path to the house, which was on stilts. An outside staircase led to the living quarters. He could hear men talking loudly about alcohol that friends were bringing. It seemed that Kun and his companions were about to have a party celebrating his thirty-fifth birthday. Cavalier was on edge as he reached a point about thirty metres from the staircase. There seemed little opportunity to confront Kun without having to deal with at least six men, and perhaps others who were expected. Then he heard female voices. He could see a girl dancing on a balcony at the top of the stairs. Another woman joined her. Food was being passed around. Minutes later, he had to rush to cover in shrubs by the track to the house as two motorcycles roared off the main road. Each male driver had a woman perched on the seat behind him and they carried about a dozen bottles of Thai whisky.

Cavalier thought he had no chance of isolating Kun. He lay where he was, watching the party. Reluctantly, at 10 p.m. he began to make his way stealthily back to his bike. He was halfway to it when he was forced to hide in the scrub again by two more bikers with passengers. They roared past him. Cavalier had resumed his retreat when shots were fired, which cause him to fall flat on the ground. He looked back at the house. Two men with automatic rifles on the first-floor balcony were firing into the air. The birthday celebrations had begun in earnest. A man moved down the staircase and into the yard. Cavalier could see from his hand movements that he was urinating on the front lawn. The man had to dodge spit, which two of the men on the balcony launched at him, bringing much mirth to onlookers. The man finished relieving himself and hurried up the stairs, hurling abuse at the spitters.

Cavalier hesitated a few minutes before another man ventured into the garden and, wishing to avoid being spat on, moved behind the thick trunk of a plane tree. Kun was leaning over the balcony laughing at his companion. He spat and hit the tree. Cavalier eased along the path closer to the house and hid behind scrub and trees only a few metres from the yard.

The party continued over the next half-hour with dancing, drinking and more wild automatic-weapon gunfire. A fight broke out between Kun and another man. Kun hit him hard. His opponent rocked backwards down the stairs. Others applauded as two women rushed down to attend to the uncon- scious man. Kun walked down, kicked the stricken man and wandered into the garden. He stopped near the plane tree about four metres from Cavalier. Two men on the balcony began spraying bullets that whistled above Kun's head. He stopped fumbling with his fly and waved a fist at the gunmen.

'Hey! That was close! Stop that or I'll come and smash you!' he yelled.

The firing stopped. Cavalier crawled in the shadows to the plane tree, gun in hand. His heart was pounding. Kun began urinating. The two men on the balcony took the moment to fire above Kun's head. Cavalier jumped to his feet and aimed at Kun from three metres. He fired two shots which were drowned out by the sporadic spray of the automatic weapons. Kun fell to his knees and then toppled over, his face in a puddle of his own making.

Cavalier kept in the shadows and hurried away from the house. The laughing and gunfire continued. He reached his motorcycle and hauled on his backpack. The partygoers were scurrying down the stairs. Cavalier started the bike and kicked away, gunning the machine as fast as he dared along the road. He heard other bikes at the house starting up. They were giving chase. Cavalier's bike was smaller, and as fast as he pushed it, the other bikes were soon gaining ground.

He raced through the checkpoint before a barrier was lowered. He ignored border guards who shouted for him to stop, then blocked the following bikes at the barrier. The security guards insisted on examining the riders' identity documents. It gave Cavalier just enough distance from them as he reached the bus terminal and hid the bike behind a closed market. The last night bus back to Chiang

Mai was just starting up and the passengers were climbing on board.

He scurried through trees to the small airfield. A Cessna was standing near the wooden hangar and terminal. Cavalier could see the bus pulling out, just as the two chasing bikers reached the area.

Cavalier jumped in the cockpit. Flight plan papers were sitting on the seat. He started the engine, revved it briefly, taxied to the makeshift, part-dirt runway and took off. On the ascent, he could see the bus stopped on the road. Kun's companions were gesticulating with the driver, who would not let them on the bus.

Cavalier headed due north at a 10,000-feet altitude that would allow him to easily clear the mountains, which could be seen in the moonlight. There were no other planes flying as low and he was able to relax on what became an enjoyable flight. Cavalier began radio contact with Chiang Mai airport after two hours and was given instructions for his approach. He landed at 4 a.m. and killed time playing pool at an all-night go-go bar on the Chiang Mai Land Road. At 6 a.m. he was ravenous after his sleepless night of exertions. He ate some pork fried rice from a street vendor.

At 7 a.m., about the time he would arrive if he'd come by bus, he reached his flat. He rang Pin at the hospital, but she was in the emergency operating room. She would phone him when she could. Cavalier decided to get some much-needed sleep. He was woken mid-afternoon by a call from Pin.

'I can't believe what I've been told!' she said in a strange voice. 'Kun was at a party last night and was either in a fight or was shot by accident. He's dead.'

'Dead! Are you sure?'

'Certain. The police came around to question my mother. She has Far. She went to the school in the hope of seeing her, but Kun and his mad mates were not there.'

'You said he was shot …'

'In the chest and head, the police told me. Apparently, his mates were skylarking about and firing their weapons!' Pin's voice was excited. 'They haven't charged anyone yet. It may be judged as an "accidental homicide".'

'Far is okay?'

'Fine. She's with my mother. They will take a bus that will arrive here arrive here this afternoon.'

'That's wonderful!'

'I told you Serena would bring me good luck. It's amazing!'

'Oh, yes the ghost doll.'

'No, she is my *angel* child.'

'Hmm. Have you done anything about medication?'

'Not had time.' Pin paused and asked, 'You think I'm mad and this love for Serena is part of it?'

'No, I can separate the two. I still want you to see a specialist. You may find that you're a better doctor for it.'

'I know as much as anyone about the side effects of drugs prescribed for my condition,' she said. 'They can retard you.'

'Let's talk about it tonight after you're reunited with Far.'

'I suppose you don't wish to be with me now.'

'I want to be with you. I believe you have to do something about your mood swings.'

After a long silence, Pin said, 'I'll see a specialist tomorrow.'

*

That day Cavalier put the Glock 17 gun and the eighteen remaining bullets in a padded bag and placed it in a bank deposit box.

*

A local coroner's report, six months after the turbulent events in Mae Sot, caused Pin to quiz Cavalier about how he had exited Mae Sot on the night of the killing. The report suggested the bullets that struck her former husband were not those from the weapons of his friends firing drunkenly into the darkness. There was also the evidence from two of them that they had given chase after an 'unknown assailant'. The police view was that one of Kun's friends had used a handgun, not an automatic weapon like the others, and had accidentally hit him with two shots. The police claimed that the gun had then been either hidden or destroyed. The coroner accepted their evidence and recorded 'death by misadventure'.

'You went to the bus terminal on my mother's motorcycle,' Pin said one morning over breakfast at his flat, 'but did you take the bus or not?'

'Of course, why?'

'My phone recorded you calling me at 7 a.m.'

'After the bus arrived in Chiang Mai, yes.'

Pin paused and eyeballed him.

'Why did you tell my mother to meet Far at the preschool, knowing that Kun would pick her up?' she asked.

'Your mother told me that he didn't always turn up. He neglected her. She said the teachers sometimes were forced to take Far to their homes to look after her.'

'But Kun could have attacked my mother.'

47

'I don't think so. The police came to her home the night before. They said they were going to talk to him ...'

'They had *already* spoken to him,' Pin interrupted.

'No, they were going to speak to him. Your mother was hostile about them not doing something about him.'

Pin pulled an expression indicating she was unconvinced. She rested her hands on her baby bump and probed further.

'You told my mother than you thought Kun would be with the police,' she said.

'Yes, they said they would interrogate him.'

'My mother said you took her bike in the evening at about 8 p.m. She couldn't remember the time exactly. The bus didn't leave until closer to midnight.'

'About 11 a.m.'

'That is a gap of about three hours.'

'I went for a long ride on the bike. I do that to clear my mind.'

'Kun's mates said that the man they chased after Kun was shot was not on the bus.'

Cavalier shrugged. 'Okay, but *I* was on the bus.'

'Hmm,' Pin mused, while keeping her eyes on Cavalier.

'I was right about Kun,' he said.

'What?'

'He *was* with the police the next day.'

'What do you mean?'

'He was in a makeshift morgue at their station. It was in the coroner's report, remember?'

The comment startled and confused her. Before she could reflect on the remark, she had one more query: 'I bumped into Char when I was seeing my family last week.'

'Char ...?'

'You know, the guy who sold me the gun.'

'Oh, yeah.'

'He was so excited about Kun's murder.'

'Killing. The coroner judged it was death by misadventure.'

'Ok, whatever. Char has taken a step up in the Mae Sot underworld because my ex was eliminated as a rival. He is very happy.'

'So?'

'He was most deferential in his remarks about you. He asked about you in an odd way. Said he hoped to see my "doctor friend" again.'

'That *is* strange.'

'He wanted to offer you a share in a bottled-water business,' she said, watching his reaction closely, 'on very good terms indeed. Are you interested?'

'No. I have a golden rule. Use contacts in the criminal and espionage world for information, but never do business with them.'

Although not entirely convinced by Cavalier's plausible responses, she relaxed her expression and poured them both coffees. She looked at her watch.

'Damn! I'll be late for work.'

'Aren't you relieved that Kun has gone?'

'Yes …'

'That is what you and your mother were plotting, right?'

'Yes, that is true.'

'Then providence or the Buddha or both conspired for you.'

'And Serena,' Pin said, kissing him and reaching for her bike keys. 'I asked for her help too. She had more influence than anything.'

*

Over the decades, Pin's mind turned to the questions about that fateful night whenever Cavalier left on 'assignments', allegedly for his newspaper, and would not discuss them in any detail. It gave her pause over what he really did on his missions, and what he may have been involved in at Mae Sot when Kun was shot. Char's continued deferential references to Cavalier whenever Pin bumped into him also raised her suspicions. Yet she never mentioned the killing with either man, preferring to accept her good fortune, or Cavalier's extreme measure in his protection of her and her family.

PART TWO
2016

7

A NEW IDENTITY

Cavalier met his good friend from the Australian Federal Police, Tommy 'Wombat' Gregory, at Melbourne's Lindrum Hotel and challenged him to a game of pool. They were both exceptional players. In the best of three, they were one-all and it was down to the last few shots of game three to decide the winner. Gregory had only to slot the black to win. Cavalier still had three balls to put away. It was his shot.

'I need to put two away at least with this,' he said, indicating two pockets at one end of the table.

'I've seen you do that once before,' Gregory said. 'It's not the equivalent to a hole in one in golf, but close. Two hundred says you won't do it again.'

'You're on. Don Bradman did it four times in six games when I played him at his home.'

'You're not the Don, Vic.'

'Granted.'

'Did you beat him?'

'No. I lost six-oh,' Cavalier said, lining up the shot, 'got close in two games. He had the best eye I've ever come across in any sport.'

'That was his secret, wasn't it?'

'Yes, coupled with his powers of concentration. Never met a competitor so focused. He was in his late eighties and I was forty years younger when we played.'

'He would have made a wonderful assassin.'

'Without doubt,' Cavalier said with a laugh. 'Now you're trying to put me off.'

The shot needed an exceptional ricochet off the target balls close to each other and at forty-five degrees to the pockets. He took two minutes to size up the angles, then played the shot. Both balls slid into the intended pockets but to the surprise of both, Cavalier's third ball was also hit. It trickled into a pocket at the other end of the table.

'Mate! I have never seen a shot like that! A triple!'

'I can assure you that the third strike was a fluke.' Cavalier pocketed the black to win the best of three.

'The Don would never have made that shot,' Gregory said, shaking his head in disbelief.

'I wouldn't bet on it.'

They took the elevator to Gregory's suite, which he used as on office when away from his home town of Mandurah in Western Australia.

Cavalier had been lying low in the eight months since returning from Vietnam, Cambodia and Thailand after he had assassinated Leonardo Mendez, the head of one of the world's biggest drug cartels. Cavalier had been given a video that convinced him that Mendez had murdered Cavalier's and Pin's daughter Pon by guillotining her. It was the grotesque recreational habit of the drug boss and his henchmen. Pon had been trying her hand at freelance journalism and had been captured by the cartel in Mexico.

Cavalier had tracked Mendez in Thailand, eventually isolating and killing him at the notorious Nana Plaza in Bangkok's red-light district. He had escaped Thailand by flying to Phnom Penh, and then taking a boat down the Mekong River to Vietnam. Cavalier had been pursued by Mendez's top hitman, Jose Cortez, who wanted revenge for Mendez's assassination. Cortez backed off, however, when Cavalier warned him by phone that if he and his two henchmen dared pursue him into the Mekong Delta hinterland, Cavalier would easily pick them off in the jungle.

Once in the suite, Gregory made him a coffee and told him: 'You'll have to disappear. Jose Cortez has put a contract out on you. If he doesn't do it himself, he'll hire someone in Australia. We believe it's worth more than a million.'

'Perhaps you should take it up,' Cavalier said with a grin.

'Vic, this is serious.'

'Who is the source?'

'Our American cousins. Their contacts within the cartel are most reliable. Since the demise of his boss and very close friend Leonardo Mendez, Cortez has become convinced you murdered him. It's not just business; it's personal too.'

'What does that mean? Cortez is the most effective contract killer in the world. Eighty kills. It doesn't compute. There must be something else.'

Gregory shrugged. 'Whatever it is, he is coming after you.'

'I expected it.'

'Does it scare you?'

'Makes me alert. I am used to death threats. It helps that you have forewarned me; thank you.'

'I know better than most how well you can handle yourself. But here you won't know where the killer will come from.

They'll be able to track you easily. It would be advisable for you to "depart". Do what you do better than anyone else: become someone else and stay blended in.' Gregory paused and added, 'Please do it, Vic.'

'Where would you suggest I go?'

'Wherever you feel comfortable; I'd suggest you leave Australia.'

'For how long?'

'Six months at least. In that time, the cousins should have acted against Cortez. Remember his kill list is mostly Americans, some of them agency people. He is their most wanted man since Osama Bin Laden. They are finally going after him with force.'

'A Seal op?'

'Could be. The cartel has a considerable armed outfit. Our cousins believe he and it will be most vulnerable while they are in Thailand. The cartel has pulled out of Chiang Mai and moved to Bangkok.'

Gregory took a package from a briefcase.

'I have a few presents for you,' he said, handing it to him. 'I hear your eyesight is failing.'

'Who told you that?'

'Only kidding. I believe you broke your own range record. Congratulations—20/20 vision at your age is a modern wonder!'

'Thank you, I think. I hate the cliché corollary "for your age".'

Gregory handed him a pair of nerdy-looking, square, dark-framed glasses that had sides like small blinkers.

'These will help. Very special ocular enhancements. They can make out more than just shapes from two hundred metres.'

'Infrared?'

'Part of it, yes. CSIRO developed these especially for us. They give you more than just sight in the dark.' He demonstrated two tiny buttons on the thick frames. 'There is a special feature I love. Gives you the high-tech equivalent of eyes in the back of your head.' Cavalier put them on. 'If you press the left button, and tilt the glasses a fraction, you obtain a clear view of what is happening behind you.'

'Hmm,' Cavalier said with reserved admiration, 'interesting. Have to try in the field.'

'It's called "real-time video". Tiny cameras and mirrors take a video of what is going on behind you. It is played for your viewing in the glasses with a delay of a fraction of a second.'

'Are our operatives using them now?'

'No, they are prototypes. Operatives will practise with them and report on their effectiveness.' Gregory handed him a second pair. 'Here, have these for luck. They have a third function, which allows you to depict colours in the dark.'

Cavalier tried them.

'These are confusing,' he said. 'The colours fuse. I can't distinguish shapes ...'

'They work well in the dark. In any case, you're a guinea pig. I'd like a full report on them on their respective efficiencies, please.'

Gregory handed him a third item in a small plastic box. 'You might as well have these too.' He lifted the box's lid to show him what appeared to be normal mobile phone earpieces. 'These are called extrasensory earpieces—ESEPs.'

Cavalier put them on and adjusted the volume.

'You'll hear a mouse fart with those,' Gregory said. 'Just plug them into your phone as if you are listening to music. You can pick up a conversation at fifty metres.' He pulled out two further small items from his satchel. 'Just a couple of other things that may be of help. Straight from the CSIRO's special ops department.'

'Didn't know they had one.'

'They don't. I call it that because our agency has pinched some of their best scientists.' He opened a small box. 'I love this one too. It's an all-purpose key. Makes the old Allen key look ancient by comparison.' Gregory removed a small, thin key. 'This will open anything. It has "thinking" chips that will calculate in milliseconds how to crack a lock. Just flick it against an electronic lock, or shove it into an old-style one. Works every time.'

Cavalier picked up the key, walked out of the suite and tried it against the electronic lock. It opened it.

'Like it,' he said, re-entering the room, 'and thank you. You've become Q, as in the Bond movies.'

'Not the latest ones,' Gregory said with a grin, 'the new young Q character is way behind the eight ball. The technology for field operatives is becoming better and better.'

*

Cavalier did not take long to work out where he should hide out: Chiang Mai. He was familiar with the city and its Northern Thailand surrounds. He had stayed a few days at Centara, a central tourist hotel since renamed Duangtwan, in the previous year when tracking Mendez. Thirty years earlier he had remained in the city with Pin, now his ex-wife, for several months. They had lived in other cities such as Chiang

Rai, and over the years he would stay with her when she occasionally did locum work in Chiang Mai, if he were not in Australia or on another assignment.

Cavalier believed that the last place Cortez and his henchmen would expect him to be would be Chiang Mai. The Mexicans had left their massive bunker outside the city and were going to escape Thailand, or at least that was the most up-to-date intelligence. Nevertheless, he would live a low-key existence for several months.

Cavalier rented an apartment in the Riverside Condo on the Ping River, with a view from its three fourth-floor balconies that would inspire any painter. Looking left he could see trees and the river just fifty metres away, where it wound its way south-east around a small green island. On the other side of the hundred-metre-wide river there were a few unobtrusive and abandoned houses, half-hidden pagodas, more trees, and the mountains beyond. To the right he could see the white railings of the Meng Rai Bridge where he had witnessed Pin's motorcycle accident thirty years earlier.

The place was quiet. Every morning he awoke to the cry of an orange-feathered crow pheasant. He rolled up the blinds to the sight of sun on the still river and peaceful surrounds. In late afternoons and evenings, the sun fell in a splash of red into the mountains.

The position of the apartment was pertinent. It was just outside the south-east corner of Chiang Mai, and far enough away from the more central location of incidents that nearly cost him his life six months earlier. It was also conveniently located with a Caltex fuel station and an upmarket 7-Eleven store called Tops across from the condominium entrance on the Lamphun Road. The area was mostly inhabited by Thais with few foreigners in sight outside the condo itself and the Holiday Inn next door. His new 'home', or 'writer's retreat' as Cavalier liked to call it, was the best in Chiang Mai of twenty he had looked at on the net. The modest rental price was within his means, given that he had received a redundancy package from his newspaper.

The condo had good security. There was only one way into his place and that was by a solid front door. Leaving the elevator, the apartment was at the end of a fifty-metre-long corridor, which was marked by a permanent smell of marijuana coming from a room halfway along. Cavalier had studied the condo's exits and entry points from lifts and stairwells and was satisfied that he could come and go without being seen. He judged that in an emergency he could even use a sheet tied to a balcony rail to rappel down a few metres to the abode on the floor below, and so on down to the ground. With that in mind, he had a hardware store three hundred metres from his condo construct a five-metre-long rope ladder.

He was very well aware that an assassin could strike onto his balconies from across the river, and it would not be a difficult shot of about two hundred metres. Cavalier used his new ESEP glasses to scour the opposite bank and the mainly obscured buildings every morning if he had breakfast on a balcony, and left the lights off if he ate outside at night.

It was an idyllic setting, into which he could fade with a new identity. He had taken the name Laurent V Blanc, which was an amalgam of two close French friends' names. Cavalier had two false French passports and two Australian (one false), but had only changed his identity for the purposes of travelling in and out of a country. In a second French document, as Claude Garriaud, he wore his glasses, wig, false moustache and goatee beard. When using the second Australian passport, as Bert Trumper, he would have to present a totally different look: bald and with brown contact lenses. He'd worn a moulded plastic 'cap' to look bald in the photo but knew he couldn't get away with this if interrogated face to face. He would have to shave his entire head of thick salt-and-pepper hair, which he detested the thought of doing.

Once through borders he shed his disguises, even dropping his French accent most of the time, only being careful when meeting some Europeans and Australians. He had chosen French because of his fluency in the language, even the nuances of colloquial speech. If he met French speakers, he would be Australian. If he met English speakers, he would be French. His Thai was good, but his height, fair skin, blue eyes, slightly gnarled nose, and square jaw prevented him from trying to pass as a native of his part-adopted country.

On his first day in the condo he wandered into the local Nong Hoi market, with its enticing smells dominated by chicken, fish, a variety of spices, and strongly scented flowers. He bought two coloured face masks—white and red—which were legitimate in fending off the vehicle pollution, one of the few drawbacks to living in the area. Whenever he walked down the street he wore cap, sunglasses and mask, which allowed him to meld into the local population scarcely identifiable as a farang. He did not himself recognise anyone in the market, which he had frequented in the distant past.

On one occasion, when he removed his mask and glasses, a middle-aged, corpulent woman named Coo kept her eyes on him as he walked away. He noticed her and did not make eye contact.

The second time he wandered near Coo's food stall she called out, 'Vic? You Vic?'

Cavalier was shocked that someone had recalled him decades after he had lived in the area, especially as his looks had changed and matured. He pretended not to notice, later buying pork and salad from her.

While Coo was scooping it into plastic bags, she said in Thai: 'You look like a handsome Australian farang from a long time ago.'

Cavalier said in French and with a charming smile: '*Merci,* Madame, my name is Laurent,' and then shook hands with her.

She said her name and frowned, still uncertain.

'Not Vic?' she said.

'Laurent,' he repeated. The name 'Coo' resonated. Despite her face not being familiar, he recalled using the image of a pigeon to remember her name. Cavalier was glad of the face mask just in case others in the four hundred metres of street stalls and cafes had excellent memories.

His main concern would be coming to the attention of Chiang Mai police or some of the enemies, particularly anyone from the Mendez Mexican drug cartel company—Golden Eagle Constructions—who might be left over in Chiang Mai while the rest of the gang had moved to Bangkok. He had hired a car to drive out to the company bunker, which had an abandoned look. There was security at a boom gate leading down the track to the underground entrance, which seemed to be closed and boarded up. Seeing this eased his fears, but not his alertness. Yet it confirmed that Chiang Mai was the best place for his temporary relocation, at least until he heard that the Americans had moved on the cartel's people in Thailand.

Cavalier was sometimes on edge in the street, despite his mask. During the morning he would have coffee on the Lamphun Road, which led south to the quaint city of the same name, at one of three welcoming shops run by three sets of Thai sisters. He would randomly rotate his patronising of these cafes to avoid familiarity with the women, none of whom interfered with his privacy or asked questions beyond the normal niceties about where he was from and what he was doing in Chiang Mai. Cavalier would remove the mask and sit inside to avoid the endless stream of vehicles, which were ten times the number of thirty years earlier, belching out contaminants.

Occasionally a bike would roar up to the front of the cafe. He would look up at a helmeted rider, unable to know in a split second if it were an assailant or not. Always in his mind was the possibility of an attempt to murder him. An assassin in Thailand could be hired cheaply.

8

DISTANT ACQUAINTANCES

Cavalier was cautious about speaking to anyone. Chiang Mai, similar to any remote outpost in any country, had a small repository of people on the run from something. It might be a mass murderer, or a petty thief; someone deserting a family; another person wanted for tax evasion in his home country; a drug runner owing money to another; and so on.

Only three people at the cafes and restaurants at different times had attempted to engage him in conversation. One was a strange forty-year-old alcoholic American-Israeli calling himself Guy, who twenty years ago had acted as a military adviser and arms supplier with rebels in Myanmar, formerly Burma. He approached Cavalier in the restaurant at the front of the condo one night and asked too many questions for his liking. Guy claimed to be a protégé of former CIA deputy director Bill Young, who was buried in a nearby cemetery. From then on Cavalier avoided Guy, who was usually too drunk to notice Cavalier stride past.

Then there was a Frenchman, Albert, who chain-smoked overpowering Gauloises cigarettes and drank black coffee.

He too had an unusual past, including a stint with the French Foreign Legion, which he tried to cover up. But the Frenchman underestimated his coffee companion by mentioning the towns and cities in North Africa he had 'visited'. Cavalier saw a pattern that few would pick up and was certain of his membership of the Legion.

'Did you enjoy the Legion activity?' Cavalier asked Albert once.

The Frenchman blanched and went silent. Cavalier had taken a chance in his discussions with him, but Albert was a character almost certain not to report on Cavalier, mainly because he was in a similar position. There was a cautious rapport between them without the exchange of numbers or email addresses. They never planned a meeting. Cavalier called himself just 'Laurent' and said he was Australian. He liked the Frenchman's thinking; he was intelligent, well-travelled and humorous. But soon after Cavalier's question about his past, he disappeared. One of the Thai women running the cafe told Cavalier that the police had asked questions about him.

'Albert was wanted for something in France,' she told Cavalier.

The third person with whom who Cavalier let down his guard was an eighty-year-old American, who had been living in retirement nearly two decades and was contemplating going home to Maryland, probably to die. Ted Baines was tall and lean, with a grey moustache. Cavalier thought he looked and sounded like a long-ago actor and World War II bomber pilot, Jimmy Stewart.

'Not sure I agree with that,' Ted laughed when told.

'Ok, you have a better jawline and no tremor in your voice.'

'As an actor, he made a good bomber pilot. Ended up a brigadier general.'

'I thought he was a fair actor.'

'Maybe.'

Ted would roll up in his wheelchair, read the *Bangkok Post* and *Nation* and chat with Cavalier, who liked and respected him. Ted also lived in the Riverside Condo. He sometimes left his wheelchair, which could collapse to half its normal width, under a canvas sheet among the scores of bikes outside the front of the condo. He would struggle on crutches from the elevator to the wheelchair and battle to open it to its full width. He would be grateful for help in this action, and also in climbing into the chair. On occasions Cavalier would leave the condo heading for the Chang cafe at the same time as Ted. He would assist Ted on the precarious two hundred and fifty-metre roll along the road of broken pavement, with close-running vehicles and bikes.

Cavalier found the American was sagacious and well read, quoting Oscar Wilde, Shakespeare and Churchill with an easy facility. Ted said he always filled in immigration cards asking if he had anything to declare with 'nothing but my genius'. He was also well travelled, having been a merchant seaman most of his life. Each day they happened to coincide at Chang, he would tell Cavalier an anecdote about his travels around the globe on all kinds of vessels, from grain transporters for free distribution in India in the 1950s, to destroyer escorts in the 1980s and 1990s. His speciality was as a radio operator and he had moved up to sophisticated listening apparatus by the time of the 1991 Gulf War. He had been brought up on a farm and had graduated from high school in Gaithersburg, Maryland. Ted spoke Thai and was proficient in Mandarin, as was Cavalier, so on occasion they would speak Chinese.

Cavalier let the friendship grow and often brought him food from the market and did chores for him, such as fixing a broken washing machine and installing Wi-Fi so he could watch American football. Ted was most grateful. It saved him many trips in his wheelchair and gave him some pleasure and security. His third long-term spouse, his Thai wife (his third long-term spouse) of fifteen years, had died a year earlier, and he himself was ailing from unspecified medical conditions. He had nothing to do with his family in the US.

Cavalier took notes in private, recognising that Ted could be a good character to emulate in a novel. Still, there were gaps in the old man's narrative. Cavalier's experience and detail-sensitive training made him mull over the possibility that Ted had a long-held dark secret or two, similar to Cavalier and the French Foreign Legionnaire.

After several months when a strong, if guarded, friendship had developed, Ted asked Cavalier to renew two passports (which he had to do each year), through two different lawyers in Chiang Mai. The name on one passport was Ted Baines. The other said 'Edward Blenkiron'.

'You noticed the names on my passports?' Ted asked Cavalier after he had happily completed the minor task.

'Yes,' Cavalier replied, but not in a tone that said he expected an explanation.

'Don't ask about it,' Ted said with a nervous smile.

A few mornings later, Ted asked Cavalier over coffee, 'Have you ever killed a man?'

It shook Cavalier, but he recovered in a split second by saying with a laugh: 'Do I look like I might have?'

'Not really. But those wristbands you wear give you a certain understated warrior look. Have you ever been in the military?'

'I was a trainee in the Australian Air Force.'

'You look combat-ready.'

'I keep in condition.'

'I know. I see you coming in from those early-morning runs along the river. How far do you go?'

'Ten K, every second day. I'd do it every day, but for a weak Achilles, which I must manage with massage and manipulation.'

'Do you know any martial arts—Muay Thai?'

'Only Korean karate, which I learnt in my early twenties. Couldn't fight my way out of a paper bag now.'

'Some modern paper bags are unbreakable,' Ted said with a knowing look, and then changed the subject to the ongoing presidential election.

'Are you following it?' he asked.

'I watch CNN in the condo. I covered the last month of three elections as a journalist—Carter in 1976; Reagan in 1980 and 1984. After that I lost a deep interest although all the presidents since then have in some way fascinated me—Bush Senior, Clinton, Bush Junior and Obama.'

'What's your take on Trump?'

Cavalier smiled. 'America has become the love child of the man and Kim Kardashian,' he said.

'Pardon me?'

'They are the product of reality television. The more outrageous they are, the more people tune in to watch them.'

'They appear so dumb!'

'Reality stars aren't supposed to lift us or add to our knowledge. They are there to entertain. Candidate Trump doesn't have to understand the fine detail of foreign policy. He only has to say he will make American great again, just like Reagan did with an actor's skill.'

'You don't think he can win, surely?'

'It's like that Jim Carrey movie *The Truman Show*. We'll all tune in to find out.'

A few days later at the cafe, Ted said with a slight quiver in his voice: 'I have been hiding something for forty years. About time I told somebody.'

Cavalier waited.

'I trust you, although I am guessing you are hiding things yourself.'

Cavalier smiled without acknowledging the veracity of the remark.

'I killed a man,' Ted said, blinking several times. 'It was the Austrian lover of my second wife, a Cambodian woman. It happened in Saigon near the end of the Vietnam War. Have been running from the incident ever since.' Ted blurted out the circumstances and how he had got into an altercation with the man before shooting him, 'before he shot me'.

Cavalier listened with a sympathetic ear.

When Ted finished his tale and dabbed his eyes, Cavalier touched his arm. 'About time you forgave yourself,' he said. 'It was self-defence.'

'I suppose you won't want to associate with me any more?' Ted said, his voice unsteady.

'*Noscitur a sociis*,' Cavalier said with a smile.

'I know that Latin expression—"a man is known by his associates".'

'And I am pleased, no, *honoured* to be associated with you.'

Ted began to cry. Cavalier comforted him, paid the bill and wheeled him back to the condo.

'That is why I acquired a false passport,' Ted said when they reached the elevator. 'They were really easy to obtain forty years ago. I've kept them both up to date. In the States, I use the false one, just in case. But no one has ever come after me.'

'Did your wife know you killed the man?'

'No. We split soon after the incident. I haven't spoken to her since.'

'Have you told anyone else?'

'No.'

'Then I doubt anyone will ever come after you.'

This revelation made Cavalier think again on his own situation. He felt uneasy and vulnerable, just at a point when he was beginning to consider himself safe.

9

BACK TO SCHOOL

'Would you be interested in some easy money?' Gregory asked Cavalier over the phone.

'Thanks, but no thanks. I am trying to avoid …'

'I don't mean using your usual expertise, only part of it.'

'You know I don't take commissions.'

'I thought now you had left the paper, you might be more open to offers.'

'No, but what's the project?'

'We know of two probable terrorists living in Chiang Mai. They are Indonesians who planned to bomb the MCG. We were onto them but they escaped Australia via a boat from Darwin to Timor two years ago. We suspect they are involved in something big in Thailand. Not sure what. They have been based there as sleepers for a couple of years, most likely ready to be activated for something. They are going to the trouble of learning Thai.'

'What would you want me to do?'

'Go to school with them.'

'What?'

'They have enrolled for an intensive high-level three-week course in the Thai language at the Pantip School in Chiang Mai. They have been on two other such courses in the last year.'

Cavalier was silent. Then he said: 'I was thinking of doing a refresher course now I'm here for a while. What would you want?'

'A report. Anything you can discover about them.'

'Bit risky, given my ...'

'You don't have to become their new best friend. If you were to learn any travel plans they have, that sort of thing.'

'I've only been here a few months. I was hoping to stay out of circulation for another three or four weeks. Are the Thais aware of them? Are you collaborating with the Thais?'

'No way. I wouldn't ask for your help if they were. It's our project. The fact that they are lying low in Chiang Mai was too good an opportunity, seeing you are there.'

There was another pause.

'How did you know they were enrolled at the school?'

'It's run by an American, Pedro. He told our American cousins who, knowing of my particular interest, informed me. I'll buy you a beer if you do this.'

'This must be important to you.'

'We had them cold in Melbourne. Yet they slipped the net. They shot and wounded one of my people.'

'Hmm. Don't tell anyone—Pedro or the cousins—that I will go back to school.'

*

The Thai class was held on the fourth level of the Pantip building, a department store on the Chang Klan Road, and a few kilometres from Cavalier's apartment. The complete floor was given over to language schools and nurseries.

There were just seven students apart from Cavalier, who was acting as the Australian Bert Trumper, but without shaving his head to look like the passport photo: an attractive Scottish woman, Rebecca, in her early thirties; two big men in their mid-forties—an Englishman, Paul, and a bearded German, Joachim; an eighty-year-old Welshman, Anthony; and a fit, bespectacled man in his early fifties, Geoff, who had a broad Alabama accent. The two Indonesians, Irina and Doug, wearing American baseball caps, were in their early twenties. Even within the confines of the small classroom, they somehow managed to keep to themselves, except when exposed to the directness of the exceptional Thai teacher, Wee. She was a tiny, energetic twenty-three-year-old, with a lively sense of humour.

Aware that most of the class had more than basic Thai, she asked them to explain, in English and Thai, the reasons they were doing the course, and why they were in Thailand. Cavalier and Anthony claimed they were retired and just wanted to improve their language skills. Paul told the class he was the part-owner of a bar with a Thai girlfriend. They were in the process of opening a cafe. Joachim was married to a ladyboy from Bangkok and wanted better communication with her; Rebecca had a Thai boyfriend. She brought a roar of approval from the class when she said in her slight Scottish brogue, 'He is so handsome and lovely and I will do anything to keep him.'

Only the Indonesians were less forthcoming. They claimed they were from Bandung, Java.

'How long have you lived here?' Wee asked in Thai.

'Eight months,' Irina replied.

'What work do you do?'

The Indonesians glanced at each other before Irina said, 'We are computer programmers.'

After a week, Cavalier, who had made an effort to charm Wee, took her aside before class and suggested she ask each student what travel plans they had.

'Very good; that's a good idea,' Wee said.

'I have heard them all talking about where they are going,' he said with a relaxed smile. 'I think you could really push us for explanations.'

Wee questioned each student. Most gave clear answers, except the Indonesians who fumbled responses and looked at each other for support.

Wee pressed them with her usual smiling yet incisive style: 'Okay, you are going to Bangkok and then Malaysia and Singapore, but how?'

'By … by train,' Irina said. She was the couple's spokesperson. Doug rarely made eye contact and always seemed shy, or nervous.

'Very good,' Wee said with a lilting Thai upward inflexion, 'which train into Malaysia and Singapore?'

Irina pulled a face and opened her hands.

'We don't know yet,' she said, nervous at this unexpected round of queries.

'There's a real good one,' Geoff from Alabama drawled in Thai. It's called the *Bangkok Express*. Is that the one you all have in mind?'

The Indonesians frowned and indicated they couldn't

understand the question, or Geoff's sharp accent. Wee repeated the query. They said they weren't sure.

'Very good,' Wee said. It was her 'tick' remark to take back control of the class or move it on.

'Is your real name Doug?' Geoff asked harmlessly. The Indonesian looked flummoxed.

Irina responded, 'We both have Western nicknames. Our real ones are too long for Western consumption.'

That drew a laugh from the class and diffused a tense moment after Doug seemed angry at the light grilling.

'Very good,' Wee said. 'I have a name that is both Thai and Western.'

This drew more laughter, even a smile from Doug.

Their mirth was short-lived after class when Cavalier insisted on taking photographs. He snapped them all in a group before the Indonesians could protest.

That night in his apartment, Cavalier made a report for Gregory, with photos attached, suggesting that the Indonesians could well be preparing for an assignment of some sort.

'I would not discount their intention to commit a terrorist act,' he concluded.

'This is brilliant work!' Gregory texted him. 'I suppose a passport copy or two would be out of the question?'

'Yes, it would.'

'There are more beers in it for you.'

'You are so persuasive! I thought my schooldays were through.'

It had nagged Cavalier that he could not secure their real names and so Gregory's request resonated with his own sense of what was lacking from a complete report. He had made a note of the staff office equipment and filing system in the room next door to the classroom. At 10 p.m. he returned to the Pantip building and had a late meal in the canteen on the fourth floor, forty metres from the school. Cavalier hid in the toilet and waited until the lights were out. Cleaners were working their way up the building, floor by floor. Cavalier put on a face mask and, wearing the glasses Gregory had given him, moved to the school office. Using his special laser key, he opened the lock. Cavalier shut the door and searched in drawers for the handwritten information on students. Within three minutes he found the four pages of files, including passport copies, for the two Indonesians. He used his phone to photograph all the information, and was careful to replace the files as he had found them.

Cavalier slipped out of the office just as the lights went on. Two cleaners were coming up the escalator. He scurried out of sight, and made a quick circuit of the floor to a back service elevator. He still wore his glasses and mask as he moved out of the building into the hot night. An hour later he had emailed Gregory attachments with the files and passport details.

'You're terrible, Muriel!' Gregory said, which was his usual comment to express astonishment at Cavalier's exploits. 'Terribly efficient.'

'It wasn't my toughest assignment, but thank the Buddha I won't be going back to school,' Cavalier said. 'A week was enough.'

10

DARK SECRETS

The more concerning moments for Cavalier were at night. If he ventured back to the condo late, he would be vigilant just outside the entrance, in the foyer and in the corridor to his apartment. This caution made him think about obtaining a weapon. He had his disassembled high-powered rifle inside Big Betty, the hollowed-out over-sized cricket bat, but it was for his other professional work, which he had stepped away from while in hiding. He thought about the Glock 17, which he had placed in a safety deposit box so long ago. He still had the key and the receipt for the box at the Bangkok Bank, but under his real name. After some research, he discovered that the bank branch he had used had been moved to the Airport Plaza, along with all the deposit boxes.

He found the bank's new address, but was apprehensive about entering it as Victor Cavalier. To his surprise, he did not have to show a passport or any ID to visit his box. All he needed was the receipt and the key. He took the package from it and later, in his apartment, unwrapped the weapon.

Cavalier took it to a firing range in south-west Chiang Mai, but was not allowed to use a private gun. A day later at dawn, he rode up Doi Suthep mountain to near a bend in the road three-quarters of the way up and found a secluded spot in the rainforest evergreens, He walked well into the wooded area, marked two thick tree trunks and fired off six shots from twenty paces.

At first, Cavalier was unsure if his aim was off or the gun needed calibrating. After some adjustment with a screwdriver and knife, he judged that the plastic had deteriorated a fraction, enough to spoil a perfect shot. Six shots more at the second attempt were satisfactory and he was pleased with his aim and the gun's proficiency. He carried it from then on in his brown valise, and felt more secure.

In his first few months, not even some of Cavalier's long-term friends would see him before he became comfortable in the new environment, or heard that Cortez had been dealt with by the Americans. He considered writing a book about his life in the demi-monde of spies and his clandestine assignments. Yet every time he thought of a narrative in non-fiction, or even fiction, it covered terrain that he could never publish. Apart from the possibility of incriminating himself, Cavalier knew too many secrets about intelligence services in many countries, including Thailand. This left him with his freelance journalism, with outlets in France and Australia. He would use Chiang Mai as a base, as he had thirty years ago, with more and easier access to ten different cultures within three or four hours' flight. He had applied for a long-term visa on his false passport and was using a precocious young English lawyer to obtain it for him. Technical help from among

Gregory's contacts had set him up so that he used an Internet server based in Russia. He could browse using an assumed Internet address that assigned his location to a country other than Thailand and Australia. Without any particular outlet for his writing, Cavalier had to be content with a false byline and the choice of mostly apolitical colour features. He knew the income stream would be meagre to begin with.

He thought about contacting Pin, but they had been divorced several years and he had not been in touch, even when he believed their daughter, Pon, had been murdered in Mexico. She had always believed this anyway and he judged that telling her of the distressing video, which appeared to show Pon had been decapitated by Mendez, would only be bad for her bipolar condition. It had flared when she was under stress, and the video of Pon being dragged into a dungeon, having her head placed on a block and the guillotine coming down would have been too much for her.

Pin believed that her special angel doll Serena, which she'd had for three decades, had protected Pon as she journeyed into the 'next world', as she called it. Soon after her disappearance, this had been a contentious subject between Cavalier and Pin. He stopped short of calling her more than 'irrational' for her faith in Serena, the 'inanimate piece of hideous plastic'. He had grown to appreciate Thai culture, its beliefs and superstitions. He had studied its roots and had kept an open mind about the prevalent concept of ghosts and spirits, mainly because of two inexplicable experiences he'd had, decades earlier in England. Yet he could not justify the doll worship as anything beyond mumbo jumbo. And he could not understand why his exceptionally intelligent wife had such faith in it.

Cavalier had kept contact with his stepdaughter Far, who was a thirty-four-year-old doctor married to an American television talk-show host and living in New York. She and Cavalier had a good relationship, and he felt an unspoken bond with her because of his effort to save her from her father. Cavalier had made sure she had a good life and education through university. Far had been unaware of the extreme step Cavalier had gone to on her behalf. He couldn't even foresee himself making a deathbed confession about killing her biological father Kun, whom she hated even as a toddler. Cavalier did not see the point.

*

Dwelling on Pon's fate, along with Ted's disclosure, had caused more sleepless nights. He'd had intermittent nightmares in the last year over the video depicting his daughter's murder, even after he had himself disposed of her apparent killer Mendez. There was always a different dream version that had not been appeared in the actual video. In one, Mendez held up the severed head of his daughter, who pleaded for help. In another the head smiled at him and he woke up thinking instantly that she wasn't dead. In a third horror reverie, he saw the guillotine slam down and blood everywhere. But instead of his daughter's severed cranium being lifted from the floor, it was that of Serena the doll. It also spoke, but not to him and without saying anything intelligible. After that he awoke in a terrible state of shock at 3 a.m. and could not go back to sleep. Instead, he poured himself a strong double malt whisky and sat alone on the balcony trying, and failing, to make sense of what his inner mind was regurgitating.

11

THE PROPOSITION

The next morning was not the best moment to be flying into Myanmar for an interview with Aung San Suu Kyi, three decades after they had first met. Yet the need for him to be alert sharpened him. The daily routines of exercise and two cups of black coffee at the airport helped him submerge the subterranean-mind horrors of the night as he prepared for a meeting with a person for whom he had the highest admiration. Suu Kyi had reached her aim to 'bring democracy' to her country as leader of her National League for Democracy party, which seemed on the surface to have dislodged the military in running Myanmar. He kept the story as colour rather than political, and the experience made him temporarily forget his nightmares.

The best he could do to stave off such hideous distraction was to bury himself in challenging work. This led him back up the Suu Kyi story in a sweeping interview with a long-term friend and senior judge in Hong Kong. The judge gave him an insider's view of the changes going on there with the mainland Chinese turning the screws on the former

British colony. Cavalier planned to vary his articles as much as possible to avoid anyone doing analysis on his work and writing style, which could be done by a computer app capable of comparing articles over time and picking out patterns and the possible authors.

His pieces had been published in several countries under the byline 'Laurent V Blanc'. They had brought him satisfaction but he was finding it tough as a freelancer, especially as the costs of obtaining these types of stories was always greater than the income from them. All his career, he had been under the umbrella of a major newspaper group. There had always been a pay cheque, even when it had dwindled to that of a three-day-week wage later in his tenure.

He had eaten into his redundancy package with a big splash-out on a powerful new Harley motorcycle, similar to the one owned by his Thai former special police operative acquaintance Jacinta Cin Lai, of Thailand's Special Investigative Unit, that nation's elite police operation. Half the adult population of Chiang Mai seemed to have a bike—many owned smaller models, yet with the growing affluence in this city of nearly three million, plenty of the bigger, more expensive variety were evident, so much so that the Harley company had just opened an office in Bangkok and a distribution centre in Chiang Mai. Cavalier felt he owed himself a luxury present. To avoid being conspicuous, he had special mufflers fitted that toned down its roar, and only took the bike out late at night, or very early in the morning when there was little traffic. Otherwise he travelled by taxi, red car or tuktuk.

Cavalier's most recent assignment to eliminate Leonardo Mendez had led to a narrow escape from the Bangkok scene of his kill, when a police net almost closed on him. He had made it to Cambodia, then managed a boat trip down the Mekong River to Vietnam only with the aid of Jacinta Cin Lai. When he refused to be arrested by her and three Mexican thugs, including the assassin Jose Cortez, who pursued him on the river, Jacinta managed to aid his departure by bluffing the Mexicans into believing that Cavalier was leading them into an American trap, which Cortez wished to avoid at all costs. He was the most wanted man in the US with more than eighty assassinations to his credit, most of them American citizens. Cavalier had had just as dangerous escapes in the past. Now he thought it might be time to give away his special contract work. He'd rarely needed help before, and the fact that Jacinta had intervened secretly on his behalf made him reconsider such precarious work—it was all too fraught with hazards and he was not getting any younger or quicker. His nerves held on the Mendez assignment, but he had been mentally exhausted by the experience.

Just as he becoming concerned about how he would eke out some sort of reasonable existence, he had a phone call from Gregory.

'One of our cousins is very keen to meet you,' Gregory told him. 'They have been fascinated by Cortez's determination to eliminate you. They had heard rumours about your work. I am not talking about your journalism. I gave them nothing. They have put two and two together and reckon you dealt with Mendez. We have neither confirmed nor denied it. And of course, we can't. We do not know.'

'Why do they want to meet me?'

'A proposition, I guess. Our cousins love to hire consultants. I would imagine your knowledge of Thailand and the cartel would mean that you would be useful in advising them. Really just a guess, mind you. Will you meet them? The cousins are in Bangkok now, tracking the cartel and Cortez.'

'I'm not going to Bangkok; too risky.'

'They'll come to you.'

*

Cavalier booked a table for two at Chiang Mai's David's Kitchen, which was a ten-minute motorcycle ride away from his condo hideout. Most nights he had either eaten food from the market or had frequented one of the many stalls or cafes. This stepping out after several months was a sign that he was gaining confidence in his reclusive existence.

He would be dining with a woman from the US Drug Enforcement Agency, Melody Smith. Gregory had been most impressed with her when she had visited him to find out more about Cavalier and his whereabouts.

'She is something out of the box,' he said, 'in a couple of senses. She is from Central Casting for female news anchors on American networks, especially Fox News: blonde hair, tall, long legs up to her throat. Extra good looks. Not quite up there with the exotic princess Jacinta, but who is?'

'At least Ms Smith won't stand out on the streets of my adopted city,' Cavalier said cynically, with a short laugh.

'Good point. Make sure you meet her somewhere upmarket where there are rich foreigners. And be ready for a big freeze. Has had a personality bypass. Not many laughs in her. All authority and business.'

The restaurant, offering a French-style menu, was modern with a large clay pots at the front, green hanging plants inside and a fresh, modern atmosphere. The clientele was split between European holidaymakers, judging from their casual attire, and better-dressed Asians, mostly Thais. There was an awkward moment for Cavalier when the manager asked for his Christian name and that of his dining partner. He declined at first to give them. The manager explained that there would be an encased printout of the names on the table. Cavalier didn't wish to make a fuss, so he changed his mind and agreed.

He was seated at a discreet table and a nameplate with 'Laurent and Melody' was placed in front of him. Soon afterwards, Melody Smith, wearing a grey cotton suit, dark-grey hat with a red band and black high-heeled shoes, strode in. She knew him from photos; he recognised her from Gregory's description. Melody was a power dresser in a powerful position. Cavalier noted her sinewy, gym-honed upper arms and lower legs. He guessed she had put in a lot of work to stay looking in her early thirties when she had tipped into her forties. Cavalier noticed the lack of movement around Smith's eyes when she smiled and her mouth when she spoke, indicating that she used Botox. Yet within these observations, Cavalier agreed with Gregory: she was a most handsome woman; lean in appearance and by vigorous body language and manner, hungry for 'success', whatever that meant in the world of a senior operative of her well-funded American Drug Enforcement Agency (DEA).

They indulged in small talk, with Cavalier giving nothing away as he helped her with the menu. She 'weighed' every course, discussing them in terms of 'carbohydrates', 'sugar', 'protein' and 'calories.' She was persuaded to take the lobster bisque without the white port to start, and the grilled duck as a main and 'definitely no dessert'. She refused buttered mashed potato. Cavalier asked for the onion soup with 'extra gruyere cheese', homemade gnocchi 'with twice the normal number of almonds', and a sticky date pudding 'with two serves of ice cream'.

Smith winced at the mention of all his choices, which prompted Cavalier to say, 'My taste buds will never forgive me if I don't make these delicious choices. Besides, I let loose with food once a week. Otherwise I'm disciplined.'

Smith refused any alcohol, but Cavalier ordered a bottle of his favourite Margaret River sauvignon blanc. Her demeanour sharpened. He could see she wanted to dispense with chitchat.

Cavalier asked her why she wanted to see him.

'Everything we discuss is confidential, right?' she said, dropping her voice. 'Mr Gregory assured me of that, right?'

'Of course, it works both ways. And by the way, you never met me.'

Smith looked perplexed.

'It's what my contacts in intelligence often say,' Cavalier said lightly.

'I am not in intelligence,' Smith said, her green eyes flashing with indignation.

'But you were, what, five years as a "researcher" in "Special Operations"?'

Smith went red.

'Come, Miss Smith, I have done my homework on you, as you have on me. I have very good contacts in the agency.' He sipped his wine. 'Why did you want to see me?'

The entrees arrived. Smith took a deep breath before saying: 'We have a special mission in Bangkok. We want to apprehend Jose Cortez.'

'How?'

'We have a plan in operation.'

'Then you don't need me.'

'We expect an extended project. We would be pleased to have you on board as a consultant; even part of the team.'

'I am not a great team player. I like to work solo.'

'We can offer you $100,000 for your input.'

'I need to know your plans.'

Smith studied his face. She kept her voice at a near whisper. 'Cortez is the de facto head of the cartel's operations in Thailand,' she said, 'although we don't think he'll last long in that position. We believe one of Mendez's two nephews will take over. They want their operations out of Asia and back with the main business in Mexico and the States. They wish to keep the big drug deals going, but at a distance. They want the organisation to look legitimate through property and company acquisitions, and Wall Street.'

'Nice background. The plan?'

'We know Cortez's personal interests. He plays chess at a high standard. He loves the violin, and he likes playing women like one.'

'Meaning he is a womaniser.'

'He has a Thai girlfriend, we believe. She is a pianist.'

'We know he is besotted with Talia Cruz …'

'The pop singer?'

Smith nodded. 'We believe he has funded her tequila business—Talia's Tequilas. She wants to branch into movies. They chat to each other on the phone, and the net. We've monitored it for six months. He has promised, now he is in charge of the cartel's South East Asian business, however temporarily, to put up a hundred million for a movie she will star in. He has written the script himself.'

'He was a paid assassin working for the cartel, not one of its directors.'

'After the demise of Mendez, the cartel was leaderless in Asia,' she said, eyeing him intently for any reaction. 'Then Cortez took over. In its desire to leave Thailand, the cartel has collected all the drug, gambling, people trafficking and prostitution proceeds in the region over a decade now. They have bought gold with it.'

'On the official market?'

'Some. They also have had plenty of people buying gold from the local village sellers, where, as you know, it is pure.'

'Smart. Gold holds and increases value. You can't go wrong by investing in it.'

'The Mexicans bought out complete shops' stocks in one burst of purchases. Maybe a hundred retail outlets' worth. An American with a Thai wife in the gold-selling business told him, and he informed us. That's how we learned about the bullion they have piled up.'

'Must weigh a tonne or two.'

'Or a lot more. We believe they may try transporting it to Mexico by cargo ship or plane. At the moment, Cortez is protecting the bullion. He has boasted to Talia Cruz that he can pay for the movie in gold.'

They concentrated on their soup for a minute before Smith said: 'Talia Cruz is coming to Bangkok to meet Cortez. We aim to isolate him from his bodyguard and arrest him.'

'Is Talia in on your project?'

'No. She has no idea. She will travel with a close friend, the

American actor Tyrone Risk. Risk is boasting to his associates that he will arrange an interview with Cortez. They arrive in Bangkok in a week.'

'How will you tackle it?'

'Cortez has already asked her to join him for dinner at, quote, "Thailand's most romantic restaurant".'

'Which one?'

'He hasn't said, yet.'

'In Bangkok that would be Gaggan or Nahm,' Cavalier mused, and added with a smile, 'if Cortez has a sense of humour, he may choose Eat Me.'

'Our sources suggest Gaggan.'

'Why would Talia want to mix with such a low-life as Jose Cortez?'

'It is weird. The fact that they are both Mexicans from the same region is part of the attraction. Notorious underworld figures in the States and Mexico seem to have an appeal for her.'

'The allure of bad guys is common; same as wild rock singers. But Tyrone Risk seems smart. Why is he involved?'

'He is on some sort of crusade to expose DEA as doing deals with the cartels,' Smith said with a cynical roll of the eyes. 'He thinks if he makes a documentary, with him interviewing Cortez, it will somehow expose this connection. It will be a specious doco if he achieves it, but it will give him much needed publicity. His wacky politics are turning off Hollywood film-makers. He hasn't made a good film in five years.'

'Are Cruz and he helping or hindering you?'

'They are not *intentionally* helping, but they are creating a way for us to isolate Cortez.'

Their main courses were served. They both made approving noises about their choices. At Cavalier's suggestion, they swapped small portions and made further appreciative grunts. Smith was careful to sample only the tiniest of morsels from his plate, yet appeared to be relaxing a fraction.

'You'll have to clarify how you would wish me to help,' he said, as a waiter filled his wine glass.

'In this case your special services will not be required. We just believe you'd be an asset in handling this. Your input would be appreciated. You know Thailand, the language, the Mexicans ...'

'Is the DEA handling this alone?'

Smith blinked and seemed reluctant to answer.

'I take it the *other* agency is in it?' Cavalier prompted.

'There are several in the game.'

'Hmm,' Cavalier leaned forward. 'I don't like too many operatives. I should imagine there will be more than a hundred personnel on this.'

'That's a reason we want someone with an overview.'

Cavalier gave a hint of a smile. 'Let me remind you of Operation Bomb-Bast,' he said. 'I take it you have heard of it?'

'Go on,' Smith said noncommittally.

'I am speaking about something most of your key people know anyway. "Bomb-Bast" was set to eliminate a certain leader in South East Asia who was rumoured to be close to developing an H-bomb and long-range missiles that could hit the west coast of your country. I was approached. I declined becoming connected. As it turned out, someone was shot but not the target. Hollywood heard rumours and made a comedy about it. It was a farce.'

'This won't be a farce,' Smith with a brisk shake of her head.

Cavalier paused. 'I know how your big agencies operate,' he said. 'They are very well funded and staffed. They have to spend huge budgets to justify allocations in the next financial year. Everyone wanted to be a player in removing that Asian leader. And this was an issue. Too many chiefs operating at cross purposes. You could see problems coming, and they came. The leader is still in power. His country is closer than ever to having a nuclear weapons system to attack the US.'

'The DEA is a major player on the current assignment.'

'You must liaise with the CIA, and as an educated guess, the NSA. Many people want the prize of Cortez's scalp.'

Smith sipped her herbal tea, no sugar, before saying, 'I lost two close friends to Cortez.'

'I am sorry to hear that. You want him badly. I believe the CIA lost operatives to him too.'

'It's more personal to me,' she said with a grim look, 'and it should be for you. Surely you are motivated? Cortez told the Thai police he has sworn to avenge Mendez's death.'

Cavalier ignored the inference. Perhaps she'd heard a rumour. Only one person really knew he had assassinated Mendez, and that was Jacinta Cin Lai. Even then, she had no concrete proof, only circumstantial evidence, which hinged around Cavalier avoiding police and escaping Thailand.

'I'm sorry. I can't operate with a cast of thousands and with some committee's plan. Your agencies like big productions. Cecil B DeMille, stand aside.'

'Is it money? Can we offer you more?'

'No.'

'I am authorised to pay what it takes on this project. Would $200,000 be of greater interest?'

'No. Frankly, I can't take the risk of going to Bangkok.'

'I can make an educated guess why. It's a reason I am speaking to you now.'

Cavalier did not respond. Instead he raised his glass and said: 'Naturally, I wish you the very best of luck.'

12

THE TAIL

After the meeting with Smith, Cavalier rode his Harley towards his condo building. He kept his speed down, aware that his bike would attract police and the usual on-the-spot fine, which the cop would pocket. He had also consumed enough alcohol to be over the limit. Cavalier had been caught once without a helmet and had paid a smaller fine.

It was after 10 p.m. and traffic was light. He could see a car in his mirrors, which had been on his tail since he left David's Kitchen. Instead of going straight to the condo, he stopped at Escudo, a nightclub on the river with attractive views. He sat in a dark corner with an eye on the door and fiddled with his phone, which was what six other diners were doing a discreet distance from him. He ordered a malt whisky.

After twenty minutes he left the club and rode on. The car, a new-looking Mazda, had waited for him. He rode past his condo and parked his bike near a 7-Eleven. Cavalier scurried down back lanes behind the local Nang Hoi market and waited across the Lamphun Road from his condo. The Mazda was not in sight. He moved along another hundred metres, crossed the road and made his way around the Holiday Inn to the Meng Rai Bridge. He straddled the fence, climbed onto the two-metre-high wall of white sandbags along the riverbank, and made his way two hundred and fifty metres along the wall to the Riverside Condo's car park.

Cavalier entered the building, nodded to the security guard and took one of the three inside elevators to his apartment. He kept the lights off and rummaged in a drawer for one of the two pairs of glasses that Gregory had given him. Cavalier tried them on and made adjustments. He eased onto a balcony and zeroed in on the bank opposite. He was amazed to be able to discern rodents, squirrels and even a snake when they moved. It was overwhelming at first. The bank of grass in front of buildings and pagodas seemed alive with squirming, writhing life and it took him several minutes to achieve a more discerning view. He was distracted by a car pulling up the other side of the Meng Rai Bridge, at the intersection where Pin had her accident.

He adjusted the glasses again. Two men emerged on the road behind buildings and then disappeared. Cavalier waited, scouring the area. He noted two figures moving into one of the open pagodas. They both had binoculars, and were looking into the Rajavej Hospital, Holiday Inn and the Riverside Condo.

Cavalier bent low and moved back inside the apartment. Using the glasses, he could still see them through windows. They did not appear to have weapons, at least not long-range rifles that could target him. He took his valise with the handgun and decided to confront these two pursuers. Cavalier hurried down the street to the 7-Eleven and drove his bike at speed over the Meng Rai Bridge. The Mazda sped off seconds before he arrived and he tailed it. He manoeuvred close enough to get glimpses of the men. He guessed they were Smith's men, and they certainly looked the part: Caucasian and in suits, which were rarely seen in Chiang Mai, especially in late March when the weather turned very hot. He had eliminated in his mind the other two outside possibilities from his encounters in the city on this trip. If the Mexicans were somehow onto him, they would not bother with the niceties of casing his apartment building, and they would be carrying weapons. If the two possible Indonesian terrorists had managed to learn his identity—which seemed an impossibility—they too would not concern themselves with surveillance.

At the lights leading to the main thoroughfare, the Chang Klan Road, he pulled up next to the car, and lifted the visor on his helmet. The two Caucasians in the vehicle were startled. Cavalier signalled for them to wind down the passenger window. They refused and drove on, trying to lose him, but he stayed right on their tail until they were stopped again at lights near the Chiang Mai night market. They lowered the passenger-side window.

'What do you want, Pal?' one of them said, his accent American.

'Tell Melody Smith to use professionals to tail me,' Cavalier said.

He then wheeled off in the direction he had come. Looking back in his mirror he could see the Mazda disappearing in the other direction. Cavalier was disturbed by this spying on him, but on reflection believed he understood the reason Smith would be creating a file on him for any number of reasons, not the least being that she would want something to have over him just in case he was ever to disclose anything of the discussion they'd had. Jacinta was ex-CIA, and he had dealt with them, indirectly and on two occasions directly, over thirty-five years. Cavalier knew the narrow and broad sweep of the agency's mentality. He now regretted having agreed to meet Smith. It manifested a sense of siege in him.

13

THE BEQUEATHING

Cavalier didn't see Ted for three days running. The wheel-chair had not been moved in that time. He made enquiries at the condo reception and was saddened to discover that Ted had died. The next day Cavalier found a brown box outside his apartment door, marked to his attention. He emptied the contents on a table, including ten thousand American dollars cash, another hundred thousand cash in Thai baht, Ted's two passports and other older ones, bank account booklets and other personal items. There was also a note from Ted.

Dear Laurent,

I am writing this before I am unable to write anymore.

You now have my personal effects. Whatever you find in the box is yours. I have notified my Thai lawyers of this.

As the sandwich board says, 'the end is nigh'—for me at least.

I have few regrets. I have been seeing out time since my beloved Rana died this time last year. I have never been one for much sentimentality.

I bored you with my travel stories but you can see from my passports that the locations were right. You'll notice too that my real name was not Ted Baines but Edward Blenkiron. So, in an odd way the real name will live on, while "Ted Baines" will leave this mortal coil. I told you the reason I took another ID. I was ashamed but your comments helped me transcend the guilt, at just the right time before I meet my maker, if there is one. You also helped me overcome worrying about what my action will mean to my reincarnation. Although a Buddhist, I've had my doubts about reincarnation. If it's real, I'll be sent back as a rat, maybe? I'd like to be a black cat, if I have a choice!

My Thai lawyers will be in touch over my meagre Estate. Spend it wisely Laurent, because there is not much of it!

I wish to thank you for enriching my last few months with your intelligence, friendship, kindness and humour.

I believe the Thais have gotten it right about Karma.

Have a good life,

Ted.

Cavalier found the American a warm, sagacious figure. The sadness was compounded by the sight of Ted's wheelchair, which he saw every day when he used the outside elevator that overlooked the condo's bike parking area, or when he jumped on the Harley standing next to it.

There was a poignant reminder in the chair's emptiness.

*

A week later, the two English-speaking Thai papers had stories about a gangland-style shoot-out in Bangkok's Klong Toey slum. At first, Cavalier thought nothing of it, but the newspaper and Internet coverage made him curious. It emerged that Americans were part of the incident; then Mexicans were said to be involved. Next, a major story broke that the Mexican singer Talia Cruz had been a victim in the shoot-out, taking a bullet in one of her long legs, which fortunately were well insured. She was under care in a Bangkok hospital. The actor Tyrone Risk had received a superficial bullet wound to an arm.

That was more than Cavalier needed to know. The stories grew and it was soon disclosed that Cruz and Risk had made contact with Jose Cortez. He had given Risk an interview and later dined with the 'stunning, quixotic' Cruz, as one paper described her. Unattributed net items speculated that these two showbiz people had been part of a DEA/CIA sting to snare Cortez.

Fascinated, Cavalier contacted Gregory by text to obtain more details. Gregory replied:

We understand it was a botched scam.

Any casualties?

No details but DEA lost two agents, CIA one.

Not the lovely MS, I hope.

No, she is okay. In fact, she is back in a bigger saddle.

Meaning?

The CIA ran the show. Because it failed, she and the DEA have taken charge of nabbing JC. I hear you knocked her back, correct?

How could anyone refuse her?

Seriously, Vic, she will be coming after you with an offer you can't refuse.

I've had them before. In any case, I'm retired.

This episode should please you on one level. All the key people—the thugs—from the cartel are certainly now all out of Chiang Mai. Still wise you stay incognito until the cousins can clean up the cartel mess.

Mess-up!

Yeah, but at least they're working on it. When and if they nab Cortez, you can consider coming home.

*

Cavalier arranged Ted's funeral in line with Buddhist traditions, on the seventh day after the death, at Wat Umong, a seven-hundred-year-old monastery located against the mountains of Doi Suthep, about a kilometre south of the main campus of Chiang Mai University. After the cremation, Cavalier watched monks chanting, wondering if he would be expected to join in the ritual of placing the small porcelain urn in the temple's beautiful gardens. A whiff of incense drifted through the building as Cavalier waited.

When it became apparent that he would not be needed, he joined the handful of people from the Riverside Condo, who filtered out of the temple. He decided to walk the grounds where monks were on benches reading, in clearings meditating, or feeding deer who roamed the gardens.

Cavalier felt a real peace in a moment of solace for the first time on the trip. He reflected on a friendship cut all too short and then attempted meditation, which he'd promised himself to re-engage with on this stay but had so far failed to do. He had been taught a twenty-minute version of basic transcendentalism by the mother of a former Indian woman friend. He realised his mind was in a state of flux and he couldn't keep certain thoughts from intruding. Ted, and his admission about having killed a man, was one. Cavalier reproached himself for not being more of a help by soothing the American's mind about this deed of so long ago. Maybe, perhaps he could have helped his will to live, and to enjoy life without the nagging, slow-burning guilt that Ted had admitted at times consumed him with grief and regret. But Cavalier had held back from speaking to him further. It brought up his own killing experiences that did not bother him, but which he'd rather not dwell on. Thoughts too of Pon encroached. He imagined her lying in some shallow Mexican grave with a thousand other victims of the drug cartel's inhumane activity, similar perhaps to the ones she had videoed herself in her proud declaration to him that she would become, like him, an investigative journalist. A third invasion of his meditative state were thoughts of Irina and Doug, the two possible Indonesian terrorists he'd spied on.

After a failed attempt to concentrate, he fell asleep.

14

RESURRECTION

By instinct or otherwise, Cavalier awoke and glanced at his watch. He had been asleep in the shade of a plane tree for two hours. He looked up and noticed a tall woman, her head covered in a green scarf and wearing large dark glasses, walking his way. Cavalier waited. She had to be coming to him; there was no other person within forty metres. He recognised the woman's lithe, sensual movement, yet could not place her. He reached for his valise, slid a zip to open it and reached in to grip the Glock 17. Its normally cold plastic handle was warm.

It wasn't until she was fifteen metres away that he recognised Jacinta Cin Lai, the former agent for the Thai Special Investigative Unit (SIU) with whom he had a loose, unwritten and unsaid alliance in his pursuit of Mendez. He eased the weapon from the valise and held it so she could see it. She stopped where she was, and slowly removed her glasses.

'I've come to help you,' she said. He scoured the area, his keen eyes searching for hidden accomplices. 'Don't you trust me?'

'I can't afford to trust anyone.'

Cavalier was mindful that last year she had been assigned by her former boss, Police Chief Aind Azelaporn, to protect Mendez, who over time she realised was Cavalier's target for assassination. She had been conflicted. Her two closest friends, one woman and one ladyboy, both Thai courtesans, had been murdered by the Mexican when he had brought them to Mexico for his nefarious pleasure. She had been their bodyguard on the trip and had failed to protect them from being guillotined.

Once she believed Cavalier may have been on a journalistic mission to investigate and expose Mendez for the murder of his daughter Pon, she had drawn him to Thailand where the Mexicans were in business. Jacinta wanted revenge for the deaths of her friends, which meant that she and Cavalier had more or less the same aim. At a critical point in Bangkok, she paved the way for the possibility of Mendez's liquidation. After a successful assignment, Cavalier made his escape to Vietnam with Jacinta devising a high-risk plan to facilitate his exit. Now, a year later, she had found him in his Chiang Mai hideaway.

Her manner was pleasant. He had seen her show aggression in the ring and elsewhere, but her body language was now unthreatening, even languidly relaxed.

She stood stock still, looking as stunning as ever in a white silk blouse that fluttered in the breeze, light-blue slacks and flat-heeled white shoes. Jacinta held a businesswoman's maroon-leather shoulder bag.

'Empty it on the ground,' Cavalier said, indicating the bag and remembering that she usually carried a small handgun in it. She obeyed and he stepped close to inspect the contents strewn on the grass.

'I'm unarmed,' she said and repeated, 'Victor, I've come to help you.'

'Drop your trousers,' he said.

Jacinta at first looked defiant. She glanced around her. A monk was walking in the other direction about forty metres away. When he waved his gun at her, she slowly undid the trousers.

'I am shy,' she said. 'I'm not wearing knickers.'

'Drop them,' he repeated.

Jacinta obeyed, pulling down her shirt so that it just covered her private parts as the trousers dropped to the grass, exposing her long legs. He moved closed. With the gun trained on her, he slipped his hand under her buttocks and inside her thighs.

'See, nothing to declare,' she said, and with a nervous giggle added, 'nothing.'

Cavalier motioned for her to pull up her trousers and to replace the bag contents. He put his gun back in the valise, but did not zip it, mindful of her incredible Muay Thai boxing skills. Before he could react, she had stepped forward and kissed him on both cheeks. Cavalier gave a nervous smile as he looked around.

'Don't worry, I'm alone,' she said, placing her arm in his and beginning to walk. Jacinta scrutinised him.

'Hmm, you are looking good, considering,' she said with a sensual smile, 'if I may say so, "the life you have been leading has etched itself into your face".'

'Where did you get that line? It's a cliché.'

'I read it in three of your biographical books on war generals. You said in an interview I picked up on YouTube that it was your signature cliché in all your tomes.'

'How did you find me?' he asked, perplexed and still cautious.

'It wasn't easy,' she said, removing her sunglasses again. 'I figured you'd keep writing. I scoured Australian papers and found the byline Laurent V Blanc. It sounded like a French name. There was never a source for his—your—online articles. I did a bit of hacking; a lot actually, over about six weeks. I found a server in Russia. I didn't think you'd be there. Then I had the tough task of tracing your hidden ID. I figured you were either in Australia or France. When digging with this premise I ended up nowhere. Then I had a lateral thinking whim: where would anyone tracking you least expect to find you? *Thailand,* of course. And going along that path further I began to scour Chiang Mai.'

Cavalier shook his head in amazement. Jacinta continued:

'I knew you wouldn't stay at Centara Hotel again. That would not be smart. Remember, I am an expert hacker. No one has my skills, certainly not in Thailand. I knew you would have Wi-Fi—to watch cricket on TV. I guessed you would have the same signal for your personal computer and not just use hotel or condo lobbies. You engaged a Thai provider. Then bingo! I found you! Well, nearly. You had to be receiving signals in either of three buildings—the Rajavej hospital, Holiday Inn or the Riverside Condo. I started with the Riverside Condo and the very helpful lady agent there named Joy told me there was only one person fitting your description in the apartments. I flew in this morning. Joy told me you were at a funeral here.'

Cavalier had rarely felt more vulnerable.

As if reading his mind, Jacinta added: 'You shouldn't worry. First, the hacker-tracker has to be looking for you. Second, they have to have my skills; and third, they need educated, very good luck. Who else, for instance, would know of your fluency in French and Thai? You are safe, my friend, Khun Victor.'

'You went to all that trouble to trace me,' he said, his eyes still scanning the monastery grounds. 'Why?'

'I had a very good reason,' she said as they hesitated outside a 'spiritual theatre' of paintings, which depicted floating, yellow and purple-robed monks floating in an azure star-studded universe. They had a quick look inside before walking in a field of reproductions of ancient Indian Buddhist sculpture. Jacinta guided him to a stone bench and invited him to sit with her. She took a folder from her satchel, removed photographs from it and handed them to Cavalier.

'You know who that is?' she asked, pointing to a female practising piano with a lean violinist, who had his back to the camera. Cavalier blinked, held the photo close and exclaimed:

'It looks like ... it could be ... my daughter Pon! The hair is shorter ... different colour ... her face is fuller ... but it is nine years since I've seen her; seven years since she disappeared.' Cavalier stared at Jacinta, his expression demanding an explanation.

'Please stay calm, Victor,' she said softly. 'It was me who sent you that terrible video, which made it look as if Pon was executed.

'Beheaded!' he said, his voice trembling.

'Yes. I believed it was genuine. But I've since learnt that it was doctored by Mendez and Cortez to make it *appear* as if Pon had been murdered, and then passed on to me via Mendez's cousin Ronaldo. She wasn't killed. Cortez wanted to make it seem as if she were dead. He was desperate to take her for himself. He figured this would stop anyone, such as an investigator like you, coming after her.'

'Pon is with Cortez?'

Jacinta sighed, looked him in the eye and nodded.

'How do you know?' he demanded.

'I don't want you to judge me, please.'

'Just tell me,' he said, looking around. He was on edge in a surreal moment.

'I had a hunch that you were a professional and could deal with Mendez. You did.' Cavalier kept his eyes on Jacinta, looking for integrity in her words, or something else. 'This time I have the true evidence about her with my own eyes. I took those photos. She plays piano with him. She is a captive.'

'Go on,' Cavalier urged.

'When Police Chief Azelaporn was fired by the junta for corruption, just after you escaped to Vietnam, I was dismissed a fortnight later. I was out of work for nearly a year, until Azelaporn offered me a job recently.'

'To do what?'

'Act as an escort.'

'A high-class hooker?' Cavalier asked, his words laced with sarcasm.

'No, a security job. Azelaporn was hired by the Mexicans to help exit Thailand with their gold. He hired me to assist him. I had sent all my money back to my family. I needed work. I did not want to box again.'

'You're protecting the bloody Mexicans?'

'My job is to help facilitate their exit,' Jacinta said defensively. 'I hate what I am doing; it's a short-term project. I need the money.'

'How will you get them out?'

'Cortez was petrified that Seals would be used to attack him. He will not leave the hotel he is in. He has a phalanx of bodyguards. He won't go near an airport. Azelaporn suggested two choices—by ship and by train. He has chosen the latter—a train to Singapore. From there he will load the gold—the proceeds of their activities in the region—into a frigate owned by his cartel, which will take him home.'

'Which train?'

'There is only one that could handle the consignment: the *Bangkok Express*. He has bought two carriages at the rear where the gold will be stored and his bodyguard will stay. He has booked a further carriage for his own use.'

'You are saying that my daughter is alive and well? Please don't play with this, I beg you.'

'I never have "played" with you.'

'How is she?' he asked anxiously. 'She looked a lot different.'

'She is so beautiful, but I fear ...' her voice trailed off.

'What?'

'She really doesn't engage. Stays in the background. I think he keeps her drugged. But she plays the piano like an angel. She seemed on a real "high" when I watched a performance at the Millennium Hotel.'

Cavalier sat with his head between his hands.

'She is his personal chattel; his prisoner?'

'It seems so.'

'You think she is drugged. On what?'

'You name it, the cartel has it. They are in the business.'

After a several seconds' silence, he asked: 'Why are you informing me of this?'

'Would you expect me to hide it from you?'

Cavalier seemed shaken and bewildered. Overriding this was the elation of knowing that his daughter was alive, if Jacinta was telling the truth. He had no real reason to doubt her, given their connection over the assassination of Mendez. Jacinta had not aided and abetted Cavalier's mission. Yet she had facilitated it and had helped protect him during his escape. He had faith in her. Yet there was a flicker of caution in his mind. She was now being paid to protect the man who had taken his daughter captive.

'Can I trust you?' he asked, searching her eyes.

'You have before,' Jacinta said, touching his forearm. 'If Cortez and Azelaporn knew I was here, they would kill me, no question about it. I'm on a secret trip. No one knows where I am.'

Cavalier was quiet for several minutes, watching a monk feeding a deer.

Jacinta could sense the dials of his braining spinning. She filled the void: 'There's another thing. In the two weeks after Azelaporn was fired, I was unofficially in charge of the police while the junta figured out who would replace him. I had you and all the other suspects, including your aliases, taken off the wanted lists. You are no longer officially wanted for anything in Thailand, although keeping a disguise is a wise move while you're here. Azelaporn still has strong contacts inside the Force. If he could somehow nail you as Mendez's killer, he would be hoping to restore his image and reputation, although I doubt any government, especially a military junta, would ever allow him back in the Force. The police are their main rivals.'

Cavalier had been listening, yet was preoccupied by the news about his daughter.

'Give me time to digest this,' he finally said. 'Where are you staying?'

'With you perhaps? That is, if you have a spare bed.'

'I do. Would that be wise?'

'Not if you secrete me in your apartment.'

Cavalier considered her for a moment.

'I have a flight back to Bangkok tomorrow morning,' Jacinta said. 'It would be better if I were not registered somewhere or seen staying in a hotel.'

He continued to stare.

'I asked you twice before if you trusted me,' she said.

'Trust? Trust is instinctive, don't you think? It is not something divisible. Either you do or you don't.'

'And?'

'I am concerned that you are back with that dangerous sleaze Azelaporn. *And* you are protecting Jose Mendez.'

'I am sorry if you feel that way. But I have a big family to support. I once could do it with my police salary and the annual boxing match. Not now.'

'Didn't you get a good payout from smashing that Russian last year?'

'I gave it all to my family and the families of my two murdered friends.'

'Guilt money for not protecting them?'

'Something like that. This assignment is for just a few weeks. After that, well, I won't ever work for Azelaporn again.'

Cavalier nodded. He seemed to be softening.

'I may be able to help you save your daughter,' she said. 'You must understand that we Thais can separate payment for necessities from moral imperatives and loyalty to those worthy of it, or otherwise.'

'Hmm,' Cavalier mused.

'Did I not assist you in Bangkok when, if I had wanted money, I could have arrested you? Even Azelaporn would have given me a bonus. And then there was your escape last year ...'

'Okay,' he said with the hint of a smile, 'and anyway, knowing you are in the apartment will allow me a decent night's sleep.'

'Thank you.'

'I will never forget the way you despatched four thugs in my front garden in Melbourne. Not to mention that Russian twice your size in Bangkok.'

'And I shall never forget the way you despatched Leonardo Mendez in Nana Plaza,' Jacinta said, holding his arm and searching his eyes for a reaction.

'That wasn't me,' he said, deadpan.

'You are not saying it was that Swede, Lars Nystrom?' she asked.

'No, I don't know anyone by that name,' he said, 'but clearly, he was your number one suspect.'

Despite his remark about Jacinta's presence allowing him to sleep, he hardly had a wink. The news that Pon was alive caused him to be restless for most of the night as he wrestled with what he could do to save her. Related, deeper thoughts intruded. Cavalier tossed and turned over the final reason that he and Pin had split. Their relationship had been fractured, but not completely broken. They had drifted apart. Pon, their one biological child, had been the glue when their work and interests had caused suspicions. Cavalier wondered about his wife's relationship with a medico-colleague, who seemed to have become more than a companion. And Pin had worried about the clandestine nature of Cavalier's work beyond journalism. They were both workaholics. His lengthy time away from Thailand on assignments—and his need to keep his Melbourne base—did not help. Pon's apparent demise had led to their differences becoming irreconcilable. Seven years later, there was no going back.

Yet now that it seemed Pon was alive, he mulled over the what-might-have-beens. Since the split he had not taken up seriously with anyone else. His professional activity and travel were always the excuse for avoiding intimacy or commitment. There was now a void in his personal life. He wondered if he were capable of filling it again. Yet relationship concerns were now a minor distraction from the task at hand, which would need all his focus: how to save his daughter.

15

TRAIN OF THOUGHT

'What are your thoughts about Pon?' Jacinta asked, when they sat down at a breakfast cafe outside Chiang Mai after taking different taxis from the condo.

'I am going to rely a lot on your intelligence,' he said. 'Where does the *Bangkok Express* run?'

'From Bangkok west to Kanchanaburi, then south through the Thai border with Malaysia, on to Kuala Lumpur and finally to Singapore.'

'What dates?'

'It leaves Bangkok on 24 April and runs for three nights, ending up in Singapore on 27 April.'

'That's in less than two weeks. What do you know about the train?'

'It's run by a French company, the Belle Époque Group, which has hotels and trains in many countries. The Express is very upmarket. It has magnificent dining. They do their best off-train—with stops in Kanchanaburi, Penang and Kuala Lumpur—to enhance the experience and also justify the expense.'

'Which is?'

'For the best carriage births, thirty thousand dollars for the three nights for one.'

'Not cheap.'

'The clientele are well heeled.'

'Retirees ticking off a bucket list?'

'That, and a curious variety of others.'

'Could you send me a guest list?'

'I'll see what I can do. The train is not filled yet,' Jacinta said.

'Could I make the trip, do you think?'

'Passports will be examined very thoroughly. Cortez is paranoid and Azelaporn is not much better after your handi-work last year.'

'You mean that of Mr Nystrom?'

'Pardon me, yes. I hear they will interrogate every passen-ger before boarding. Of course, it will be light.'

'You believe passengers will put up with that?'

'They'll have to,' Jacinta shrugged. 'Most travellers are used to all sorts of privations with terrorism everywhere these days. This will be sugar-coated, with champagne and snacks served beforehand.'

'Hmm. I'll need detail on the train. Where was it built?'

'In Thailand in the late nineteen-sixties. First run as the *Eastern Spirit* in Northern Thailand. When Belle Époque took the train over in 1990 it went through an extensive internal rebuild and fit-out.'

'Who designed the new version?'

'His name is Paul Witowski. He managed to create a blend of Asia and colonial pomp. He was inspired by the 1932 movie, *Shanghai Express*, starring Marlene Dietrich.'

Cavalier interjected as his brain raced ahead:

'I'll need detail about carriage hallway widths, carriage sizes, if there are adjoining berths with a common door. I want to know if there is an observation car.' He looked at her intently. 'I want to know if it is feasible for a man to move outside the carriages; how many train guards there will be and how they are armed; that sort of thing.'

'Could you text me a list of your requirements?'

He nodded and asked: 'Are you completely with me this time?'

She smiled and touched his hand.

'I am,' she said.

'It will be trickier than last time. Make sure Azelaporn pays you up front.'

'I already have.'

'Good. May I ask how much?'

'Eight hundred thousand baht.'

'You have all of it?'

'Half.'

'Okay. If I decide to do anything, I'll pay you at least twice as much for your assistance.'

'You don't have to …'

'Oh, yes I do. I am sure to need you. And you are putting your life on the line.'

16

SECOND PITCH

Cavalier was in an agitated mood in the evening. He watched an old YouTube interview with Sean Connery and listened to an Astrud Gilberto album in an attempt to relax. At midnight he dressed and took his Harley on a traffic-free ride into the notorious bar and massage parlour area of Chiang Mai's Loi Kroh Road. He found the Coyote bar owned by the Englishman, Paul Biggs, whom he'd met at Thai language school. He was drinking with the big German, Joachim. They greeted him cordially. Cavalier ordered a beer. Adele was on three TV screens singing 'Skyfall'. Three women in the bar were quick to join him, but he was in no mood for carousing.

The news about his daughter had disturbed him greatly, coming so close to the death of Ted. First and foremost, he was elated to learn she was alive. The second, nagging thought was that she had been a captive of Cortez for seven years. Cavalier knew that she was partial to drugs and had experimented, much against his wishes. He reflected that she could be impulsive, similar to both him and her mother. He feared that Cortez had taken advantage of that.

Cavalier downed the beer and asked for another. He told the bartender to play Leonard Cohen singing 'Dance me to the end of love'. The women circled again, hoping that he would take one of them for an hour, or the night. He offered a drink to one, called Tuk. She wore a long purple dress and was more mature than the others. Cavalier danced with her and then invited Tuk to play a game of billiards. A Russian, about a hundred and ninety centimetres tall and around a hundred and twenty kilograms, watched the game with growing agitation. Tattoos covered his every limb and throat, which featured a prominent, ugly swastika.

Cavalier played a slack game and let Tuk get close. At the end of it, the Russian shouted at Cavalier: 'My woman!'

'Tell you what, sport,' Cavalier said, 'I'll play you for her.'

Both Paul and Joachim made signs that he should not further antagonise the Russian, who grunted, ignored Cavalier's offer of a handshake and prepared the balls for a game. The Russian indicated he wanted to play Tuk. She shook her head.

Cavalier tapped his own chest and pointed to the Russian, who begrudgingly agreed. Cavalier indicated the Russian should break first, and then asked the bar woman to play 'Uptown funk' on the videos over and over during the game. He began to dance with another of the girls while the Russian slotted two balls and missed a third. Cavalier stopped dancing and took so long surveying the table that the Russian complained. Much to the appreciation of onlookers, Cavalier then proceeded to slip around the table in rhythm with Bruno Mars on the screens, while slotting every ball with a mix of aggression and subtlety that had every person in the bar watching and applauding.

After every pocket, he would glance at the action on the screens. Finally, he potted the black for a win. The Russian again refused to shake hands.

'Where did you learn to play like that?' Paul asked.

'It's obvious,' Joachim said. 'Bruno Mars taught him.'

They all grinned.

'That sort of stroke play looks professional,' Paul persisted. 'C'mon, where'd you learn?'

'You saw the movie *Casablanca*?' Cavalier asked. The others nodded. 'Remember when Rick said, "Of all the bars in all the world, you had to come into mine"? Well, I've been in most of those bars that had pool tables.'

Tuk moved towards Cavalier. The Russian manhandled her, then pushed her hard in the chest. Cavalier stepped between them. The Russian picked up a pool cue and swung it at him. Cavalier ducked and was caught a glancing blow on the back with a force that snapped the cue. The Russian lumbered at him, shoving him into a corner. After weaving away from the heavy-armed lunges, which demonstrated the Russian was more thug than fighter, Cavalier let go two snap punches in the Russian's big stomach. It winded him. Cavalier stepped side on and hit him hard in the right ribcage. The big man wheeled around, trying to face Cavalier, who had outmanoeuvred him again. Cavalier struck, this time in the left ribcage.

The Russian was almost immobilised. Even through the alcohol haze, he was hurting. Cavalier slapped him hard across the left cheek, then the right. He slipped behind the big man and kicked him in his huge derrière. The Russian went down on all fours, gasping. Cavalier moved side on, and pushed him in the side. The Russian rolled onto his back and was not able or willing to get up.

Two of his mates approached Cavalier, without any enthusiasm for taking him on, having witnessed his restrained demolition of their larger companion. Paul—known in the bar as 'Bigus'—and Joachim, both nearly as large as the Russian but much fitter, intervened, stopping the altercation going any further.

Cavalier's first inclination was to leave, but Paul and Joachim insisted on buying him a drink. He was distracted by the Russian's mates demanding beer for them and a black coffee for their stricken companion.

'Ask politely,' Paul said. 'Put your money on the table and I'll consider your request. Oh, and the pool cue will cost you another two thousand baht.'

The Russians paid for the cue, put their hurt mate's arms over their shoulders and dragged him away.

'Have the police been called?' Cavalier asked, loudly to be heard over the blaring music.

Paul ordered that it to be lowered and replied with a laugh: 'Good heavens no. This happens almost every night.' He handed Cavalier a beer. He had only taken a few sips when three local 'tourist police' arrived to investigate.

'They must have been informed by a rival bar,' Paul said to Cavalier. 'Let me handle it.'

Paul told the police that it had been a minor scuffle. He slipped them five hundred baht not to make a report. The police left.

'You can handle yourself, my friend,' Joachim said.

'He was drunk,' Cavalier said.

'You toyed with him.'

'He'd had a skinful. His blood pressure would be low. A solid punch to the jaw, or his head hitting the concrete, could have killed him. When the blood doesn't have the force to reach his brain, he's in trouble.'

'If the blood could find it,' Paul laughed, raising his glass to Cavalier.

'He is a really big, nasty guy,' Joachim remarked. 'Paul's had trouble with him before. They are Russian mafia from Pattaya, trying to muscle into the bar business here.'

'Do you box?' Paul asked Cavalier.

'You sound like Ernest Hemingway,' he said with a smile, as Paul's attractive, ultra-shapely partner and bar owner, Oh, snuggled up to him.

'I have just started learning Muay Thai with Joachim in the early morning at the boxing ring here,' Paul said. 'You should come.'

'Hmm, might join you.' Cavalier got up to leave and shook hands with them. 'Thank you for intervening.'

Cavalier walked down a dark alley, ignored offers from street girls and jumped on his Harley. As he adjusted his helmet, he heard a roar of bikes at the top of the alley. The two Russians who had come to the aid of their companion when he was felled called out to Cavalier. In a split second, he made a decision to take flight, not fight, knowing that a second brawl could be dangerous for him if the police arrived again. He rode off. The Russians gave chase. Cavalier picked up speed and headed for the motorway that took him north out of the city on the way to the mountains. The night air was cool as he built the bike's speed.

Cavalier shook off his pursuers after about ten minutes. He kept the speedometer hovering at a hundred and ten kilometres an hour until he reached a lake that he had visited before. It was surrounded by huts, which by day made an open-air restaurant.

The place was deserted at night. He stopped his bike near the water's edge and lay on his back in one of the huts. Cavalier glanced at his phone. There were messages.

The most important was from Gregory, who had sent a text: 'MS wants to talk to you again.'

'After that botched sting?'

'It seems. She sounded on edge. Do you want to see her?'

'She should book in at the Holiday Inn on Lamphun Road. I'll find her.'

'The CIA director of that project is out. She is in charge of a new operation and she has a big DEA war chest. If you decide to do anything, you may name your own price. Of course, I never told you that.'

Cavalier switched off his phone. He took a jacket from his bike and decided to cat-nap in spite of the protests from a score of croaking frogs. After an hour he drove steadily back to the condo without incident. He parked his bike as usual next to Ted's wheelchair. A black cat was curled up on the seat. It stood up and greeted him as he dismounted the Harley. Cavalier stroked the cat. He smiled to himself as it preened, arched and meowed enough to show it was a good communicator. It brought back the words from Ted's note about his desire if reincarnated:

'I'd like to be a black cat.'

*

Two days later, Melody Smith returned to Chiang Mai and booked into the Holiday Inn. She was doing a workout in the gym there when Cavalier came in. He switched on one of the TV monitors, flicked to a US news channel and turned it up. The presidential election was on. Loud cheering and clapping accompanied a speech by a Republican front runner. Cavalier climbed onto a cross-trainer two metres from Smith, who was working hard on a stationary bike.

'Oh, you are staying at the hotel?' she asked, climbing from the bike and wiping sweat from her brow. She moved close to Cavalier, wiped her face on a towel and shook hands. Cavalier could smell her perspiration, mixed with too much of an expensive perfume.

'Why did you have me followed?' he asked.

'I wanted to keep track in case we could rethink a deal. My agents were most impressed. After our dinner, you disappeared.'

'They nearly found me.'

'Yeah,' Smith said with a half-smile, 'makes me think you'd better help apprehend Jose Cortez before he tracks you down.'

Two Japanese men and a European couple entered the gym and began working out.

'Can you meet me in the pool area after the workout?' Cavalier asked. 'It's cool today. Only a few will be swimming at this hour.'

A half-hour later, they met by the hotel pool, Cavalier still in his gym gear and Smith in a one-piece swimsuit. The sun had peeped through the cloud. Two Chinese guests had moved into the pool area wearing their hotel dressing gowns. They shouted in Chinese at the door and were soon joined by a teenage boy. A Thai waiter brought Cavalier and Smith black coffees. The aroma was strong. Cavalier savoured it as if it were a top wine and smiled.

'I love the smell of coffee in the morning,' he said, 'much better than napalm.'

'Guess you read about the Risk, Talia Cruz event,' she said, ignoring his light remark, and keeping her sunglasses on, despite the sky being grey and cloudy.

'Reads like another failed operation,' he said.

'Not all of it.'

'Should have used the Seals.'

'It was not their kind of project. They can't barge into a foreign country and densely populated area and take on a force of armed desperadoes.'

'They could have been isolated at an airport, or a road ...'

Smith shook her head.

'You don't know the terrain, the logistics, the circumstances. It needed special agents. It was a big op.'

After a pause, Cavalier asked: 'Why didn't it work then? Too many chiefs?'

'There is only one now ... me,' Smith said in a half-acknowledgement that Cavalier was correct. 'I want you on the team.'

'Told you, I'm not a team guy,' he said, and then, as if it was an afterthought, added: 'I'd consider working with you, and you alone. It would have to be my plan.'

'Can't do it,' she said, biting her lip.

'Then there is no deal.'

Smith sipped her coffee. 'May I ask what changed your mind? You were set against a few days ago.'

'That's my business.'

'I can offer you a lot to be in on this,' she said. 'We need a good squad.' She paused. 'Look, you can be my number two, okay? This means I will be acting extrajudicially. We are not, by law, allowed to hire mercenaries.'

'I am formulating a concept. It needs just one operative.'

'You have a plan?' she said with a half-laugh of cynicism.

'I'm working on it.'

'Cortez is in Bangkok. How can you—?'

'I know how he is going to leave.'

Smith removed her glasses.

'How?'

'That stays with me at the moment. I have someone on the inside.'

'You're bluffing!'

'You think so?' Cavalier put down his coffee cup. He stood and added: 'The figure is two million US dollars for my services.' Smith's expression twitched between shock and disdain, 'one million up front and another million once the job is done, with seventy thousand expenses on top. Take it or leave it.'

Cavalier half-bowed, left the pool area and returned to his condo. Twenty minutes later, he had another text from Gregory.

'MS is very steamed up about you. She wanted more information on you. Gave her nothing, of course. But she wants you, I ascertained that. Whatever you said, hang tough. She asked me twice if I knew how the Mexicans were leaving Bangkok. She is the top dog on the project. It puts her under pressure to deliver. I'm told that she presented such a strong case to control the show that she now must deliver, or be sidelined to a dead-end street, career-wise.'

'How long should I give her to respond?'

'She'll have to gain higher approval, whatever your demands, and especially if you want to go solo.'

'MS mentioned my request to go it alone?'

'Yes. I told her you only operated that way.'

'Thank you.'

'I also said you were the best in the business.'

'That deserves a beer or two.'

17

SWEET & SOUR MELODY

Melody Smith agreed to Cavalier's terms with one caveat: that he committed to involving her team at some point in his schemes.

'You'll need back-up,' she said in a face-to-face meeting, sitting on a sofa in the lounge of her Holiday Inn suite. 'You can't go it totally alone.' She switched on her phone recorder. 'Must have this for legal purposes.' She asked for his bank details.

Cavalier didn't react, but he was uncomfortable. He took a notepad from his valise, wrote the details on a page and handed it to her, saying, 'As soon as I know the first tranche is in the account, I'll implement the plan.'

'Are you going to say how the Mexicans are leaving Thailand?'

'Have you considered the options?' Cavalier asked.

'We figured they'd use a vehicle convoy to a port some-where. Bangkok would seem the most obvious point.' She looked at Cavalier. He remained impassive. 'They couldn't do it by plane unless they left the gold, or used a squad of trans-porters to drive it out.'

'I'll let you know in a week, maybe two. It's going to take that long for me to put something in place.'

'I have thirty agents ready. We need to know from a logistical point of view.'

'Your aim is to eliminate Cortez, right?'

Smith pointed to the phone, indicating her remarks would be for the record. 'The priority is to apprehend him and his men. Given his record of extreme violence, we must be prepared for casualties in any encounter.'

'Meaning you will take him and them dead or alive?'

'No, that is Wild West talk. We must work within the letter of the current law.'

'Ok, I think I understand,' Cavalier said, nodding and pointing at the phone, 'and you wish to grab the gold.'

'"Grab" is not a word we'd use,' Smith said with manufactured indignation.

'Secure the gold then?'

'That contraband has been gained from illegal drug deals, people trafficking, prostitution, arms deals and even gambling. Some of the drugs end up in the United States, which comes under DEA jurisdiction.'

'Even though all the cartel's deals are done outside the US, in this case?'

'The role of the DEA is to bust the big illegal cartels, if they have anything to do with the US, period. The Mendez cartel is still the biggest player in the US. If we break it and round up key operatives within it, then we are doing our job.'

Smith sounded as if she were making an Agency political broadcast. Cavalier had no doubt the recording would be used to impress DEA lawyers and DEA chiefs, or even politicians at a future Congressional hearing.

'Let me say this,' he said, picking up on the political theme as he leaned forward and spoke closer to her phone. 'Once my plan is in place, I'll let you know what is happening, even if you are not needed for the prime objective.'

They chatted for another half-hour, Smith attempting to lead Cavalier into talking about his achievements, which was to reassure both her and her superiors of his capacities, especially with the funds that would be invested in him. He divulged nothing beyond his travels as a journalist.

Frustrated, she asked him straight out: 'Did you assassinate Leonardo Mendez?'

'Why do you ask?' he replied with a calm expression.

'We were informed on good authority.'

'By whom? Where?'

'I can't disclose that.'

'You have to be careful of rumours.'

'The Thai police say it was an incredibly well planned hit. They think the Mexicans know who did it. Cortez, we hear, believes it was an Australian posing as a Swede, who stayed at a hotel looking into the Bangkok's Nana Plaza where Mendez was assassinated.'

'What evidence is there?'

'Cortez learnt it from the former Thai Police Chief Aind Azelaporn, whom he has hired for protection in Thailand, and, we assume, to deliver him out of the country safely.'

'And how did you learn this?'

'From contacts in the Thai police,' Smith said. Scrutinising him, she asked: 'Did you, or did you not, eliminate Leonardo Mendez?'

'No,' he said, staring her down. She stopped the recording.

'I was kinda hoping you'd say "yes". But you would say "no", wouldn't you?'

'Sorry to disappoint. I'm just a journalist. Have been for more than thirty-five years.'

'Nice cover,' she said, with the only unforced smile he'd seen from her. 'Just like Clark Kent, mild-mannered reporter for the *Daily Planet.*' Cavalier still gave nothing away. 'Can you give me some idea of your plan?'

'I'll divulge more when the first tranche is in the account,' Cavalier said, 'in addition to the seventy thousand expenses, as agreed.'

'You must itemise all expenses,' Smith said, 'and collect receipts.'

She took a small plastic pack from her bag and handed it to him.

'You'll need this,' she said, 'for verifying you have completed your project. Its nickname is—excuse the expression—KK, for Killing Kit. It has been perfected ever since we destroyed Bin Laden in Pakistan.'

Cavalier opened the pack.

'Has a very new feel about it,' he said, 'fresh out of the oven.' He wrinkled his nose. 'What's that smell? It's like formaldehyde.'

Smith smiled. 'The first of its kind the DEA has had,' she said, 'and yes, the plastic cover has a special cleaning preservative. Makes it fingerprint-proof.'

'How?'

'You'd have to grip it very hard with your fingers to leave a print.'

Cavalier was impressed.

'It has three syringes of different colours, two swabs, a small camera about half the size of a mobile phone and two pairs of surgical gloves,' Smith said. 'The swabs are for wiping the inside of the target's mouth for DNA verification. The yellow syringe is a tranquiliser; the red syringe is for a blood sample; and the blue syringe is for a lethal injection.' She took a breath. 'We'd prefer you acquired both a mouth swab and blood sample, but either will do. The camera is fairly new. If you press the button marked "1" you make the shot on the screen, just like a mobile phone camera. The innovation is button 2. If you press that from about one metre above the body, it will photograph the entire body of a person up to two hundred centimetres, regardless of whether it is the frame or not. We need photos of the face, profile and body to complete the ID.'

Cavalier exhaled audibly. 'That is going to take a few minutes,' he said with a grimace.

'It must be done,' Smith said. 'We prefer you used the blue syringe—'

'For the kill?'

'It is preferable to a bullet. If you shoot him in the head, it may make recognition difficult.' She paused and eyeballed him. 'The person who liquidated Leonardo Mendez gave new meaning to the term. I'm told face recognition was not possible. He did not have one.'

Cavalier smiled thinly.

She added coldly: 'Also gives new meaning to the expression, "saving face".'

Smith kept staring, always assessing. If she wasn't probing with questions, her eyes were forever exploring, looking for the 'give', the tiny mannerism or twitch that would expose a weakness, or the truth.

'May not be able to reach that close …' Cavalier muttered.

'You'll have to, for full recog and photos.'

'Hmm,' he said, 'I'll work it out.'

'As soon as you can, email us the photo of your success and guard the swab and/or blood sample.' Smith was enjoying Cavalier's uncertainty. 'You have used a syringe, I take it?'

He nodded.

'You find a blood vessel in the crook of the arm—' Smith began.

'Not the easiest place,' Cavalier interjected. He was imagining himself in the dark somewhere, 'but it will all right on the night.'

*

At just before midnight, he felt like a bike ride to Wat Phra, the temple sixteen hundred and fifty metres up at the top of the rugged mountain Doi Suthep. He liked to wai the Buddha at the 24-metre-tall gold-plated monument, one of Thailand's holiest sites. At this late hour, there would be fewer worshippers in attendance. The space, speed, and lack of traffic on the exhilarating ride always allowed him to think his way through issues. He wore a black jacket, helmet and night goggles and placed his Glock 17 in an inside pocket.

Just as he was driving off he noticed he was nearly out of petrol, so he turned into the Caltex station opposite his condo. One of six attendants filled his tank and Cavalier was about to leave when two farang bikers slipped in, next to two other bowsers. He was adjusting his helmet when he realised the new arrivals were the Russians who had chased him a few nights earlier. Cavalier's first instinct was to ride back across the road and into the safety of his condo. But if they spotted him, they would know where he lived. He turned his back on them and strode into the Tops store to buy a bottle of water. When he came out after a few minutes, one of the Russians pointed at him. The two Russians conferred as Cavalier strode across the petrol station forecourt. They seemed to have made up their minds that they had recognised him when he jumped on his Harley. One began running at him, knife in hand. Cavalier kick-started his bike and burst past the yelling Russian. Cavalier glanced back to see them giving chase. He hugged the river and ran two red lights in a scramble to reach the highway running north to the base of the mountain. The Russians nearly collided with a truck in their scramble to catch him. On the earlier pursuit, Cavalier had done everything to avoid confrontation so soon after he had manhandled their companion. This was different. The threat was not going away unless he took action. He began the mountain climb with the Russians only seventy or eighty metres behind. Cavalier put his foot down as he wound the bike up the steep slope, leaving his pursuers two hundred and soon three hundred metres behind. The road had tight turns and sharp inclines. It had him cornering at forty-five degrees, past a dog lying perilously close to the road's edge, and two young farang on foot. He took a risk on a blind turn, speeding past a taxi red car, which struggled through the gears. Its driver hugged the low left-hand railing that formed a flimsy barrier to a cliff edge leading to an abyss of heavy, tangled undergrowth.

The Harley's lights bounced over a large billboard picture of Thailand's king and queen and a dirt road leading to a small temple. Cavalier slowed the bike near a bend in the road where he had stopped months earlier to do some shooting practice with his Glock 17 in the rainforest. He then braked hard, skidded off the road and scrambled behind a two-metre-high rock.

Cavalier waited, heart pounding. He could hear the whine of the two bikes as they strained up the mountain. He moved from behind the rock, and took aim at the bikes as they drew close. He fired twice. The first shot hit the front tyre of the lead bike, bursting it and throwing the driver onto the road. The second shot smashed into the back tyre of the second bike, shattering it, and causing the second rider to slam into the rock. Both the Russians lay prone in the road, holding their helmets, for more than a minute.

Cavalier walked to his bike, drove it fifty metres down the road, parked it in front of the clearing in front of the royals' billboard and waited to see the result of his ambush. Both men got to their feet uncertainly. They looked about but could see no one. From their nervous words to each other, Cavalier believed they were concerned they would be killed. They gingerly removed their helmets and dragged their broken bikes clear of the road.

Cavalier mounted his Harley and drove slowly to within ten metres of the stricken men. They backed away. Cavalier removed his gun and aimed it at them.

'I won't direct bullets at your bikes next time,' he said. 'If you chase me again, it will be your last rides.'

With that, he revved the bike and drove off down the mountain. He would have to wait until another night to wai the Golden Buddha at mountain top.

18

THE SILENCER

That next day, Cavalier walked home from a quiet cafe on the Chang Klan Road near his apartment after a light meal of duck and mixed vegetables, and water. In his mind the project was almost certain and this meant lifting his regimen to what he noted in his dairy as 'SAS-level'. He would increase his running, gym work, yoga and aerobics to two hours a day, cut his sugar and alcohol intake to zero and reduce his daily meals. He also went to the local shooting range for practice, especially with handguns. On his second visit, he engaged the manager, who called himself 'Maverick'. Furtive and gaunt-faced, he wore dark mirror glasses. His otherwise bald head had a foot-long ponytail and a smaller rat's tail at the base of his skull. Cavalier said he wished to buy a silencer.

'We can make them to specification,' Maverick said, seeming to look directly at Cavalier. 'It must be recorded, along with all your details.'

Cavalier took out his wallet and laid a thousand baht on the counter.

'Could it be done *quietly*?' he asked.

The Thai nodded, looked around and pocketed the money. 'I'll need the gun,' he said.

Cavalier took it from his satchel and handed it over.

'Hmm,' the manager said, 'haven't seen one of these for a long time.'

'It works.'

'May I ask why you need a silencer?'

'Are you a red shirt?' Cavalier asked, referring to the main political force in Thailand's north.

Maverick took off his glasses and blinked in surprise.

'I am, yes,' he said.

'I am going to chase yellow shirts with it.'

Maverick stared for a moment, forcing Cavalier to say: 'I'm only joking. I don't want to wake up the neighbourhood, if I use it.'

Maverick gave a short laugh, exposing a big gap in his teeth.

'I'll need it for forty-eight hours,' he said, and scribbled down his address, 'could you come there at say nine p.m. in two days?'

As requested, Cavalier gunned his Harley to the manager's smart, two-level home in the Serene Lake Estate close to Chiang Mai airport. The noise from planes taking off was barely tolerable. The fumes from jet fuel were noticeable.

'All the houses around here are empty,' Maverick volunteered. 'The owners have been driven away. This makes it easier for me to do my other business.'

'Which is?' Cavalier asked, as he was led down steps into a large basement with weapons-making and -repair equipment, and target boards. An array of guns, in various states of dismemberment, were scattered on benches. Two crates of automatic weapons sat in one corner.

'I think you can work that out from this,' Maverick said, sweeping his hand around the room, 'many people want arms. It is very handy to be close to the airport for shipment. And buyers come from all over the world to inspect my handiwork and products.'

'You live alone?' Cavalier asked casually.

'Yes. I take girls here when I want them. But only for a short time. They snoop around, smell the cordite and ask too many questions.'

'Some are buried in the back garden, no doubt,' Cavalier said, more as a statement than a query.

Maverick tugged at his ponytail and was speechless for a moment.

'Now look here,' he said finally, 'are you some farang cop or something?'

'No, no, of course not. Your burial rituals are safe with me.'

Maverick was now uneasy.

'Relax, Pal,' Cavalier said, 'I'm only kidding. And I don't care even if you have gold buried in the back garden. It's not my business.'

After making direct eye contact for the first time since they had met, Maverick considered him with a nervous expression for a few moments.

'The silencer?' Cavalier prompted.

Maverick sighed, picked up Cavalier's Glock 17, placed four bullets in the chamber and fired at a human-like wooden target with painted-on eyes, nose and mouth. Its dents made it appear from ten metres like Emmental cheese. The gun made a soft 'phut' sound and splintered the wood around the chest level. Maverick handed it to Cavalier. He aimed and fired twice.

'You missed!' Maverick said, squinting at the target.

'Don't think so,' Cavalier said walking to the target, 'the eyes have it.'

Maverick was staggered by the accuracy as he put his finger into the holes where the fake eyes had been.

'You're a professional,' Maverick said, trying not to sound in awe.

'Just a better than average shot.'

Cavalier pulled out his wallet.

'How much?' he asked.

Maverick blinked. 'For a professional like you, just five thousand baht. That includes twenty bullets, gratis.'

Cavalier counted out five notes.

'Of course, you keep this business quiet,' he said.

Maverick took the money, looked at the floor and said, 'Well, that depends.'

'Depends on what?' Cavalier asked as he picked up his gun and slid it into his satchel.

'Nothing, really.'

Cavalier smiled, but not with his eyes. He mounted his Harley.

'Just remember I know what is buried here,' he said with a sharp grin, before revving the engine. Its roar, despite the special muffler, blanked out that of a plane taking off.

*

Cavalier had a love–hate attitude to the rigour of his training, and he likened it to slipping into the zone of writing a book. He hated the isolation and the high level of discipline, but loved the endeavour with the prospect of a successful operation. He would have worked just as hard to free his daughter for no payment at all, but with his shaky finances, the prospect of a big payday was an additional, if less emphatic, motivation. He believed he had stayed within his own moral code of not being able to be bought for an assignment. Cavalier would have planned this current mission regardless of the DEA's payment. Taking such a fat fee was a welcome bonus. He was careful not to admit to his personal motivation, which he believed would have given Melody Smith an upper hand in the 'project'.

His few months stay so far in Chiang Mai, as low cost as it was, made him realise that his freelance writing and newspaper severance payout were not going to give him much of a living. In the past, while employed by his newspaper, he had avoided even taking a bus ticket for his secret work. Cavalier could not be suborned. He took quiet pride in no one being able to 'buy' him. Now it was different. He had actual formal contract work for the first time in a long career. It was on his terms and in that respect, he was keeping his independence, although he did not delude himself that there could be consequences for accepting payment.

All his energies had to go into the assignment for which he had only partly formulated a plan. He had spent every day mulling over it. Jacinta had sent some good information on the train and its design, which he would follow up on with a phone call to the engineer. These, plus details on how the Mexicans would use the train, along with passenger lists, were just a few of the issues he had to factor in. The main question to start with was, how would he board the train? Booking and appearing as Cavalier was out of the question.

He reached the condo after his meeting with Maverick and was alert to any movement in the car and bike park surrounding the ground level. He put on his special glasses and was again overwhelmed by the movement they picked out, especially of rodents in corners and near drains. The biggest animal was a cat. It tripped across his path. Cavalier took off the glasses to observe it. Was it the black one he had seen sitting in the wheelchair? It did not stop to communicate as the one on the chair had. Cavalier parked his bike next to the chair, always a forlorn reminder of his departed friend.

He made a mental note to ask the condo management what it was going to do with it.

*

In the late afternoon of the next day, he ventured for the first time in daylight to a favourite eating place, the Garden Restaurant on the Loi Kroh Road, not far from the Duangtwan Hotel, formerly Centara, where he had stayed on previous visits. He had spent four months holed up at the condo and venturing during the day only into the local market, and cafes, in a radius of three hundred metres from his apartment. Even his Thai language course at Pantip Plaza had been in night classes. Cavalier had been feeling claustrophobic and he decided to take a risk of being noticed by someone in the more central location frequented by foreigners and Thais alike. He ordered coffee from a cheerful mama-san and went again over how he might carry out a scheme to save his daughter. As hard as he thought and sketched things in a notepad, he could not figure a way to do this on the *Bangkok Express*. The venture seemed next to impossible to achieve, even if Jacinta could manage to assist. He kept thinking he had to be on the train, but was tormented by how.

Just as he reached a mental impasse, he sipped his coffee and looked up to see a couple across the road moving past on the broken footpath. They were in animated discussion. It was Doug and Irina, the two suspected terrorists. They happened to glance at Cavalier, but looked away and avoided further eye contact. He wondered what they might be up to and whether Gregory would take action against them. He finished his coffee quickly and left. The sighting had put him on edge again and he regretted leaving the condo and village area.

19

SCORES OF
A PSYCHOPATH

That night Cavalier had the most powerful dream since his nightmare about decapitation. This one had him waking up feeling disquieted. He stepped up to the front door of a house and could see his mother and father inside talking to each other and acting as if they were expecting a visitor. Cavalier woke up before he entered the house. Both his parents had been dead for some time. Cavalier's first fully conscious thought was that the dream was forewarning him, or forecasting that he would soon be joining them, in death. That shook him. He never considered that he was dicing with his own demise. He had always believed that he took calculated risks and prepared for any mission so well that he invariably limited the chances of ultimate failure. He never thought he had nerves of steel, and that was why he did everything to remove the major risk elements from any assignment. He did not think his courage had been corroded by too many dangerous projects, although he admitted to becoming unhinged after or before the odd project. On these rare occasions, as with the believed beheading of his daughter in the previous year, he turned to the bottle for solace.

Unlike his late friend Ted, he had never been tormented by a kill. Cavalier's golden rule had always been that if he did not execute, then the proposed target would go on destroying others. He told Tommy Gregory it was his 'Pol Joe Adolf' rule. If someone had assassinated them—Pol Pot, Joseph Stalin and Adolf Hitler—before they did damage, hundreds of millions of lives would have been saved, not to mention the untold misery that enveloped families and friends of all those who died or were injured by these monsters. He felt not a second of remorse for his targets before or after his work. Not even the murder of Pin's husband caused him a moment's anguish.

Cavalier as a boy was the family executioner if a beloved pet or a farm animal had to be put down. He told his diary that he had more feeling for those animals than he ever did for his human targets. He had recurring nightmares about a cat he had to chloroform and bury when it was half-crushed by a car. He was then fifteen. He cried as a twenty-one-year-old after he had to take the family dog to the vet when it was crippled by arthritis. At fifty, he recalled the look of safety and security in the eyes of his mother's dying poodle when he held it as a vet injected it into oblivion. That minute stayed with him for years, and it hurt. Those events lingered around his psyche for decades.

In more recent human projects, a success only raised his heartbeat to about a hundred and twenty. In his earlier projects, his rate soared as high as a hundred and ninety and he admitted being afraid to the point of shaking, even losing control. Over the decades, he learnt how to prepare himself for the emotional reaction of a kill. He factored in the fear element and how to manage it.

Gregory once asked if he ever had self-doubt about a project, or a moment when he wanted to pull out.

'Of course,' Cavalier replied. 'In recent years, I've overcome this by telling myself an aphorism expounded by a great football coach, who happened to be an atheist: "If it is to be, then it is up to me." No superbeing's will, or anything else, comes into it. This simple but wonderful line has always bolstered me, sometimes just before the end of an assignment. I have always done the preparation, justified in my own mind by what I am about to do. I don't need to go over all the reasons. I just recall that line and go on with it.'

In the last twenty-five years, he could not recall his heightened emotion ever spoiling his aim or intent. His physical recovery from a mission was quick, as it was from exercise. Cavalier had built an exceptional constitution into his body, which he believed kept his mind active and sharp.

A year earlier he had wondered if he were a psychopath, although he never enjoyed actually killing. Cavalier treated it simply as a job, and he did it as well as he could. He had studied psychopaths and serial killers and had done all the tests (under the supervision of psychiatrists and Gregory) to calculate if he were, indeed a cold-hearted, mental defective of some sort.

'You scored a miserably low score,' Gregory told him when they reviewed his test results, 'six out of forty. This means you are the opposite of a psychopath. Our analysis and yours came up with similar figures and the mean was six. Under "glib and superficial charm" you score nought. On "grandiose self-worth" you failed to register. None of the shrinks or I, who studied you, ever heard you brag or pump yourself up.'

'I must have hit the scoreboard on the category "need for stimulation"?'

'Do you want to be known as a psychopath?' Gregory asked with a grin.

'It would be kind of fun to know one, wouldn't it?'

Gregory chuckled. 'I believe you've eliminated quite a few,' he said.

'Didn't really know them, though.'

'True, true …' Gregory said, as he adjusted his glasses and looked at the result sheet, 'you scored on "taking chances and doing risky things". Yet psychopaths have low self-discipline. I don't know anyone with your level of self-discipline. You follow through. You are dogged even when the routine is dull, such as when you impersonate someone else over a certain period of time.'

'That's because I want a successful end result.'

'Psychopaths don't have that capacity. They fail to finish tasks.'

'So sad,' Cavalier said with a mock frown.

'You are not a good liar either, Vic. Psychos are.'

'The category mentions "shrewd, crafty, cunning".'

'Okay,' Gregory conceded, 'you have those traits on the job.'

'You once called me a cunning linguist.'

Gregory laughed. 'You do have language skills!' he said.

'The lying category also covers being "deceptive, deceitful, underhand, manipulative and dishonest".'

'So?'

'I can be all those things on assignment. I often behave unethically and misrepresent myself to acquire information. I receive a few points there, don't I?' Gregory tilted his head in a further sign of concession. 'And how about "lack of remorse and guilt"?' Cavalier added. 'What if a killer doesn't care about his victims?'

'Yes, okay, agreed. But in your case those victims are worthy of elimination.'

'Semantics! I am dispassionate and cold-hearted. I have disdain for targets.'

'You really want a higher score, don't you?' Gregory said, observing him over his glasses with a slight grin.

'I don't like being outscored by anyone, even psychopaths.'

Gregory shook his head and laughed. 'You're a real competitor, Vic. Okay, you gained a point for "impulsivity".'

'That's not a word. Sounds like an American management school make-up.'

'It is.'

'No credibility.'

'Where do you fit into this?' Gregory asked. 'It says, "unable to resist temptation, frustrations and urges".'

They looked at each other and laughed.

'Well?' Cavalier said, 'and how about "foolhardy, rash, unpredictable".'

'Yes, but that is in relation to "erratic and reckless", which is decidedly not you.' He paused. Then, with a more serious expression, he asked, 'Is it?'

Cavalier ignored the question and remarked: 'I've had trouble in long-term commitments.'

'You're only thinking of your relationships with women. You are very committed in all other things.'

'True. But you must give me a point here.'

'Half a point, maybe.'

'Thank you.'

'The doctors and I wondered about the only two answers you did not respond to. The first was: When did you know you were cut out for your kind of specialist work?'

Cavalier paused before responding: 'Mark Twain once said: "The two most important days in your life are when you are born, and when you discover why you are here".'

'When was that for you?'

'On my first project.'

Gregory pulled a face, and looked as if he might want to know more about this.

Before he could, Cavalier asked: 'What other thing didn't I respond to?'

'The question was, do you have any fears? Psychopaths often don't, and certainly not concerning the consequences of their actions.'

'I would fear being eaten by a shark or a croc.'

'That's not a serious answer, Vic. No one, not even psychopaths, put that down as a "like".'

'I used to really hate jumping out of planes during air force training.'

'You had to do that? Doesn't say much for the instructors and pilots.'

Cavalier laughed. 'All the blokes wanted to show how brave they were. We all went skydiving. I reckon I feared it most. But I did my best not to show it. In fact, I did it *because* it gave me the yips so much.'

'How did the "yips" manifest?'

'I would not sleep all night before going on a dive. I would wake in a pool of sweat. I would sometimes vomit in the clubhouse toilet before getting in the plane. Everyone joked and larked about before they jumped. I was silent. I jumped purely on adrenaline.'

'How'd you overcome it?'

'Never did. I just confronted it by jumping more often that anyone in the group. They all thought I was a daredevil. I even went gliding a few times, jumping off cliffs above the sea. It was my way of taking it on.' Cavalier shuddered at the memory. 'All in the name of machismo!'

'Anything else that scared you?'

'Public speaking.'

'Huh! It's often said to be worse than the fear of dying.'

'I'd put it on a par with skydiving.'

'But you are very good ...'

'I wasn't a natural. I look back at cringe at my early efforts. I worked at it. Now I enjoy it.'

Despite Cavalier's mild tongue-in-cheek protestations, the doctors and Gregory concluded that he had almost nothing in common with psychopaths and serial killers, except a body count.

*

'Who do you regard as true psychopath?' Cavalier asked Gregory a year later.

'Your current nemesis, Cortez, although he does break the mould here and there. The CIA has done as much profiling as possible on him. He is a narcissist, who seems to enjoy murder.'

'But he's a contract killer. That work needs planning, following through.'

'Correct. This is where he varies from the stereotypical psychopath, but he still seems to want direction. You are a classic instance. He has designated others to track you, rather than go after you himself. Hence the big price on your head. Cortez, we believe, has promised to fund your elimination.'

20

BLACK CAT CROSSING

Cavalier had another strange dream a day after the first. It involved Ted, his wheelchair and the black cat he had seen in the week since the cremation. Cavalier was flying in the wheelchair, the cat on his lap, racing over the Chiang Mai district of Mae Rim, a beautiful cultural destination. He discovered he could make the wheelchair fly faster, especially when he was being chased by a motorcycle gang. The cat took it all in its sitting position, and merely meowed its approval as Cavalier propelled the bike faster and higher. Then he woke up, his heart pounding. He lay in the bed, trying to make sense of the pacy reverie, before falling asleep again.

In the morning, he thought about the wheelchair. He was still not fully awake when an idea struck him; at first, he considered it an epiphany triggered by the dream. He had Ted's passports. There was the wheelchair. He would board the train as Edward Blenkiron, who was still 'alive', for all bureaucratic and border-crossing purposes. In Cavalier's experience, all brilliant ideas like this needed a time of filtering and consideration. By the end of the day he dared to think this radical concept might work.

Cavalier would have to look two decades older. He had pictures of Ted. He blew them up on his computer, printed them off and studied the look in detail. Ted kept his good head of grey hair short and combed it over in an attempt to cover the hint of a bald patch. Cavalier's thatch was thick with pepper-and-salt streaks of grey. Ted was a bit taller at a hundred and eighty-six centimetres, but their facial structures were similar. Ted wore prescription glasses. Cavalier had learnt enough about make-up over the years to do the touches that would make him look older. The only major difference was in the hair, which needed to be cropped. Cavalier needed an older male barber who knew about short back and sides, not a female 'artist' who would make him look young and modern. He found the right man down a side street next to the local market, and was given a cut even shorter than one he had in Bangkok in the previous year. It reminded him of his air force days in the early 1970s, when everyone else had long hair.

He had just stepped out of the barber's shop when another black cat sauntered into his path. He bent down and beckoned it to him. It turned, swayed over and rubbed itself against Cavalier's calves. He patted and stroked it. If the cat was an omen, he was going to take it as a positive one.

*

With Jacinta's secret assistance, he tracked down the designer of the *Bangkok Express*, Paul Witowski, a seventy-year-old Cambridge University-educated Pole who was working on a job in Melbourne. It helped Cavalier ease into a conversation with him.

'You claimed to have implanted a few "signature" inclusions in your work,' Cavalier said. 'I'd love to know what they were.'

'Is this for publication?'

'Not in a newspaper. I am writing a book on "signature" items in everything from house designs to movies; what directors, for instance, put in all their films and architects put in their buildings.'

'There is a market for that?'

'Small. With photos and good illustrations, it will make a quaint niche-market product. A coffee-table book.'

'I'm not sure I could do that.'

'Why? Your trains have been running for more than forty years.'

'Well ...'

'Okay, I understand if you built in a feature on the train that was dodgy or something ...'

'It wasn't dodgy. I'm not even sure it would be on the *Bangkok Express* now, although it should be.'

'Can you talk about it? Was it a hidden camera? A two-way mirror?

'Good heavens, no! Nothing like that. It was a door catch.'

'A door catch?'

'It was in every presidential suite in each carriage. It was on a door that linked to an adjoining compartment or so-called state cabin. The catch was in the catch. It was hidden and only worked from the presidential suite side of the door.'

'You say hidden ...?'

'You have to slide a finger down the left side of the door until you touch a slightly raised button five centimetres from the floor. Press it and the door latch is unlocked. But it has not been used since the *Bangkok Express* was constructed. The owners believe the door is a sealed-off partition.'

'Nice signature.'

'Thank you. It's in some form in every train I engineered.'

They chatted for an hour on the phone, Cavalier taking copious notes about a wide range of details on the train, from its brake design and emergency exits to the possibility of a man riding atop the carriages.

'Why would you want to know that?' Witowski asked, with a trace of suspicion.

'I don't know. It may be useful to include ...'

'An average-sized human could ride lying flat. He could also move along the outside. There are foot ledges for repairmen in the case of breakdown.'

'Is there a special quarter for guards?'

'Funny you should ask. I was recently contracted to reconfigure two of the carriages for storage. The Express often carries cargo in them for extra revenue.'

'Any idea of the cargo?'

'That is confidential.'

'Can you talk about it off the record?'

'Completely off the record, the company has doubled the Express's armed guard. No one is allowed to use mobile phones or any sort of computer equipment en route. Its public relations people are saying that they wish to give "a timeless experience, reminiscence of the 1930s and the Shanghai

Express". This is bulltish. They are more than concerned about a terrorist attack.'

'Concerned? Something is imminent?'

'I was just doing the engineering, remember, but the way the train company's people spoke about it, I'd say they have some intelligence that has put the wind up everyone.'

'Hmm,' Cavalier reflected.

'Are you considering a trip?'

'I was thinking about it, to take pictures for the book.'

'I wouldn't. It's just too dangerous.'

21

SPIES ON THE STATION

Jacinta emailed Cavalier the lay-out of the eight-hundred-metre-long train. There would be thirty-four carriages. It had sixty-nine airconditioned cabins, as well as a saloon, three dining carriages, a library and two bar cars. There were kitchen carriages and another three were for dining with different themes that would be used each night of the trip. There was also a long bar–lounge in the centre of the train that would be used for speeches, Thai dance performances and a classic music recital, which were open to all.

Two carriages near the train's rear, 31 and 32, would carry the bullion, watched over by the dozen armed Mexicans. They would always have six on watch either end of the two carriages to guard the chests of gold ingots and jewellery. Another two Mexicans were in carriage 30, where Cortez and his companion had a state cabin suite to themselves. The penultimate carriage, number 33, was the observation lounge. It led into the last, the observation car, which was furnished in gleaming brass and varnished Burmese teak. The last two were for use by all passengers, who had to make their way down the passageways of the two Mexican carriages.

Cavalier looked up his bank account on the net and was pleased to find that his first tranche of a million dollars American, and an expense allowance of a further seventy thousand dollars, as requested, were in his account. Unless there was some unforeseen circumstance, his mission was now unofficially on. He made his bookings in a first-class carriage on the night train from Chiang Mai to Bangkok, and on the *Bangkok Express*.

The *Express* would begin in Bangkok on 24 April, his daughter Pon's twenty-seventh birthday and one he could not forget. The first night's stop would be in Kanchanaburi, right opposite the major cemetery for British Commonwealth graves from World War II, which Cavalier had visited the previous year. The second day and night of 25 April would be spent travelling through to Southern Thailand. There were scheduled stops at Penang and Kuala Lumpur in Malaysia. The third night would be spent in that country before crossing into Singapore.

Jacinta was able to send him the guest list of a hundred and twenty people apart from the party of fourteen Mexicans, which included Cortez and a woman travelling under the name of Fai Tang, who Jacinta said was Pon. They were in a special double-bunk cabin with an outsized lounge set up in carriage 30.

'I have to vet them all on paper,' she told Cavalier in a phone conversation that was secure due to her skills in creating a firewall around her communications. 'When they come on board, I'll be in charge of the face-to-face discussions. We won't interrogate. We will tell the guests that we are doing routine questioning in line with international rules due to increased pressure from terrorism.'

'Will Azelaporn be doing that too?'

'I doubt it. He's too lazy. He'll be on board because he is contracted to do so by the Mexicans, despite hating trains. He can't stand confined spaces for too long. This will be for him like a three-day plane trip with stops. He doesn't like French food either, although the train's master chef offered to give him Thai food every day. Azelaporn's only joy will be with a couple of Chinese courtesans donated to him as sweeteners in business deals. They will accompany him.'

'What's he doing with the Chinese?'

'Offering protection and facilitating introductions. They want property or to buy into operations, such as his bars and prostitution. He was fired by the junta for corruption, but that has not stopped him from having contacts everywhere. His power has barely diminished since he was sacked as police chief.'

'Anyone else I should know about on the guest list?'

'Just one superstar who everyone in Thailand knows: Dr Topapan Makanathan.'

'The DNA specialist. Why is she making the trip?'

'The form she filled in said simply "tourism", which hardly seems likely. She's a known workaholic. She will be travelling with her husband, Dr Marc Makanathan, a former Vietnamese heart surgeon who has the cushiest job in the junta-controlled government. He oversees Tourism, Sports and Arts. They make a true power couple.'

'I'll avoid them.'

'Would be wise. In an emergency, she would rank higher than anyone on the train, even if there were police on board. She solves crimes, particularly murder.'

'What sort of emergency are we talking about?'

'Say a passenger died from food poisoning. She would take change of any investigation, and could overrule everyone else, especially with her husband there too.'

'A sort of coroner?'

'Something like that.' After a pause, Jacinta said, 'How do you plan to board the Express?'

'Like to say, but better I don't.'

'How will I help you if I don't know who you are posing as?'

'You are being most helpful in your current position. I need to make it through the vetting.'

'Will I recognise you?'

'That will be interesting, won't it? But either way it will solve the first problem I have—actually boarding the train. If you *don't* pick me, then that will absolve you of any connection to what will follow.'

'And if I do recognise you?'

'That's up to you.'

'It's high risk.'

'Is there anything we both do that is not hazardous?'

'I will have ten security people under me; not to mention the Mexicans. They will protect Cortez and the gold. He is obsessed with it. He uses a calculator every day to measure the gold's value. Cortez is an unemotional type, but he does become stimulated about the Chinese and Indians buying gold and pushing up the price.'

'He seems to have been excited about my daughter too.'

'Please don't do anything that will put you into a direct confrontation with me and my guards. It was bad enough last time when he chased you down the Mekong River when you were escaping. Cortez was hell-bent on killing you. I had to restrain him. Then you bluffed him in that phone call, which left me with palpitations.'

'And him. How'd he react?'

'He showed no emotion. Just wanted to murder you. It wasn't until he thought you were leading him into an American trap that he backed off.'

'Why did he think that?'

'I made him believe the Americans were waiting for him.'

'I should thank you for that.'

'This time we have a far more dangerous situation, in confined spaces.'

'Not on the stops at Kanchanaburi, Penang and KL.'

After a long pause, Jacinta said, 'You plan to—'

'I have options,' he said, cutting her off. 'That is all I know at this point. I really won't formulate anything until I'm travelling.'

'You will bring your weapon? The one you carried in that oversized baseball bat?'

'Cricket.'

'Will you bring it with you?'

'The bat, no.'

'You would use a rifle on the stops—?'

'As I said, I'll have options.' He changed the subject. 'Anyone else of relevance among the guests?'

'Not really. They are mainly retirees from England, France, the States and Australia. There are about six Chinese, of course they are everywhere; and two Japanese couples.' Jacinta pondered for a moment. 'There is one interesting Australian female psychiatrist from Brisbane travelling with her twenty-six-year-old adopted son. He has Down syndrome with autism.'

'Hmm,' Cavalier said, 'where will your security people be?'

'They will be mainly at the tail end of the train in carriages 28, 29 and 30.'

'Protecting the Mexicans?'

'I had no choice,' she said defensively.

'I expected that. I just want to know where they are.'

'They will be between the Mexicans and the rest of the passengers.'

*

At 3 a.m. on the night before the *Bangkok Express* was due to leave platform 11, Hua Lamphong station, Bangkok, a truck backed up to the thirty-first carriage. Ten Mexicans surrounded the vehicle as its loud 'beep-beep-beep' split the hot night air. Three of them held AK-47 automatic rifles as if they were ready for combat. Under the curt direction of a nervous-looking Jose Cortez, the Mexicans were alert to the unlikely event of an attack as a hoist on the truck lifted steel crates up, over and into the opened carriage roof. Cortez paced back and forth, like a boxer just before an event.

'Fast; efficient!' he repeated several times, 'move it!'

Across on platform nine, the Indonesian couple Irina and Doug, dressed in tight-fitting black hats, pollution masks, jeans and running shoes, were watching through binoculars from behind the last carriage of another train. They put down their glasses, and using their phones, filmed the action on platform 11.

Ten crates took about forty-five minutes to be dropped into the carriage. Its roof was then rolled back, closed and locked by maintenance men on ladders attached to the Express. Irina climbed onto the train on platform 9 to gain a better video picture. She was spotted by a worker on the platform. He yelled at her. This caught the attention of the Mexicans two platforms away,

'Chase them!' Cortez ordered as the two figures could be seen scurrying along platform 9. 'Take them!'

Two of the Mexicans propped, fired and missed. Their bullets bounced off the train as the spies stayed close to it. Two of the armed men ran to the end of platform 11. By the time they reached the station exit, the Indonesian couple had hopped on a motorcycle and roared off. The Mexicans fired wildly, narrowly missing people walking home from a nearby nightclub, homeless people lying in streets and startled prostitutes doing late-night deals with customers near the station entrance.

'Do you get them?' Cortez demanded.

'No,' one of his deputies said, 'there were too many people. They were on motorcycles.'

Cortez looked fit to explode. His men gathered around him like a football team with their coach during a break. They hung their heads, not wishing to make eye contact.

'This means,' he said, pausing to control himself, 'somebody is aware of our shipment. You and the others will guard the bullion around the clock. I mean sleep with it!' He paused to wipe his weeping good eye and temper his outburst. 'I will see if we can limit the number of stops on the trip.'

22

THE SCREENING

Melody Smith's American DEA agents staked out the Riverside Condo for twenty hours a day and noted Cavalier's movements. They arranged video surveillance from a local Thai detective operating in the hours 2 a.m. to 6 a.m. from a van in the car park. Smith had become increasingly nervous about Cavalier's reluctance to lay out his plans. She did not think for a moment that he would debunk to Brazil with his first tranche payment. Yet she was concerned that she was losing control of the overall operation to apprehend or, under extreme circumstances, liquidate Jose Cortez. Her bosses in Washington were beginning to harass her about the project, in response to her stalling on information while waiting for Cavalier to tell her more.

At 5.30 p.m. on 23 April the sun was beginning its lazy descent into the mountains and was obscured by an early wet-season torrential downpour. A taxi van pulled up at the condo, among a never-ending stream of tuktuks, cars, red cars, taxis and trucks entering and leaving the condo grounds. In a flurry of movement in the rain that reduced visibility to a few metres, a wheelchair-bound elderly man in a rainhood and coat was being helped into the van. A backpack and suitcase were placed inside it, and the wheelchair was lifted mechanically into the vehicle's rear. The agents monitoring the condo's entrances took no notice. Cavalier was more than able-bodied. They had all seen him since early in the morning of the previous day when he had been on a long run and had worked out at the Holiday Inn gym. Late morning, he bought the papers and had coffee at the Chang cafe. At about 7 p.m. he had strolled past the market to a restaurant specialising in duck. An agent doing an overly diligent job had parked himself in a noodle cafe opposite and used a powerful long-range camera to pick up Cavalier's order. He diligently recorded it as '*pat pak muan* and *moo*—mixed fried vegetables and pork; water, no alcohol'.

Cavalier had seemed in no hurry. The agents noted that he stopped to talk to two people, both Thais, on the way back to his apartment. His Harley, a plastic cover over it, was sitting all that day and the next in its usual spot in the bike park in front of the condo facing the Lamphun Road. There was nothing out of the ordinary, the agents reported to a now worried Melody Smith. She tried to contact Cavalier. He wasn't responding to phone calls, texts or emails, except to send her a text at one point saying: 'The project has begun. Stand by for more information.'

This only upset and frustrated Smith even more. She had returned to Bangkok to brief her team without anything new to report. They had to cool their heels at hotels and rented apartments awaiting directives and monitoring the Mexicans, who had dispersed in small groups to apartments on the upmarket Soi 24 off Sukhumvit. Smith and her entourage thought this might signal that they were going to split up in an attempt to leave Thailand by several routes with sections of the bullion.

Video footage of everyone leaving the condo was sent to Smith's computer and she and other DEA agents spent hours poring over images fast-forwarding out of the building. No Caucasians looked like him. Blown-up stills of males run against his photo proved not to be Cavalier. Only a few people could not be seen clearly in the video, either from headgear or because of the rain, or both. One was the man in the wheel-chair, who had been helped out into the taxi van.

On the afternoon of the day after Cavalier left the condo, Smith became suspicious that the man in the chair might be him. Inquiries were made at the condo at 5 p.m.

Agent 3815 Ralph Bozer reported to her in an email: 'The condo manager told me that a Frenchman, Monsieur Laurent Blanc, had inherited the wheelchair since an American named Ted Baines had recently died and left it to him, among other personal effects. We have Baines' lawyer's number but his firm is closed for the weekend. I asked the condo manager to describe Blanc. He sounded like an elderly version of Cavalier.'

'It must be him,' Smith said in a phone call to Bozer, 'but what the heck is he doing in a wheelchair, and where was he going?'

*

At 5 p.m. on 24 April, Cavalier paused in his wheelchair under the decorated stained-glass windows at the entrance to platform 11 at Bangkok's Hua Lamphong station where

163

the Express was parked. He had spent the night in a first-class cabin on the train from Chiang Mai after sending his backpack on by courier to Kanchanaburi, the train's first stop on the way to Singapore. He wheeled himself to a queue of passengers in the special lounge area next to the platform under the ancient, European-style, steel-arched roof. One by one or couple by couple, and with as much politeness as possible, passengers were called to an office and questioned by the train manager, forty-five-year old Cyril Huloton, and Jacinta, who both sat behind a plain wooden desk.

The guests were asked to sit down. Huloton, being the manager and official captain of the train for the journey, was in charge. Huloton was short and balding. He sported a grey goatee beard, de rigueur for Frenchmen of his vintage who had lived well enough to develop the beginnings of a second chin, which they wished to cover up. He continually stroked his modest moustache. Jacinta, wearing a light-grey pants suit and white chiffon shirt, looked suitably official, despite her role of escorting the Mexican contingent. Her hair was piled high, which both exposed her magnificent neck and bone structure, and made her look businesslike. Huloton was all busy apology and sweet smiles. He was uncomfortable in a role of mild interrogator and he gushed questions while doing his best not to offend.

'Monsieur, Madame,' he said to an elderly American couple, Dick Arnold Bowles the Third and his wife Ruby, 'we see you have come from New York. May I ask what your business is?'

'It sure ain't terrorism!' the big man said with a hearty laugh. He sucked on a Cuban cigar. The strong odour pervaded the office.

'I am sure, Monsieur,' Huloton said wringing his hands, 'this is just routine. By law now we must be sure of the passengers' bona fides.'

'I was in construction, Sir, and might I say we appreciate you doing this. We don't want any undesirables on board either!' He laughed again, and had trouble keeping his eyes off the stunning, although today understated, Jacinta. He kept looking to her, hoping she would ask a question. Jacinta didn't have to do any public relations. She would not waste her breath on anyone who was not of interest.

Finally, she asked: 'Have you had anything to do with Golden Eagle Constructions?'

Bowles stiffened.

'Not if I could help it!' he said with vehemence. 'They competed with me in Texas. They're a bad, *very* bad Mexican outfit. They employed really cheap labour from over the border, with the workers being promised permanent residency in the United States. There are rumours that all the corporation's base capital was generated in the illegal drugs trade.'

'Have you taken action against them?'

'We were always in the courts over something with that crooked mob,' he grumbled. 'They should not be allowed to operate in the States. I hope Donald Trump wins the election and builds that goddam wall he promised. I really do!'

Jacinta made a note and thanked the couple, who went away muttering to each other.

'I think you upset Monsieur,' Huloton whispered.

'He was quite hostile about Golden Eagle,' Jacinta said.

'So?'

'They are the ultimate paymasters for Cortez and his men.'

Jacinta scrutinised everyone's passport and paid attention for the first time to a solid, urbane and tanned Australian of about 60 years, who put down his profession as 'Western Australian grazier'. He wore a large bush hat that had seen better days and one gold ring on his left hand that seemed far too small for his finger. He had massive forearms and hands, gnarled from decades on the land. He and his thin, regal-looking wife Annie of the same age sat impassively as Jacinta asked, 'Have you ever been associated with the military?'

'No. I missed the Vietnam War. Too young.'

'Sir, do you use a weapon in your work?'

'All people on the land have to, from time to time.'

'What sort of weapon do you use?'

'I have a twelve-gauge shotgun and a handgun. They are both licensed.'

'Do you have those weapons with you now?'

'No. They are under lock and key back at our homestead.'

'You have to ask me that too,' Annie said, her voice cultured and pleasant. 'I am a better shot than my husband. Whenever an animal has to be put down, it is my duty.'

'Er,' Huloton said, 'I take it your gun is locked away also?'

'No, it is encased under our bed, fully loaded.'

'Under your bed?'

'In Carnarvon, Western Australia.'

'Oh, pardon.'

Huloton wiped his brow during this exchange and apologised again, this time for the humidity. Jacinta kept her eyes on 'Mr Dempster' and looked down at his gait. He had a slight limp as he walked out of the room.

The next guests in—Dr Topapan Makanathan and her husband Marc—had both Huloton and Jacinta jumping to their feet and bowing deeply. She was a sparkling, lively-looking woman in her early fifties, with streaks of red and blue in her spiky hair more fitting to a teenager. A strong waft of a dated face powder, with a fruit and lavender fragrance, floated in with her.

When asked once by an interviewer why she used such an old-fashioned scent, Makanathan had replied: 'I have to go into sewers and toilets to retrieve body parts in my work. My lovely lavender blocks out the odours better than any perfume.'

Her face was all keen, sharp intelligence intermingled with infectious grins. Her sixty-five-year-old husband was a quiet, fuzzy-haired string bean with glasses.

'This is a mere formality, you understand, my good doctors,' Huloton said with another obsequious bow. Looking at Topapan, he added, 'Everyone in Thailand knows who you are.'

'What a good cover for a terrorist,' she said with a laugh, causing Huloton to grin inanely for longer than the comment merited.

'We are honoured to have you on board and hope you have a most pleasant trip,' he said, and motioned for attendants to take the famous lady and her husband to their suite in carriage 16.

Huloton ran a pen through their names, leant across to Jacinta and remarked: 'That's two we don't have to worry about.'

'It still leaves one hundred and thirty or so to watch,' Jacinta replied, 'some closely.'

23

THE CHALLENGED

Huloton was embarrassed with the entrance of the American 'Edward Blenkiron'. He appeared to have trouble with manoeuvring the heavy chair over a step. Only a train official stopped it from toppling over. Cavalier cursed under his breath as the chair was pushed forward to the table. Huloton asked a question about his wellbeing. Cavalier, wearing his darkened 'special' glasses, looked slightly to the left of Huloton, and pretended to be hard of hearing.

'Sir, I do apologise for this routine,' Huloton said, moving around the table to clasp Cavalier's hand. Glancing at Jacinta, the Frenchman added, 'You have poor eyesight?'

'What?'

'Er ...' Huloton began raising his voice, 'we will do everything we can to make your trip comfortable. Is your eyesight not so good?'

'Not the best, no. I need these glasses, you know,' Cavalier said, his drawl as much like Ted's as possible, 'it's gonna be a race between me goin' legally blind or bein' dead!'

He laughed at his own joke, which brought a wince from Huloton and no expression at all from Jacinta.

'I can see shapes at night but it's better in the day, mostly,' Cavalier said more soberly. 'Depends on the weather and how I feel. We're all organic, ya know. There are good days and bad 'uns.'

'This is trip is for pleasure?' Jacinta asked, paying a fraction more attention to him.

'Well I sure hope so, Ma'am,' Cavalier said, 'don't want it to be business or boring. I have promised myself this train trip for twenty-five years since it first started. I'm doing it because, well, frankly, I don't have long to live and I just wanted to. The mystery of the Far East and all that. I've read Conrad and Orwell. Two of my favourite authors.'

'You booked one of the only two presidential suites, specifying carriage 29,' Jacinta said. 'Any reason for that?'

'I want to be close to the observation car. Means I don't have to go so far.' He paused and turned more towards Jacinta. 'Is there a problem?'

'No, no, not at all,' Huloton said, glaring at Jacinta. 'It happened to be free. We are gratified that you have taken it.'

'I don't want to be in the way. These chairs are wonderful but heavy, and barely squeeze down the corridors. I don't plan to use the dining cars. Afraid I cause too much damned disruption.'

'We will make sure our stewards 'elp you.'

'Nope, won't be doin' it.'

'As you are travelling alone sir,' Huloton remarked, 'we will make sure you have company at lunch and dinner.'

'Oh, that won't be necessary, I have my books. If I am not in my suite readin', I'll sit in the observation car.'

'Sir, the food is exquisitely French. It is a feature of our train. We have Monsieur Charles Bonnet, the grand chef from Paris' legendary Hôtel Plaza Athénée, with us now. You will meet the most interesting people.'

'Maybe I'll have something in the suite,' Cavalier said with a tilt of his head, 'Besides, if I am stuck with someone who is not too bright, it is difficult for me to extract myself. I begin to think about the book I'm readin'.'

'Sir, I doubt any of our passengers are stupid. They are mainly accomplished couples, many of them professionals of some sort.'

'Oh, I don't mind stupidity. I just have no patience for those who are so inclined and who are proud of it.'

Huloton looked confused. Jacinta seemed amused by this eccentric comment.

'Sorry about that,' Cavalier added, 'I am a bit of a curmudgeon.'

Huloton looked at his watch. The train would be late in taking off if he didn't conduct the interviews more rapidly. He could see the next two in line. One was a short, stout, bespectacled woman of about fifty-five, wearing a long dress. She was holding the hand of her twenty-six-year-old adopted son, who had Down syndrome and autism. He looked fidgety and concerned.

'Oh, mon Dieu!' Huloton muttered under his breath. 'Must we really interrogate them? Clearly they could not be terrorists. It can't be fair to them and it is a waste of time.'

Jacinta inclined her head and gave a brief smile.

'There is no handbook for the way a terrorist looks,' she said. 'Suicide bombers are taking many guises these days.'

Huloton groaned and beckoned in the two. Then he turned to Cavalier, thanked him profusely, went through an apology routine again and called for two attendants to help him board the train.

Cavalier looked up at the video screen framed in red, white and blue on the side of the front carriage that announced on one line it was La Belle Époque Company. On the second line in capitals it proclaimed: THE BANGKOK EXPRESS, and then on lines 3, 4 and 5 it said:

To: KANCHANABURI

MALAYSIA

SINGAPORE

No mention was made of the stops at cities in Malaysia. Nor were times for arrivals in Kanchanaburi or Butterworth and Kuala Lumpur posted or in any of the literature and online brochures about the trip. Cavalier was apprehensive, assuming, correctly, that this was for security reasons. He wished he could check with one of his intelligence contacts if there were any alerts about possible attacks. Yet this would have exposed his whereabouts and he knew how fast the networks, occasionally intercepted by foreign agents, would pass around his location, even coordinates.

Cavalier rested the chair's motor as they pushed him along the platform beside the train, which was a polished navy blue with white window frames, and two lines of red completing the French and Thai tricolours. They reached carriage 29 at about five hundred metres. Four Thai attendants were needed to lift his wheelchair up the steps and into the carriage.

Cavalier, gripping crutches, was hoisted up the steps, eased into his chair and pushed along the narrow, inlaid-wood corridor.

The carriages were a mix of traditional Chinese decor, Malaysian embroidery and hand-tufted Thai rugs. Cavalier's suite of a hundred and thirty-five square feet was spacious with a muted, red-maroon colour scheme on walls, a sofa, cushions and twin beds. The low lighting created a romantic ambience. The suite was convertible, becoming a lounge during the day. Cavalier made a point of insisting that the beds should remain in the same configuration all the time.

'I will want to rest up during the day,' he told the carriage captain as he collapsed his wheelchair with grunts and groans as if it were a tough task for him. 'I sleep a lot. I don't want anyone a-knockin'.'

'As you wish, sir,' the Thai captain said.

The expensively tiled en suite bathroom was not much smaller than that of a five-star hotel. The timber-lined interior also had a stunning inlaid table that could be folded out for meals. There was a polished redwood wall desk. The wall lamps' designs were a feature copied from the Orient Express in Europe, as were other lights and *objets d'art* throughout the train.

When the attendants left the suite, he stood, locked the door, and went straight to the partition leading to the adjoining state cabin. Its latch was locked. He ran his hand down the sides of the partition. After several attempts to find the button catch that would open it, he dropped to his knees and examined the partition near the floor. He leant his shoulder against the door and it moved a centimetre. Cavalier ran his fingers around the side again, pushed a small raised button and heard an almost indiscernible 'click'. He tried the latch. The door slid across. The next-door cabin was empty as expected.

It had been booked by him in the name of Frenchman Claude Garriaud, who would be joining the train at Kanchanaburi.

*

At 5.44 p.m. to the second, a crotchety old Thai conductor called for stragglers to board the Express.

'I'm not waiting!' he yelled in Thai and English, keeping his eyes on the ancient clock mounted on the wall two metres above him. 'All aboard! All aboard!!'

He dropped his red signal flag. His shrill whistle cut the thick evening air. The Express crawled and clattered the first a thousand metres as it avoided children playing on the tracks, then it built speed on its seventeen-hundred-kilometre journey to Singapore. Cavalier was moved to wave to Thai families, backpackers and other tourists on the platform, who all gaped in admiration at the luxury train, despite its hiccups for the halting first kilometre as the station fell away behind it in the encroaching dusk. The Express built speed and more certitude and swayed rhythmically out of Bangkok's north and bound for Kanchanaburi in Thailand's west, approaching the Myanmar border.

The poor suburbs, intermingled with modern high-rises and mansions, were animated by scores of fascinated children who ran along beside the tracks waving. For a moment, Cavalier felt a pang of guilt over the luxury he was about to experience compared to the lifetime of struggle most of those kids would probably have to face. But the feeling passed when they disappeared into suburbia and the landscape changed as the colonial anachronism wandered on its way. Cavalier opened the suite's window to let in the warm evening air streaked with the smell of trackside grills, woks and make-shift stoves that would feed several million people in the next hour or so. In between these strong wafts, Cavalier caught the more pleasant aromas of flowers growing in thick clumps beside the track.

He went to the door and asked a Thai steward for 'a malt whisky with ice, stirred, not shaken'. He reflected that this might be one of the few moments of near-relaxation he would have in the next few days. After finishing his drink, he lay on the bed and was almost asleep when he heard shouting and screaming, then someone crying. Concerned, he got off the bed, placed crutches under his arms, opened the door and called to the steward.

'What's going on?' Cavalier asked.

'I don't understand,' the Thai steward said.

Cavalier was about to break into Thai when he stopped himself. 'Listen,' he said.

The muffled sound of raised voices could be heard: one that of an angry male; the other of a distressed female.

'I think you should investigate,' Cavalier said.

The Thai steward bowed and nodded. Cavalier shut the door, lay on the bed and waited.

24

THE CAPTIVE

In the very next carriage, Cavalier's daughter Pon, wearing just a bra and pants, was on her knees. She had her head over the toilet in the state cabin as she gripped the sides of the bowl and threw up.

A few metres away in the bathroom, thirty-eight-year-old Jose Cortez, wearing a white suit, was having trouble adjusting a cravat. He seemed oblivious of her plight as he cursed under his breath.

'I want you to perform at your best tonight,' he said. 'You will have an audience of maybe a hundred people in the piano bar; the biggest you have played before in a year.'

'I cannot,' she whispered hoarsely. 'Can't you see I am ill?'

'My dear, it is your condition … bulimia …'

'No! It is the drugs you give me. You sedate me. You abuse me!'

'I keep you alive.'

'I'd rather be dead!'

'So you show me with your pathetic slashed wrists.'

'I hate you! Always have, always will!'

'That's not what you say when I fuck you.'

'Rape me!' she corrected him. 'You rape me!'

Cortez tore off the troublesome cravat, pushed into the toilet and backhanded Pon across the face, sending her sprawling to the floor. Blood sprang from the corner of her mouth. He held her by the throat, causing her to begin choking. Cortez's face was demonic. He'd lost an eye in a Florida gunfight with FBI agents and his appearance was made more frightening by his tartan eyepatch slipping and exposing a white glass substitute, which bulged from the socket. His one good eye was opaque like that of a fish. He eased his grip. Pon coughed and used all her strength to release his hold.

'Now look, you stupid bitch!' he hissed. 'I promise I will murder your father if you don't do as I say. If you attempt suicide again, he is a dead man.'

Pon refrained from responding. She would never admit it to Cortez, but the only thing that was now keeping her alive was the concern that the Mexican would kill Cavalier.

'You know he is a professional like me?' he asked staring so hard that his one 'good' eye flared red, went pale again and let go a trickle of fluid.

Pon shook her head.

'You know nothing about him,' Cortez said. 'You think he is a simple journalist. It is a cover for his killing, sanctioned by the CIA.'

Pon broke down. Cortez pushed her head over the bowl and flushed the toilet. She struggled to avoid being wet.

'Clean yourself up and prepare for the show.'

Pon struggled on all fours into the shower. Cortez turned it on and left her slumped on the floor and sobbing under the cascading water. He returned to the mirror, adjusted his eyepatch and had a second try at his troublesome cravat.

*

Cavalier was unable to rest, although the sound of heated argument and worse had abated. He locked the door to his suite as the train rattled west for three and a half hours towards Kanchanaburi, where it would stop for the night. In the first hour he took out five tubes containing high-powered rifle parts from his backpack and cleaned them. He then removed his old Glock-17 handgun, put six bullets in it and placed it back in the cavity of the chair's right arm.

He refused to come out for the first dinner sitting of the trip in the dining cars. Instead, he accepted a soup entrée, which a waiter brought to his door. After devouring the food, accompanied by a glass of Chablis, he took out a detailed description of the train, studied it and placed it back in his pack. At 8.15 p.m. he climbed into the chair and began to wheel down the corridor towards the observation car at the end of the train, passing slowly through carriage 30, watched by four armed security guards, and another four Mexicans with concealed weapons under sleeveless leather vests.

Cavalier noted the door to the suite where he believed Cortez and Pon were. He pushed beyond it to the two carriages harbouring the gold and manned by most of the cartel bodyguard. He took some time easing through the doors, looking at their locks and wondering if he could cut off the guard from the rest of the train. He did not linger too long, aware from his glasses and movement behind him that he was being followed by other passengers and two of the Mexicans.

There were a half a dozen people sitting on the observation car's seats watching the passing scenery of part jungle, part rural west Thailand with its myriad villages. The end of the train was also open and three suited travellers were having an after-dinner drink. He positioned himself next to the seats in the car's centre and ordered a scotch and ice, keeping up his pretence of being both nearly blind and almost deaf. Cavalier looked out on the passing vista with his back at forty-five degrees to the door leading to the observation car.

A half-hour later three Mexicans came out of carriage 30 followed by Cortez, his eyepatch slightly askew as ever, his cravat on straight and his violin in his right hand. Pon was behind him in a long white dress, head down, and 'assisted' by two Mexicans either side of her. Despite efforts to use make-up to mask her injuries, one eye was black and slightly closed. The corner of her mouth was red and swollen.

They strode through the observation lounge. Cortez brushed the wheelchair with his elbow, cursed under his breath and glared at Cavalier as if it were his fault for being in the way. For a split second Cortez's eye flashed red, as if an oven door had been opened. It was the look of a psychopath, a person who may well have enjoyed every one of his scores of murders. He moved on into the next car.

Cavalier touched his glasses, not quite believing what his reflective lenses were showing him. The woman with Cortez looked like Pon, or a bedraggled, bug-eyed and bruised version of her. His heart raced. He gripped the right arm of his chair and had to stop himself from taking out his handgun and killing his intended victim.

Overriding his rage in the moment was a rational thought. He would be gunned down, and his daughter could be killed in the crossfire. Instead, he kept looking out at the passing parade until the Mexican contingent had a quick drink and moved back down the carriages to the piano bar and lounge.

Cavalier swung his wheelchair around, just as Huloton scurried into the car.

'Mr Blenkiron, sir,' he shouted into Cavalier's ear, 'would you care to listen to a wonderful violin and piano recital?'

'Who is giving it?' Cavalier said, attempting to conceal his shortness of breath and anger.

'Arh! A special performer from Bolivia and his Eurasian partner.'

'No, I'd rather stay here,' Cavalier said off-handedly. 'Never had much time for classical music. New Orleans jazz is my thing.'

'Are you all right, sir?' Huloton said solicitously. 'You look, if you will permit me, somewhat pale.'

'I'm okay,' Cavalier said, keeping his slight drawl and trying to calm down. 'Thank you for your concern. I have these "turns" at times.' He tapped his chest. 'Heartburn sometimes; erratic beat others. But don't worry, I take pills for it.'

Cavalier returned to his suite. He could not stop thinking about his daughter and this caused him to change his mind. Although still emotional to the point of tears of anger, he felt he had to see her again.

25

THE PERFORMANCE

After about twenty minutes, when he believed he had calmed down, Cavalier pushed down to the lounge piano bar where the performances were going on. Once there, he could not see for the throng and was embarrassed to be helped, still in the chair, closer to the makeshift stage area and the piano. A Thai female was going through a wrist-writhing, traditional dance routine. Passengers were taking photos. He could barely see the musicians, Pon at the piano and Cortez with his violin, waiting to perform. Pon was seated on a stool, her head slumped forward like a rag doll.

Cavalier could see Azelaporn, carousing with exquisite Chinese courtesan twins who wore identical neck-to-ankle green dresses, split to the hip for occasional glimpses of thin legs perched on high heels, and adorned at the back by red Chinese dragons. The former Thai police chief was enjoying himself on what he considered a cushy assignment. His hired help, namely Jacinta, was doing all the security organising. Azelaporn did not believe that there would be trouble on the train. Jacinta sat near him, ignoring his fondling of the

Chinese women. He squeezed their waists, rubbed their shoulders and cuddled them together. His groping public display was not appreciated by the women.

One commented loudly enough in English for Jacinta to hear: 'Please be discreet. We are not whores!'

That caused Jacinta to smile inwardly as she ran her eyes over the crowd, wondering if Cavalier was on the train. No one among the guests had seemed remotely like him at the boarding in Bangkok.

The audience applauded the dancing. Cortez prepared for his show. He announced in a husky, hesitant voice on a microphone that they would be playing a piano composition by French composer Maurice Ravel.

Cavalier kept his eyes on Pon. Her head remained down. She seemed to be refusing to tune up. She pouted and looked angry. Visions of the occasional spoilt child he recalled so well flooded back.

The performance began. It was soon clear that she was behind the tempo and producing the odd discordant note, including one or two off-key blunders that had Cortez glancing at her. After a minute she stopped playing and stood in front of him. She seemed ready to strike him. Cortez took a step back, his one good eye betraying the inner demon for a moment before he controlled his anger. Two Mexicans hurried forward and gripped Pon by the arms.

'Murderer! Assassin! Rapist!' she screamed at Cortez as they escorted her out of the carriage as.

Pon came close to Cavalier's chair, accidentally kicking a wheel as she was pulled from the room. She winced in pain and stumbled. For a split second she looked down at Cavalier, whose arms reached up to stop her fall before the Mexicans had pushed her on through the audience and out of the carriage. The guests were stunned into silence.

Cortez leaned to the microphone with a false smile. 'My partner has been under stress of late,' he said. 'Her father has been missing for some time. She was in a state before we began, but insisted on performing. We apologise to you and will continue.' He nodded to a stand-in Thai pianist, who seemed reluctant to go on. Only a word in his ear from Cortez caused him to start playing. Couples began filtering off to their compartments.

Cavalier backed his chair up to the exit and was in two minds about leaving. Tears were trickling down his face from under his glasses. He wiped his cheeks and looked up to see the diminutive Down syndrome man, standing by the wheelchair and staring at Cavalier from not much above eye level. His mother introduced herself as 'Janet Hinkley' and her son as 'Cowboy'. He was wearing a slouch hat, dark-blue check shirt, jeans, outsized studded belt and boots with spurs. A large sheriff's badge was pinned to a shirt pocket.

'Hi, Cowboy!' Cavalier said, reaching to shake hands. Cowboy ignored him, his round, pinched face expressionless, apart from an eye twitch.

'He was worried about you,' Hinkley said, bending down and smiling pleasantly. 'He relates to anyone else with …'

'A handicap?'

'Anyone "challenged",' Hinkley said with a sweet smile.

'Thank you then, Cowboy,' Cavalier said his voice a thin rasp. 'How'd you get that name?'

He had not taken his eyes off Cavalier. He just blinked as if it were a kind of code.

'He likes old cowboy movies,' Hinkley explained, 'don't you Cowboy?' She stood up and took her son's hand. 'C'mon, let's go to the observation car. You said you wanted to go.'

'He speaks okay?' Cavalier asked.

'Not exactly. We can communicate via a computer program.'

Cavalier had to be careful not to engage with anyone too much on the trip, just in case the merest suspicion was aroused.

'Bye, Cowboy!' Cavalier said, patting him on the back.

Jacinta had been watching the interaction. She came to Cavalier, leant down and whispered as the recital continued:

'We are sorry about the musical interruption. Can I take you back to your suite?'

'No,' he said, his voice steadier, 'I'd like to watch this violinist until he finishes.'

When the shortened performance was complete there was only about one-third of the original audience still in attendance. They clapped without enthusiasm. Cortez's apparent lack of sincere concern for the distress of his first piano accompanist had cooled their response to him.

Concerned about his wellbeing, Jacinta pushed Cavalier along the corridors despite him saying he did not need assistance. She helped him open his presidential suite door and before he could stop her, was inside the spacious compartment helping him out of the wheelchair. She poured him a drink of water.

'Thank you,' he said. 'Never seen anyone so beautiful this side of the Potomac.'

'What does that mean?'

'That you are pretty darn pretty, that's all.'

Jacinta smiled faintly. 'I did not ask what you did for a living …' she said sweetly.

'No, I don't believe you did. I was a merchant seaman most of my life.'

She sat at the chair to the inlaid wooden desk and observed Cavalier as he stretched out on the bed.

'I should have some sleep; feeling pooped,' he said.

'I'll leave you. Anything I can bring you?'

'A double malt whisky would be nice, with ice.'

'A double malt,' she repeated.

Jacinta stared at him before saying, 'Do you mind me asking why you were crying during the piano recital?'

'Was I? Gee, I didn't notice. Great music moves me to tears.'

'I thought you told Monsieur Huloton that you preferred New Orleans jazz?'

'I do, ma'am, I do. But lovely sounds like that move me. Always have and will.'

'It was hardly a great recital.'

'That I grant you, Ma'am, but still it's often the thought that counts, isn't it? I always say, if somethin' is worth doin', it's worth doin' badly.'

Jacinta frowned and continued to stare.

Cavalier manufactured a yawn. 'Now if you'd excuse me,' he said, 'I'd like that scotch.'

'I'll pass that on to the steward,' Jacinta said, standing. She added, 'If there is anything I can help you with, you must let me know.'

'There is just one thing, Ma'am. Please inform the carriage manager that I will not be leaving this suite tomorrow when you all see the Commonwealth War Graves ceremony at Kanchanaburi. I want to rest.'

'What about meals?'

'Tell the stewards to leave my breakfast outside the door. I won't be venturing out for lunch either. Food is not my kind.'

'A special meal can be produced ...'

Cavalier waved a hand. 'No thank you, ma'am,' he said, 'I'm not feeling so good.' He chuckled and added: 'Old bodies like mine need a complete rest, inside and out.'

'You may feel differently when we arrive at Kanchanaburi in the morning,' Jacinta said, now satisfied that he had settled. 'Goodnight.'

'Don't forget my scotch,' Cavalier called after her. 'I need it for medicinal purposes. It opens up the arteries.'

*

He was woken the next morning at 6.30 a.m. by a tap on the door. He hauled on pants, his cap and glasses, and balancing on crutches opened the door.

'Your breakfast, sir,' a Thai steward said, 'handing him his breakfast tray.'

'I told you to leave it outside the door, goddammit!' Cavalier said, feigning 'grumpy old man' anger.

'Sorry, sir,' the Thai in a tricolour uniform said, with a deep wai, 'I did not receive that instruction.'

'Okay, okay,' Cavalier said, juggling the tray while keeping upright with the crutches. He placed it on the table and said in a more moderate tone, 'Nice uniform.'

Cavalier handed him a fifty-baht note and reminded him to leave the tray outside the next day. He locked the door and savoured the food—fresh fruits, croissants, and strong

Columbian coffee. Having foregone the evening meal, he enjoyed the offerings more than normal, especially the rose apple and a fleshy, succulent mango, his favourite fruit.

He was just finishing the breakfast when the train began to move from outside Kanchanaburi and across the three-hundred-metre-long trestle bridge with its iron arch that clung to limestone cliffs. Cavalier had not joined the other passengers in the observation lounge and car as the train crawled over the thick wooden cross-slats.

He placed the tray outside the door.

'Not wanting to see the Bridge over River Kwai?' the steward asked.

'No!' Cavalier snapped. 'It's a goddamned tourist con!'

He stayed in the suite and watched a crowd that had gathered to view the train's arrival. He studied the faces of local villagers, hawkers, tourists, police and others. A couple caused him to do a double take. *Doug and Irina,* he thought, *the two Indonesians from Thai language class.* They were dressed in identical jeans, vests, and blue caps, both depicting the insignias for the New York Yankees.

'What the fuck are they doing here?' he mumbled to himself.

26

THE ASSASSIN PREPARES

Cavalier took a black backpack from his suitcase and placed the cylinders containing his rifle and a few other items in it. He prepared his wig and moustache for his identity as Claude Garriaud. Cavalier had trouble sticking on the small goatee beard. It kept slipping. In the end he discarded it, despite it being on his passport photo.

He practised about a hundred words of French, which he used with a Gallic flourish that was well practised. Cavalier felt most comfortable in French shoes. His accent and his command of the language were good. He had always worked hard on his Thai, French and Mandarin, as if it were an almost daily habit, similar to his physical exercise and gym workouts.

Cavalier had tested this with French native speakers, who were convinced of his authenticity as one of them. They only time he caused a minor frown or two was in his constructed biography of being born the son of a diplomat in Paris, then brought up for a decade in Australia and travelled through-out the world. He never gave details, realising that he would probably dig himself into a deeper hole of deception if he attempted to explain his fabricated background fully. He usually finished any doubts by saying that he was one of nine million French living outside their country. He was not sure if the figure was correct, but it sounded authentic.

Cavalier, wearing a flamboyant unstructured navy jacket, white shirt, light trousers and sneakers, waited until he believed almost all people were off the train, before jamming a navy-blue beret on his head and putting on expensive sunglasses, dark enough to hide his eyes. He pushed his wheelchair against the main suite door, making it impossible for anyone to enter short of breaking in, and then eased aside the partition and entered the adjoining state cabin. He poked his head out of its door and, seeing no one in the corridor, stepped from the train and headed off in the direction of the 25 April Anzac ceremony. Then he doubled back around behind the train to the office where new passengers were joining the Express at Kanchanaburi.

There were just six people. Huloton and Jacinta were seated behind a desk. Cavalier would be the last person to be interviewed. He sat next to the others outside on a bench and waiting to be called in. Those in front of him included four Mexicans, easily recognisable in their Stetsons, high-sided boots and leather vests. Cavalier glanced at the two other people waiting. Then he froze. They were Doug and Irina. Cavalier turned away so he was not facing them. Typically, they had not even looked at him, behaving as if he wasn't even there.

When the Indonesians were called in, Huloton asked about their work, and they claimed this time to be employed at a primary school. The woman, still calling herself Irina, said she was the head of the school. Her partner, now 'Nani' rather than 'Doug', was claimed to be her deputy.

'You must be paid very well to make this trip,' Jacinta said in English.

Nani didn't seem to understand. But Irina bristled.

'We have saved for two years for this,' she said indignantly, locking eyes with Jacinta, who outstared her.

'You are Muslim?' Jacinta asked.

'Is something wrong?' Nani asked as if he had learnt the phrase from a how-to-speak English booklet.

'No Monsieur,' Huloton broke in, 'we have a hundred and thirty-four passengers on board and must ask questions of every traveller. It is the law.'

Irina put a hand on her partner's forearm. 'We must comply,' she mumbled in Indonesian.

'You are both Yankees fans,' Jacinta said with a more relaxed look. 'Pity about their form. But they do have Mitchell Jones, best pitcher in the league, don't you think?'

Nani looked blank again. Irina gave a firm nod of agreement. Huloton gave them permission to board. Jacinta watched them as they made their way out of the room and headed for the train. Cavalier sat facing the other direction as a security guard guided them to their cabin.

'They are doing their best to look like Americans,' Huloton said.

'Not doing a very good job either,' Jacinta said. 'I know nothing about baseball. I made up the pitcher's name.'

Huloton glanced at Jacinta. 'We need to keep an eye on them?'

'Wise, I would think.'

They greeted the next two new travellers, a Mexican couple—Marco and Maria Rodriguez. Two hefty Mexicans, who looked like nightclub bouncers, stood at the back of the room, hands clasped in front of them as if they were part of a soccer wall defending against a penalty kick.

Marco was short, of medium height, sallow-faced and with outsized ears. Despite this, he was trim and handsome. He wore an immaculate Savile Row suit. His form said he was a 'merchant banker' and twenty-eight years of age. He claimed to be a senior vice president of Golden Eagle Acquisitions. Not on his form was the fact that his company had taken over Golden Eagle Constructions, and others with the illegal drug cartel's insignia. In the last two years, he had steered the organisation towards legal drug production, while never admitting that the illegal activity was still generating much of the group's revenue.

Dark-haired wife Maria, thirty-one, was taller and bigger than him. She had a sensual face featuring black saucer eyes and full lips. Her expression oozed boredom as she examined her nails and sat down, her sizeable derriere spilling over the sides of the seat. She fiddled with her bra, so that her ample breasts and cleavage distracted Huloton. Jacinta concentrated on her husband.

'Vacation?' Jacinta said, glancing at both of them.

'Sort of,' Rodriguez replied, 'I have been doing business in Bangkok, and will in Singapore.'

His accent was educated American; his manner superior.

'You are a banker?'

'I am. Here I am looking at property and other investments also.'

'And in Singapore?'

'The same.'

'You sound American, sir,' Huloton said. His interjection seemed superfluous, as if he were trying to assert himself, given Jacinta's control of the conversation.

'I did law at Harvard,' Rodriguez said, his chest going out, 'I was fifth in my final year.'

'Most commendable,' Jacinta said, her suspicions verified. 'You are related to another Harvard alumnus who didn't make it through law school?'

Rodriguez blinked and feigned confusion.

'Did you have an uncle at Law School, Mr Rodriguez?' Jacinta asked more pointedly.

'What has that to do with anything?'

Maria was suddenly alert. She stopped playing with her hair. 'You don't have to take this kind of interrogation,' she said to him.

'Yes he does,' Jacinta said. She turned to Rodriguez. 'Your uncle was Leonardo Mendez? Yes?' Rodriguez swallowed, trying to recover his pompous bearing. 'You're here protecting your investment, are you not?'

'Everything I do is legitimate,' he blurted, his face reddening. 'I had nothing whatever to do with my uncle's operations.'

'You are on this train to protect your investment, correct?' Jacinta repeated.

'We don't have to answer—' he began, before Jacinta interrupted him.

'You don't have to worry, Mr Rodriguez,' she said agreeably, 'I have been hired to protect Señor Cortez and his ... er ... associates. Not to forget their bullion.'

Rodriguez's look waxed between self-importance and uncertainty, as Jacinta added with equanimity, 'This means I will be protecting you too.'

He glanced at his two men, standing rigidly.

'Oh, and your bodyguards also,' she said.

After a few more questions for the couple and their protection, the four wandered off towards the train. Huloton waved to Cavalier and he entered the room. Huloton engaged him in French, asking him about his work.

'I am a teacher,' he said, 'specialising in languages—Thai, English, Chinese and, of course, our own.'

Jacinta studied the information sheet.

'You have written here that you also teach cinema?'

'I use movies to instruct in languages. I use the visuals and subtitles. It makes the students learn much faster.'

Huloton, as ever, was impatient and wished to move on.

Jacinta intervened only to ask in Thai: 'Have you taught outside France?'

'Of course,' Cavalier said with a friendly gesture with both hands, 'that is what I do here.'

'Where? Bangkok?'

'*Oui.* There is a school for French people.'

'Chiang Rai?'

'No.'

'Your address is down as being in Chiang Rai.'

'Yes, well I expect soon to take up a post at a college there.'

Jacinta's expression did not change. She held Cavalier's gaze. In a split second he realised she had seen through his disguise. Huloton, unaware of the interaction, moved to wrap up the interview session. He welcomed Cavalier to the train and called for a steward to direct him to his cabin.

'If you hurry you will catch the Anzac ceremony,' Huloton said.

'I was hoping to see the Bridge over the River Kwai,' Cavalier said with his best French pout. 'I have always been fascinated to experience it after seeing the English movie about the "death railway" that the Japanese built. I use that movie often in my lectures.'

'You can still join the boat tour down the river,' Huloton informed him, 'where an expert gives a lecture on the subject. It will sail under the bridge.'

'Will the expert discuss the fact that after the movie appeared in 1957 tourists flocked here to see the bridge, which did not exist?' Huloton looked blank. 'Will he say that there was only a bridge over the Mae Klong river? They renamed the river at the point of the bridge the Kwai Yai, or "Big River". This was of course for tourist purposes.'

'The Thais are a shrewd lot,' Huloton acknowledged with a respectful glance at Jacinta. 'This mythology has satisfied the tourists for six decades, including our trainload today.'

Cavalier walked off with a steward.

He was shown into his state cabin', next door to the presidential suite in carriage 29. Once the steward had left, Cavalier locked the main door and slid across the partition between the two compartments. He was relieved to see the wheelchair was still jammed against the door to the corridor, just in case an attendant tried to enter.

He sent Jacinta a message, using an app which didn't allow the source to be registered.

'The two new Indonesians passengers are almost certainly dangerous. Watch them.'

Jacinta was stunned by the message, to which she could not reply. Yet she felt instinctively that it had come from Cavalier. It was confirmation that he was the Frenchman.

Cavalier had not planned on the river trip, but he changed his mind when he saw the Mexicans filing down the platform. He stared when he saw Pon straggling along and looking forlorn. She wore dark glasses to hide the marks around her eyes. Then he noticed the earrings she was wearing. They were green jade, a pair he had given her on her eighteenth birthday. Cavalier looked away, took some deep breaths, slipped on his backpack, and hustled off the train. He bumped into Azelaporn, Jacinta and Huloton. Cavalier and Jacinta made eye contact and acknowledged each other perfunctorily as he walked briskly ahead of them.

'Who is that?' Azelaporn asked.

'A Frenchman who has the joined the train here,' Huloton replied.

'He doesn't look like a farang retiree.'

'He's a language teacher,' Huloton said.

'Then he's hardly in the money class of his fellow travellers, is he? Have you looked at his passport?'

'Jacinta and I have reviewed them all.'

'I'd like to see it.'

'You can when we collect them for passing into Malaysia tomorrow.'

'You know what to look for?' Azelaporn asked, almost patronisingly. 'The blurred writing, the perfection or otherwise in the rubber stamps, the traces of old gum around the edges of the photograph, the alteration of a letter or number where the paper has been tampered with ...'

'Yes, yes,' Huloton interjected impatiently, 'I have been making this type of inspection for two decades.'

'With respect, *Chief*,' Jacinta added with a tone that did not match her words, 'we are both aware of this applying to *older* passports. Newer ones from many countries use modern technology that makes it much tougher to pick forgeries. The creator has to be a software expert and an outstanding hacker.'

'Like you, my dear?' Azelaporn sneered.

Jacinta held his gaze for a moment before saying emphatically: 'Actually, yes.'

'Keep your eye on them all,' Azelaporn said, diverting the conversation from his ignorance.

'The Indonesians may be a problem.'

'Why do you say that?'

'Their behaviour was suspect during the interviews,' Jacinta said.

'They are Muslim,' Azelaporn observed with a sceptical shrug.

'They are teachers too.'

'Oh, really?' Azelaporn said with sarcastic tone, 'teaching what, Rebellion? Terrorism? Again like the unemployed Frenchman, how could a couple of Asian teachers afford such a trip? They paid upward of sixty thousand dollars for the trip. That's still a fortune for most Asians.'

'They are not imams. They claim that they teach at a Muslim primary school.'

'So they say,' Azelaporn said. 'I want you to raid their cabin in case there are bombs or weapons.'

'That would be highly irregular, Monsieur,' Huloton butted in. 'They are guests on our train, not terror suspects.'

'Let me be the judge. You run the train; I run the security.'

'Correction, Monsieur,' Huloton said, 'I run the train and its overall security. *You* are looking after the Mexicans.'

195

27

STALKER

Cavalier turned stalker, keeping his eyes on the Mexican contingent and, in particular, Cortez and Pon. They entered the Kanchanaburi Cemetery, where Cavalier had lingered in the boiling heat nearly a year earlier to kneel at the grave of his uncle, who had died in this town after being in a slave gang on the Japanese-built Thai–Burma railway.

He stayed a discreet forty metres away from the Mexicans, watching.

Pon, carrying a bunch of flowers, wriggled away from the guards, who moved after her. One held her by the arm.

'You can't stop me looking for my great uncle!' she yelled, causing several others in a group between her and Cavalier to turn their heads. Pon punched and kicked at her guards, broke free and hurried along between the long rows of memorial stones. She was pursued by four Mexicans. They scuffled near the Australian grazier, Ben Dempster. He stepped between Pon and the Mexicans, and struggled with them. Pon kept moving and squinting at the graves.

Cavalier took a few steps forward. His instincts were to help Dempster and his daughter, but he was restrained by Jacinta, who moved past, saying, 'Don't do anything.' She trotted to intervene in the scuffle.

The Mexicans pushed and shoved Dempster. One hit him with an elbow blow across the chest. The Australian threw a straight punch, hitting the Mexican on the nose and bringing him to his knees. Another pulled out a gun from a holster under a vest, just as Jacinta arrived.

'Give me that!' she demanded, pointing at the gun. The Mexican lowered it. Jacinta stood square on and repeated 'Give it to me!'

Moments later Marco Rodriguez appeared and spoke to the Mexicans.

'Show some respect in this place!' he ordered. The one who had drawn his weapon stood hunch-shouldered and crossed himself. Jacinta took the gun from him and thanked Rodriguez. While the altercation occurred, Pon kept tripping along the rows of graves until she stopped and fell to her knees. She laid out the flowers at the memorial stone for her great-uncle on her paternal side, Victor Donald Cavalier. She began crying. Cavalier, who had kept his eyes on her, took a deep breath. He felt tears welling. Every instinct was to run and hold her. Cavalier removed his glasses for a few seconds, wiped his eyes and sidled along with a group of travellers behind the Mexicans.

He felt someone beside him. It was Cowboy, wearing a big sombrero. His boot spurs glinted in the sun. He stared at Cavalier, who acknowledged him without saying his name, as he had met him as Edward Blenkiron. Seconds later, his mother arrived, apologised for her son's behaviour and marched off, holding Cowboy's hand. He kept looking back at Cavalier, his spurs jangling with every step.

Other Mexican guards caught up with Pon when she stood and walked away from the memorial stone. She pushed them away until Cortez arrived. He looked at the name on the stone at which she had left the flowers. He walked briskly to her.

'Behave,' he said. 'You are making a spectacle of yourself!'

Pon spat in his direction. He seemed ready to strike her but could see Marco Rodriguez, wearing a light-coloured suit and black tie, striding his way.

'Whose grave was that?' Cortez demanded.

'My great-uncle!' Pon screamed.

'He has the same name as your father. You continue this way and I swear I shall have his ashes buried there too!'

Pon reluctantly sauntered away, surrounded by the Mexicans, just as Rodriguez confronted Cortez, moving him aside as they left the grave area.

'What are you doing?' he asked. 'Who is this woman?'

'She is my partner,' Cortez said, wiping his one good eye, which was weeping, although not from emotion. It always leaked tears when he was stressed.

'Let me remind you, Señor,' Rodriguez said, making sure he was out of earshot of others, 'I am now in charge of the cartel. I control the bullion and you will do as I say. Is that clear?' Cortez nodded and Rodriguez added, 'It was reported that you told your *other* girlfriend Talia Cruz and the actor Tyrone Risk that you controlled the gold. You said you would use it to bankroll a movie with, what, one hundred million?'

'That's a lie!'

'Risk said it in his TV documentary,' Rodriguez said, using a pink handkerchief to wipe his brow.

'I never said it.'

'You *did* say you'd help produce a movie, right?'

'I may have said that.'

'You also funded her tequila business.'

'I was one of several investors.'

Rodriguez looked around again. His two heavies were now behind him in their usual stance, backs ramrod-straight and hands covering their trouser fronts.

'I am in charge of the cartel, now, understand?'

Cortez nodded, submerging his contempt.

*

The train party of about seventy passengers were bussed to a jetty and then led onto a twenty-five-square-metre raft boat. The Mexicans and Pon sat near the front rows of seats as an Australian historian lectured the group on the Thai Burma railway. Cavalier stayed near the rear a few rows from Jacinta, who was joined by Azelaporn. He had remained on the train until then to entertain his Chinese courtesans. He heard about the disturbance in the cemetery.

'I'll have a chat to Cortez about keeping his woman in line,' he whispered in Jacinta's ear. 'She always looks drunk.'

'Drugged,' she whispered back, 'he controls her that way.'

'It's none of our business, especially with Marco Rodriguez joining the train. He is the new "Capo". He has taken the reins of the cartel, although it's unofficial. He has control of the purse strings and is likely to invest big in Thailand and the region. Rodriguez will move out of drugs ...'

'When?'

Azelaporn shrugged and replied: 'When revenue from respectable businesses can allow it.'

'So that will be about the year twenty-one seventeen, right?'

Azelaporn glared and pretended to listen to the lecture. After another minute, he leaned to her again and said:

'This is boring, this farang history about the nineteen forties. I should have stayed on the train.'

Jacinta gave him a withering look of disapproval.

'I hope you are keeping an eye on our three teachers,' he whispered, 'the Muslims and this Frenchman. I don't trust any of them. They may be up to something.'

'The Indonesians, I admit, are suspect. They would not earn enough for this trip from their salaries.'

'I'm having their room searched.'

'Is that advisable?'

'Why?' He nodded to the right, where the two Indonesians were sitting and listening to the lecture. 'I am doing what you should have done.'

Jacinta bristled.

'And that Frenchman,' Azelaporn said, 'I want you to stay close. Watch him. There is something about him I don't like.'

'His good looks and manners, perhaps?'

'Don't be frivolous,' Azelaporn hissed. 'Cortez is paranoid about someone assassinating him. Why would a single man board the train for the second leg of the journey?'

'There are about six single men and women on board. There is an old American in a wheelchair. Perhaps we should put a guard outside his door too.'

Azelaporn was angered. Other travellers jerked their heads and gave disapproving looks.

'I am ordering you to put guards outside the Frenchman's door,' he said angrily under his breath. 'He is to be watched around the clock.'

'I still don't understand why you suspect him.'

'Instinct my dear, instinct. You recall how good, how perfect it was in our police work.'

'No, I don't,' she said with a cynical look.

Azelaporn's face burned again, but before he could abuse her, she asked, 'And the Indonesians? Do you want them under guard too?'

'Maybe. Depends on what security finds in their luggage.'

*

Early afternoon, the train chugged out of Kanchanaburi on the long leg down through southern Thailand towards the border with Malaysia. Cavalier ventured out of his cabin after a couple of hours as the train meandered on its way. He entered the library, which doubled as a massage parlour, with books lining one wall and open cubicles at one end of the carriage. Cavalier had tension in his shoulders, as he often did in the period before the culmination of an assignment. He asked for an hour's Thai massage and was handed judo-style pants and top and directed to a change room. When he returned, he was told to lie face down and found he was next to Dr Makanathan on one table and her husband on the other side of her. Cavalier wanted to avoid conversation. Apart from her unsurpassed forensic skills, Makanathan had a reputation for being an incisive researcher, interviewer and thinker when investigating crime, particularly murder.

The three of them were attended by Thai masseuses dressed in navy-blue, red and white uniforms. Cavalier, stretched out on his front, turned his head away, so that he was not facing Makanathan. She was speaking loudly enough for him to hear and seemed to be inviting responses from him with comments about the French food and chef. He ignored them, shut his eyes and drifted in and out of a half-sleep, while enjoying the massage. He jerked his head when the masseuse pushed hard on his left Achilles tendon. She apologised. When he rolled onto his back, the masseuse pushed his shirt up and uncovered four scars on his abdomen. Her eyes widened.

'Oh, sorry!' she gasped.

The Makanathans turned their heads to see what had caused the masseuse to react. Thinking the Frenchman would not have Thai, Dr Makanathan spoke rapidly to the doctor.

'Marks on his stomach!' she said. 'Injuries! I have seen wounds like that before.'

'From what?' her husband asked.

'Bullets.'

Cavalier pretended he had not understood the exchange and inwardly cursed for having exposed himself, in more ways than one.

'Arh! The man is a soldier?' Makanathan said in English for Cavalier's benefit. 'A war hero perhaps?'

'French Foreign Legion,' he said with an enigmatic look while he let the masseuse manipulate his shoulders, arms, chest and stomach.

'Arh, so I was right!' Makanathan persisted.

'I was joking,' Cavalier said. 'I've never been shot.'

'Then how did you get the wounds?' she asked, her inquisitiveness bordering on rudeness.

'An industrial accident, Madame,' Cavalier said as he shut his eyes and turned away.

'I am sorry, sir,' Makanathan remarked and let the conversation lapse.

*

Cavalier returned to his cabins and did not appear as either Blenkiron or Blanc for the rest of the day. In the evening, as the Express glided deep into Thailand's south, he applied his 'old man' make-up, dressed again as Blenkiron and rolled himself out of the presidential suite and along through carriage 30, where several Mexicans paid him scant attention.

He could hear shouting and crying coming from the compartment harbouring his daughter and her captor. He hesitated outside the door, pretending he was having trouble with the chair's driving mechanism. One of the guards glanced at him and was about to offer help when Cavalier moved on, pushing his way through the lounge into the observation car. Twenty people, including six men wearing dinner suits, were having a drink before the first of two sittings in the three dining cars, 'St Louis', 'Merlin,' and 'New Orleans.'

Cavalier, earpiece attached to a phone, sipped another double malt Scotch and ice. He watched the passing parade of paddy fields, jungle and villages that flashed by in a continuous vista, like a video on a loop, with minor variations, as the flaming ball of sun drifted into cloud behind them on the horizon. The rice fields of the central plains turned from a sunlit, phosphorescent emerald to dark green. He was feeling almost at peace when Azelaporn burst into the car, followed by Jacinta. She sat as close to Cavalier as she dared so he could hear the Thai conversation. Azelaporn gestured at Cavalier in the chair and motioned for her to ease away from him.

'Don't worry,' she said, 'he is nearly deaf.' She glanced at his phone. 'He's listening to music too.'

'I was right about the Muslims,' Azelaporn began.

'The Indonesians?'

'Don't interrupt. This is serious. We found maps and photos under the mattresses and hidden in suitcases. They are casing the train.'

'Weapons?'

'Not that the security guards found, no.'

'What are you going to do?'

'I'll speak to Huloton, but I want to interrogate them. Then I'll throw them off the train at the Malaysian border, where they probably belong.'

'They're Indonesians.'

'They are fucking Muslims.'

Azelaporn demanded a Mekong whiskey from a steward.

'Jacinta, you should have been onto them,' he said. 'I insist you find out about that Frenchman. He still worries me. Sleep with him if necessary.'

Jacinta gave him a reproachful look. Yet she had wanted Azelaporn to believe he was the one who had discovered them. Had she told him she had information on them, he would have become suspicious of her source.

'I have placed you at dinner with him, along with that revolting Mongol retard and his mother. Be sweet; be charming. Take him for a drink afterwards; find out what he is doing. If we discover anything on him that makes us at all suspicious, we'll kick him off with the Muslims.'

Jacinta began to protest, but Azelaporn stopped her.

'If you want to be paid out,' he said aggressively, 'you'll do as I say.' Then, in his usual quixotic fashion, he added what he saw as a sweetener: 'Provide some evidence that he is up to something, even a suspicion of it, and you'll receive a good bonus.'

Jacinta stood up, glanced at Cavalier, who had heard every word, and stormed out of the observation car. When Azelaporn finished his drink ten minutes later and left, Cavalier backed up into the observation lounge. He ordered a glass of water, sat in his chair with his back to the door leading into the Mexican carriages, and watched the movements for the next half-hour. He observed the changing of the guard in the carriages, and noted the slackness of the Mexicans, who laughed and joked in carriage 32.

Finally, he rolled through carriages 32, 31 and 30, and returned to the door of his suite. Signalling to a steward, Cavalier put on his cantankerous act and said, 'I am not coming to dinner. I don't wish to be disturbed. Leave the breakfast outside the door tomorrow and don't, whatever you do, knock.'

'Of course, sir. We won't do that again.'

'Make sure you don't,' Cavalier said rudely, and bumped his way into the suite, refusing help from the steward.

28

UNMASKED

Once inside and locked in, Cavalier entered the adjoining suite, showered and changed into a light white suit and purple bow tie. He shifted any possible future incriminating evidence into the presidential suite, judging and hoping that a security or any other break-in would be in the Frenchman's state cabin, and not the American's presidential suite.

A note under the door from a steward assigned him to the New Orleans dining car, and a particular seat number. That left him an hour and half to kill before eating. He wandered down to the piano bar in the lounge car, the train's social epicentre, with a book on Napoleon by a French biographer. There were five couples. The men wore dinner suits; the women were all in evening dress. He began to order a double malt whisky but checked himself. He may have been one of the few on board ordering this drink, and he had already devoured a few as American Edward Blenkiron.

Cavalier asked for a rum and orange juice and sat on a high white chair at a new marble-topped bar that had its initiation on this trip. He was joined by the Australian psychiatrist Hinkley and her son Cowboy. Hinkley was attracted to Cavalier is his guise as Claude Garriaud, and was happy to learn she would be sitting with him over dinner. She began asking him about his background and Paris.

'I'm taking Cowboy there in a few months,' she said. Cowboy was sitting, his short legs dangling, between Hinkley and Cavalier. He suddenly threw a hard punch with his left hand that hit Cavalier on his right shoulder. Cavalier pretended it had not hurt. Hinkley smiled sheepishly.

'Sorry about that,' she said without admonishing Cowboy, 'he thinks you're chatting me up.'

'Pardon?' Cavalier asked with a frown, 'I don't know this expression.'

'Um, he thinks you are flirting with me.'

'Oh,' Cavalier chuckled. He smiled at the stern-looking Cowboy and added, '*Mais,* I am not, young man!'

'Are you retired?' Hinkley asked.

'No, no, I am a teacher, looking for work at the moment.'

Out of the corner of his eye, Cavalier could see Cowboy lining up another punch. This time Cavalier swung his right shoulder back. Cowboy threw his fist and missed by a few centimetres. He overbalanced, clipped his face on the bar's marble edge and collapsed to the floor. Hinkley and Cavalier lifted him to his feet. He was not badly hurt from the hit and fall, despite blood trickling from the corner of his mouth. Hinkley whisked him off to a bathroom with a steward in attendance offering first aid.

Cavalier left the bar and settled into a chair in a corner. He began reading his book but was distracted by the histrionics of a Singaporean pianist, different from the Thai who had performed the day before in place of Pon. His speciality was ragtime jazz, with a few variations. He kicked his chair out as if he were a latter-day Elton John, and climaxed a long bracket of songs with a more than passable version of 'Rhapsody in blue'. Cavalier returned to his reading for another half-hour.

The numbers in the bar built and the pianist returned for another bracket, beginning with a not-so-good version of 'Dance me to the end of love'. The second sitting of diners drinking before the meal numbered about forty when Jacinta waltzed in wearing a short powder-blue dress and showing an impressive cleavage. The open back revealed she did not need a bra. Her high heels, adventurous for the sometimes jolting walk along the corridors, accentuated her ultra-slender legs and high calves, and pushed her height to above most of the others in the bar. Her jet-black hair, which until now had been arranged in a businesslike bob on top, was loose and touching her shoulders. She was accompanied by Azelaporn, his bull neck seeming more bulbous in an ill-fitting dark dinner suit and black bow tie. He was wearing his trademark mirror sunglasses, and looked agitated. They propped at the bar and whispered in Thai to each other.

'I've had Garriaud's compartment searched,' he said.

'And?'

'We found nothing incriminating.'

'So, he is not under suspicion?'

'No, he still is.'

'Why don't you trust him?'

'He is a farang, and French.'

'That's racist!'

'So what if I am?' Azelaporn nodded his head sharply. 'He's in the corner, reading. You must do your duty.'

'My duty? This is not for king and country.'

'I am ordering you to fuck him,' he hissed.

Jacinta shook her head and was about to leave him when he gripped her arm. 'You took this job knowing it might not be all peaches and cream. You must know that if you screw men they blab. You'll learn all we want to know.'

'I refuse to have you dictate to me with whom I should be intimate. That is an order too far.'

'You fancy him, don't you?' Azelaporn sneered, 'I noticed him watching you when we walked in.' His tone softened. 'He fancies you. Every man in this bar fancies you. You know that.'

'I am *not* one of your bimbo Chinese courtesans or bar girls! *You* know that!'

'Of course, I do. But Jacinta, it is not as if I ever asked you to do this before.' He glanced over her shoulder at Cavalier. 'Look, as I told you, if you do this I promise you a nice *extra* bonus.'

Jacinta stood and towered over Azelaporn.

'Go and play with your whores!' she said with a fierce glare. Azelaporn rubbed his face. His bullying had never worked when dealing with her. He had never pushed her too hard. He was intimidated whenever he shoved her to a brink and she answered back. Azelaporn had witnessed many times her demolition of men twice her weight in the Muay Thai boxing ring, and the ferocity of her attacks on all opponents. He turned and marched out of the bar.

Jacinta asked Cavalier if she could join him. He bounced up and in halting, yet confident Franglais ordered her a glass of Champagne.

'My boss suspects you and the Indonesians,' she said quietly in Thai. 'He wants me to be close to you; as close as I can.'

'I am sure that is not necessary.'

'I agree,' she said, holding up her glass to him, 'but I may have to do what he wants.' She sipped the Champagne and leaned in close. 'He has had your cabin searched.'

Cavalier could not quite hide his concern. His forehead stretched. He was not always at ease masquerading as other people and this was another vulnerable moment.

'*My* cabin?' he asked.

Jacinta nodded.

Cavalier was relieved. He had moved all his notes and his backpack of rifle pieces into the presidential suite.

'Hmm,' he mumbled, 'did he find anything?'

'Apparently not. But he is set against you for some reason.'

'Why?'

'Perhaps because you are a good-looking Frenchman. He hates farang.' She looked away and then locked eyes on him. 'He wants me to take action.'

'What "action" exactly?'

'Sleep with you. What do you think of that?'

'Might be the beginning of a beautiful friendship, or the end of one.'

'He suspects you of *something*,' she said.

'Of what, I wonder?'

Jacinta gestured helplessly. 'He is a supreme *ass-hole*,' she said softly, 'a dangerous man. He is whimsical and paranoid.'

'What *really* made him suspicious about me?'

'Well,' she said slowly, and began counting on her fingers, 'one: you are travelling alone; two: you are not in the same age bracket as most of the retirees; three: you look very fit, four: an out-of-work teacher could not afford the trip, and five …'

'What do you think?'

'I think you are not who you purport to be,' Jacinta said with a cunning look. 'You can drop your pretence with me. It is an impressive image, but it did not take me long to work it out.'

'What gave it away? My removing the beard?'

She shook her head. 'Your mannerisms.'

Cavalier half-smiled. It made him nervous once more, although he had trust in her not to disclose his identity.

'Also the way you walk,' she added after some thought. 'You still have that slight limp from your Achilles problem.' She sipped her drink. 'With those things in mind, I began to study your face, your body, your hand movements, your manner. You are not a great actor. A good one maybe, with your French gestures and accent, but not a great one.'

'Third-rate, I'd say.'

'No one can cover up everything.'

Cavalier felt vulnerable. He sipped his drink and changed the subject: 'What do you think about the Indonesians?'

Jacinta shrugged. 'They could have been just nosey. They might be doing some industrial espionage to copy the train's design. Then again, they had maps. They could simply be tourists.'

'Unlikely,' Cavalier said. 'Gregory had them under surveillance in Chiang Mai.'

'For what?'

'Terrorism. They had been plotting something in Australia. What if they learnt of the bullion?'

'Go on?'

'ISIS and its affiliates in the south—the Malaysians, the Philippines and Indonesians—would love to put their bloody paws on such booty.' Jacinta stared. 'The oil situation in Syria and Iraq is an issue. The fields are being bombed out of existence. If they haven't got it, they can't sell it. ISIS is on the way to defeat and running out of cash.'

'Now you have me concerned,' she said. 'What would they be up to? Destroying the train? Stealing the bullion?'

Cavalier sipped his drink as the pianist played 'As time goes by'.

'Suppose you were running an ISIS affiliate and your brothers in the Middle East put pressure on you to aid the cause.'

'They are already robbing banks.'

'Right. ISIS is also stepping up its hostage-taking. They could obtain a reasonable haul on the Express …' He paused. 'Imagine these two Indonesians were doing the reconnoitring for an attack.'

29

COWBOY AND CHAOS

Hinkley returned to the bar with Cowboy, who had a bandage over the corner of his mouth. Cavalier, concerned, stood and enquired about his condition.

'He'll be okay,' Hinkley said. 'Just a small cut. See you at dinner …'

Cavalier returned to his chair next to Jacinta, just as Dr Makanathan and her husband joined Hinkley and Cowboy at the bar.

'Huloton seated those four at dinner last night,' Jacinta said. 'They hit it off. Three specialist doctors: one in psychiatry; one formerly in heart surgery; the third in DNA. They joked that they might write a book together: *The intersection of the mind, heart and DNA.*'

The train manager took the microphone and announced that the second dinner sitting was ready. The guests began filing into the three dining rooms. Jacinta and Cavalier found their cubicle for four. Hinkley was already seated with Cowboy, who didn't seem thrilled that Cavalier was joining them, although he was soon glued to Jacinta. Introductions were made just before the overweight, over-refreshed French chef, Monsieur Bonnet, appeared. He enthused about his concoctions, beginning with warm goat cheese soufflé with asparagus and a delicate Thai curry bouillon. Cavalier's approving comments indicated he might be French. This triggered the chef into waxing lyrical about the main course of grilled snowfish with vegetables in a vermouth and soya sauce. He was interrupted by Cowboy, who brought his fist down hard on the table.

'Monsieur,' Hinkley said, 'my son wants his fish and chips.'

'Now?' the chef asked more than a little miffed. 'He does not want to try the soufflé?'

'He will not eat goat.'

'Madame, it is *fromage!*'

'I appreciate that, but my son does not.'

The chef was affronted and stormed off just as Azelaporn arrived in an excited state and whispered in Jacinta's ear: 'The Muslims have disappeared! They are not on the train!'

'You've searched everywhere? The Mexican carriages too?'

Azelaporn, still wearing his mirror-glasses, nodded vigorously.

'Calm down,' she said, staying composed herself, 'if they have left ...'

'They didn't return to their cabin after Kanchanaburi,' Azelaporn said, raising his voice.

'Your raid would have caused their departure.'

Azelaporn went red and was about to abuse his deputy when he noticed everyone staring at him.

Cowboy was disturbed by Azelaporn's anger. He began swinging his left arm into the window frame: bang! bang!

bang! Azelaporn glared at Cowboy and left. Cowboy farted, loudly enough for the next cubicle to be disturbed again. The smell caused Jacinta to cover her mouth.

'*Pardon-moi*,' Cavalier said with a grin as if he had been responsible, 'I am sorry!'

'You are so gallant,' Jacinta said with a wry smile at Cavalier.

'Oh shit!' Hinkley said. 'He hasn't had his medication!'

Cowboy kept up the steady hammering on the window and wall. Hinkley wrinkled her nose at the strong smell while fiddling in her handbag. She took out pills. 'He does that banging all night, every night. We have loud fans in the house at home to drown it out. The rest of my family can't sleep otherwise.' She lifted a glass of water to Cowboy's lips, popped one pill in his mouth and urged him to swallow his medication. 'He has broken stuff wherever we are,' Hinkley said, 'if I miss his medicine by even an hour.' She gave a short laugh. 'We are banned from two of my local cafes in Brisbane.'

Cowboy kept up his window abuse as he swallowed two more pills. People in the next cubicle courteously said nothing.

Huloton stood by their cubicle wringing his hands.

'Your boss is in a terrible mood over the "departures",' he said to Jacinta. 'He says he will fire you.'

'He won't. Let him simmer down. I shall attend to the issue when I am ready.'

Huloton dropped his voice to a hoarse whisper: 'But Madame, what if they 'ave placed a bomb somewhere?'

'You've searched their cabin thoroughly, and the rest of the train?'

'*Oui*, of course!'

'Then you have done all you could.'

Huloton retreated, dissatisfied. After a few minutes, Cowboy seemed to have settled with his medication. His mother noticed he was staring at Jacinta.

'Don't stare, Cowboy,' she said, and turning to Jacinta added: 'I'm sorry. I don't think he has ever been close to someone as beautiful and elegant as you.'

'Nor have I,' Cavalier remarked, raising his glass to Jacinta.

'No, seriously, he is intrigued, I can see it,' Hinkley said 'I've never seen him this way before.' She chortled and said to Cavalier: 'He is not happy with you; although you passed the Cowboy test.'

'Oh?' Cavalier said with a pout, 'and what is that?'

'When he struck you.'

'Oh, it was nothing, Madame.'

'Maybe. After something like that, people never come near us again!'

Cavalier smiled politely. Cowboy didn't seem to approve of the comments. He bashed the table, causing drinks to spill. A steward attended to the mess before the entrées were served.

'You communicate with Cowboy well,' Cavalier remarked. 'How do you manage it?'

'I use a special computer software package of words and pictures. He responds by pressing keys.' She turned to Cowboy. 'You've written some wonderful poetry, haven't you Cowboy?'

He looked blank, turned his head away and went on hitting the window.

'I recall reading something about that,' Cavalier said.

'It was in the Australian papers,' Hinkley said, 'where did you read it?'

'It was on a French news service,' Cavalier said with a pretend frown, 'on the Internet, I believe.'

'Oh, I didn't know that,' Hinkley said, pleased the story about her son's poetic skills had made the international news outlets. Cavalier tried to divert her from his faux pas. 'It was quite beautiful if I recall. Something lyrical about him being lost in a void, or the world …'

'Yes, yes,' Hinkley said, brightening, 'you have an excellent memory. And so does Cowboy. He will recall frightening detail about everything on this train and everything at all stops. He'll recall even the positions of pot plants and rubbish bins.'

'Does he know you are talking about him now?' Cavalier asked.

'He has an idea. He tunes in and out. Once he has seen or noticed any object, he can bring it back. It is a feature with some autistics, but not all, and it is confused by his Down syndrome condition.'

When Hinkley turned her focus to spoon-feeding Cowboy, Jacinta rolled her eyes at Cavalier.

'Maybe you are more a second-rate actor, after all,' she whispered in his ear.

'What do you mean?'

'Your enthusiasm for information on him nearly blew your disguise. But you recovered well.'

30

JACINTA'S APPRECIATION

Jacinta walked Cavalier back to his cabin after the meal.

'Are you going to invite me in?' she asked.

'If you like; a nightcap perhaps?'

Jacinta locked the door and approached him. Cavalier was surprised at her seductive manner. He was concerned not to antagonise or upset her in any way, given that she was the one person in Asia who could expose his double 'game'. In effect, she held a life or death power over him, if she wished to exercise it. It made him wary and keen to avoid intimacy. So far, Jacinta had repeated her approach to the Mendez assignment by remaining a passive supporter, who had let Cavalier use his ingenuity and experience in challenging situations.

'This is where I must find out what you are doing,' she said, 'who you really are.'

Cavalier undid his bow tie and the top button of his shirt.

'Hmm,' she said nodding to his chest hair, 'reminds me of an Australian with a similar chest full of hair.'

'Yeah, well I used to wear a gold Buddha chain around my neck to show me where I should stop shaving.'

Jacinta half-smiled. 'You're not that bad. Your chest is hardly a mohair sweater. I only saw this Australian naked once, or nearly so—in the dark at a hotel pool in Bangkok,' she pulled at his shirt and exposed his scars from bullets. 'And I never saw evidence of his past—like these.' She ran her hand over the scars.

Cavalier removed his jacket. He fixed them both a double malt whisky and ice. He saluted her as they sat on the plush sofa.

'This is what's called a "steadier",' he said, his expression more serious.

They sat in silence, listening to the train's beat before Jacinta remarked: 'This is where I am under orders to find out about you.'

'A gentle, seductive grilling, perhaps?'

'I know this expression. I think it is better to say a "slow pan fried".'

'There is not much of interest really. Just a simple French peasant family from outside Montpelier.'

'No French Foreign Legion?'

'You know about the Legion?'

'You were in it, *Monsieur Claude*?'

'I wish I had been, for a short time at least.'

'Why?'

'The experience.'

'You like to work alone, no?'

'I prefer it. I've known a few members of the Legion. They were spirited, devil-may-care.'

'Doing France's dirty work in North Africa?'

'That is the downside,' he said, 'the reason I never bothered, although I was invited to join, twice. Similar to the CIA, the Legion wouldn't give me clues as to what I'd be doing. I rejected their offer.'

'When did the CIA want you?'

'When I was a journalist in Melbourne. I was twenty-four. That was the first time. One of their reps in Australia had heard about my capacities other than in journalism. Without specifics for the job, I couldn't judge what would be expected of me. Money was enticing, though—three times my newspaper salary. The downside was that I would not have my job in journalism. I needed more experience in the writing business.'

'Did you ever find out what they wanted you for?'

'I did, actually. It brought me to Chiang Mai for the first time.'

'For what?'

'Did you ever hear of the Handy Nugget Bank?'

'Not really.' Jacinta frowned. 'Although the name is familiar. I think Azelaporn may have had a link to it, a long time ago.'

Cavalier looked out the window again.

'So what about this bank?' she asked.

'I've said enough.'

'You see,' Jacinta smiled mysteriously, 'I have learnt something I did not know about you.'

'True,' he said. He reached and pulled a curtain across to reveal a blur of jungle in the darkness. 'Is the train speeding up?'

'Maybe,' she said, reaching in her handbag for her phone and checking the time, 'it's not yet eleven p.m. Can't be in the territory yet.'

'What territory?'

'Extremists'. The train doubles its speed and more through the south of Thailand.'

'Why? Fearing an attack?'

'The Express takes no chances. It would be hard to stop it at top speed.'

They sat in silence for a few moments.

'I don't know how you plan to do it,' she whispered.

'Do what?'

'Please, Victor, don't play games.'

Cavalier did not answer. He sipped his drink and looked out the window.

'You know that there is a guard outside your door all the time?' she said.

'It's a problem, I admit,' he said.

'Do you have help on board?'

He stared out the window without answering.

'You're not thinking of—'

'There are footholds and handgrips on all the carriages.'

'You'll be spotted and shot!'

Cavalier pointed to the roof.

'You are not going on top!' she protested, 'if we go under a bridge ...'

'There are two tunnels between here and our destination. Neither would cause a person to be struck if he was prone on the roof.'

Jacinta looked concerned. 'You've done your homework. But someone is going to recognise you,' she said. 'You really should escape. The Americans will deal with Cortez.'

'Maybe they won't. In any case, it's my daughter I want to save. That's the main priority.'

'It's all too dangerous,' she hissed. 'Azelaporn is suspicious. Remember, he saw the real you in Bangkok at the Satan's Cave bar.'

'And he came to a cricket match in Chiang Mai last year. I was playing and he wanted to interrogate me.'

'Something will click in his mind. Especially if he does some recognition work. He did that last year when you escaped Thailand. He was smart enough to compare photos of you, and the Swede you impersonated. If he does that again, he will know it's you.'

'I'll take the chance.'

'Your disguise is good,' Jacinta persisted. 'However, if someone focuses on comparisons with real photos of you, they will make the link.'

'I am an illusion. I can only hope it lasts another day.'

'You love the charade, don't you?' she said. 'That performance you gave in Melbourne when we first met when you impersonated your cricket coach at an old school dinner; your taking off of a Frenchman to evade police in Chiang Mai; a Swede to carry out the liquidation of Mendez; an Englishman to escape Thailand last year; and now this, a Frenchman again. Any more characters you want to perform as?'

'Michael Caine would be cool,' he said with a slight smile as he sat up. 'People have often said I have his eyes.'

'Never heard of him.'

'He played the butler in a Batman movie.'

'Still never heard of him.'

'Do you know Mr Bean?'

'Yes. Everyone in Thailand knows and loves him,' she paused and scrutinised him. 'You look nothing like him.'

'Maybe not, but I know an English guy in Chiang Mai who is the spitting image of the Rowan Atkinson character. Every time he goes to the market, Thais point and tell him he looks like him. He becomes very angry, just like Mr Bean, and goes home to complain to his Thai partner.'

'You seem relaxed, for someone planning to …'

'I can assure it's a cover for nerves. I'm always on edge at these moments, although I am clear on what I must do.'

'Don't you fear death?'

'I try not to think about it. This is not a suicide mission.'

She looked concerned.

'I do know I don't want to be there when it happens,' he said flippantly.

'So you are scared. You can back out now. You can achieve so much more alive.'

'We all die,' he said, his expression more serious, 'but only what we die for counts.'

'Please, you should leave the train.'

'There are no scheduled stops between here and Singapore.'

'I can arrange it. Just go, please …'

'I can't leave Pon now.'

'If you manage to achieve your mission, have you an exit plan?'

'No. It depends …' He felt he had said too much. He stood up. 'I need to rest.'

Jacinta walked to the door and unlocked it.

'If you need any assistance …'

'I don't want you implicated,' he said touching her shoulder. 'If you know nothing, you can't be accused of being an accomplice.'

31
MIDNIGHT MEETING

Cavalier woke at 2 a.m. after three hours sleep and felt the Express was now living up to its name as it sped into Thailand's jungle-riven south with its interspersed rice fields and dragon rocks flowing all the way from the Himalayas, which burst up through the vegetation. He looked out the window and watched the moonlit landscape of tangled undergrowth broken by ramshackle villages or cleared field, a false green by day but black and grey at night. He concentrated on staying awake, taking a few moments to collect his thoughts. Several things conspired to lull him into further sleep: the hypnotic clip of the wheels; the reassuringly steady train movement plunging on into the dead of night; the just discernible clang of the couplings at his end of carriage 29; the unthreatening, slight back-and-forth slide of the woodwork in his cabin. It felt like a sleep-inducing womb.

The moonlight fell away as the train burst through a long cutting. The room's colour scheme seemed to change to a dark purple. It was ethereal and strange, and it brought Cavalier to his full senses just as the Express emerged back into the endless jungle.

He shook his head, breathed deeply and moved into the presidential suite, making sure to lock the partition door, especially after being told that security guards had searched his cabin. He dressed as Edward Blenkiron, edged his wheelchair into the corridor and wheeled left towards the end of the train. He could see security guards at the other end of carriage 29. Three Mexicans, all slumped in sleeping poses, guarded the corridor leading to carriages 30, 31 and 32, the observation lounge bar and the observation carriage.

Cavalier, his special glasses on and hat jammed down on his scalp, drove his chair with its faint but distinct whirring sound, which was more pronounced in the quiet of the night. The one guard fully awake barely acknowledged him.

Cavalier was surprised to see Topapan and Marc Makanathan in the observation car. They were both smoking and enjoying the cooler night air. Next to them, but not engaging with them, were the Dempsters, the Australian graziers. Cavalier rolled past them, closer to the end of the train, and ignored the other four. He sat at forty-five degrees to them.

After five minutes, Azelaporn appeared with Cortez. Cavalier froze, but had the presence of mind to ignore them. He placed his extrasensory earpieces in his ears. When they had passed, he edged his chair around so that he almost had his back to the new arrivals, who perched in the open alcove at the very end of the train.

Cavalier adjusted the sound and heard the conversation from about eight paces.

'Can that old man hear or see?' Cortez said.

'Do not worry,' Azelaporn replied with a wave of the hand, and annoyed that he had to speak English, 'he is deaf, nearly.'

'He seems to be listening to music okay.'

'With the volume up very high,' Azelaporn chuckled. His expression changed as he added, 'Don't worry about the Muslims. They are no longer on the train.'

'What were they doing?'

Azelaporn shrugged. 'No one knows.'

'And that Frenchman you mentioned?'

'He had books in his cabin, that's all. But we're watching him. I have a guard right outside his door all day and night he is inside. My deputy says he is harmless. I ordered her to sleep with him.'

'Did she?'

'Not sure. She was not happy about my directive.'

Cortez wiped his weeping good eye and fiddled with his eyepatch. He grinned and exposed uneven, nicotine-stained teeth.

'How very fortunate for him, if he did,' he observed as he lit up a cigarette, much to Azelaporn's irritation. 'Have you looked closely at all the Americans on board?' Cortez asked.

Azelaporn nodded vigorously. 'There are ten; five couples all over seventy and retired.'

'And that old prick in the chair?'

'Yes.'

There was a disturbance at the entrance to the car. Pon, dressed in a pink nightgown, was trying to enter. Cortez tossed his cigarette over the side and bustled to her.

'Take her back to the room and give her a shot,' Cortez

ordered his men. 'Lock her in and stay with her until she is asleep. Make sure she is in the top bunk.'

Cavalier twitched in his chair but did not turn his head. It was all he could do to restrain himself again as Cortez gave Pon a sharp slap across the face and hissed at her, 'Behave yourself, you drunken slut!'

Two guards dragged her screaming back to the cabin.

Cavalier kept staring out into space as Cortez returned to Azelaporn, bumping the wheelchair as he did so.

'That damned woman!' Cortez said.

'She looks terrible! I can't believe it is the same person whom I heard play in your Chiang Mai bunker last year.'

'It's sad,' Cortez said. 'She was so beautiful. It's the drugs ...'

'You should dump her. She will be trouble.'

Cortez nodded ruefully and ran his hand through his hair. 'I'd like to get rid of her, permanently,' he said.

'Not on the train,' Azelaporn said with a jerk of his head as Makanathan and her husband were leaving the carriage, 'not with that bitch on board.'

'I have read about her,' Cortez said, glancing at the doctors as they left.

'She is bad for police! I had much trouble with her. Sticks her nose in every investigation.'

'I shall attend to my girlfriend when we reach Singapore. She has passed her use-by date. Her piano performances are woeful.'

'You will ...?' Azelaporn began and made a sweeping motion across his neck.

'I have no choice. She knows too much.' He paused a few seconds and added, 'It will not be a problem. She is thought to be dead anyway.'

'You do not worry about her father, the journalist? We believed he assassinated Mendez.'

'He thinks his daughter was guillotined by Mendez. That's why he killed him.'

'You will avenge his death?'

'Huh! If we could find him. The coward has disappeared. I have my spies in Australia. They can't find him.'

Even though Cavalier could hardly tolerate what he was hearing, he had to stay and learn as much as he could. He saw Marco Rodriguez enter the carriage. He strode past Cavalier and joined Azelaporn and Cortez at the rear of the train.

Rodriguez shook hands with them.

'This is a good time to meet,' he said, 'middle of the afternoon in New York. I am wide awake.'

Cortez lit another cigarette. Rodriguez joined him with a cigar.

'The Chinese bought more gold today,' Cortez said. 'Our bullion went up $10 million.'

'*Our* bullion?' Rodriguez said, staring hard. 'It is not yours. Implant that into your skull, please. I don't know what Leonardo said or promised. But you are a salaried employee. I hope you comprehend that.'

Cortez's head movement was ambivalent.

'He who has the gold rules, eh?' he remarked.

'Yes, and it belongs to the cartel.' Rodriguez turned to Azelaporn. 'You are sure about security?'

'No problem,' Azelaporn said. 'The bullion will be met at Singapore by the bank and its security. They will take it straight to their vaults.'

'Good,' Rodriguez said, 'I'm going back to bed.'

'We have arranged a frigate in Singapore,' Cortez said.

'*You* arranged a frigate, not me. The gold goes into a Singapore bank. We are not going to risk pirates on the high seas trying to seize it.'

Cortez eye flared to his dead stare for a fraction of a second, although he refrained from arguing with his new boss.

'Let's meet here tomorrow an hour earlier,' Rodriguez said, 'say 2 a.m. All right?'

The others nodded and watched Rodriguez stride off, his heavies close behind him. Cavalier waited. He had his back to Cortez and Azelaporn and wanted to hear their reaction.

'I hate that shit!' Cortez mumbled. 'When Leonardo was in charge, we did all the hard work to build up the cartel. Now he wants to make it all legitimate. Property, stupid businesses with small profit margins, football teams, TV stations. It is not our core business!'

Cavalier rolled his chair slowly out of the car. He lingered at the door to Cortez's cabin. He watched the guards who sat between carriages 29 and 30. They were less lethargic with their bosses so close, yet there was still a carelessness in their attitude. Cavalier rolled on past the suite he was occupying as Blenkiron. One guard sat facing the door to Garriaud's cabin. He was asleep. Cavalier eased his chair forward to observe him for a few seconds. Then he backed up to the presidential suite just out of the guard's line of sight, and entered it.

Cavalier showered and worked on his plan. He looked at his phone. There were ten missed calls and messages from Melody Smith.

Sorry to have not replied,

he texted her,

but we are out of range and the train rules don't allow mobile use. Please send your team to Singapore by tomorrow afternoon. Stand by with trucks and arms, just in case. Am ready to use your special kit soon. Must do before Singapore. Wish me luck.

Smith sent back a quick response.

What train?

Bangkok Express. Pulls in about 8 a.m. on 27 April. Bullion on board. Must intercept before it goes straight to bank vaults.'

Which bank?

Don't know.

How many armed cartel?

A dozen.

Including Cortez?

No. Add two heavies with Marco Rodriguez, and his wife. She is quite hefty in a certain way.

Marco Rodriguez—Mendez's nephew?

The same.

What is he doing?

Protecting his investment.

There was a pause of thirty seconds before Smith's next text:

Why didn't you let us know about the Express?

I told you; I like solo operations.

But we could have helped you!

Just push your squad to Singapore train station on time, please.

32

LAST CHANCE

At 7.15 a.m. the next morning, the second of the trip, a steward knocked on Blenkiron's door, handed him his breakfast and, apologising profusely for the interruption, asked for his passport.

'Why?' Cavalier asked grumpily, knowing full well that they would soon be passing into Malaysia. He handed it over, shut the door and moved fast to remove his disguise before there was a knock at Garriaud's door.

'I'm in the bathroom,' he called. 'I'll bring the passport to the porter in a few minutes. Leave the breakfast tray outside the door.'

The steward obliged. Cavalier picked at both breakfasts and drank the coffee of one before leaving the trays outside the two doors. Dressed as Garriaud, he delivered the French passport to the porter.

An hour later the passports were returned. Cavalier wanted a break from masquerading as two different people. Still acting as Garriaud, he told a steward that he was not feeling well and would miss the lunch before the train reached

Butterworth inside Malaysia. He said he would consider later in the morning if he would join the tour of Penang Island. Cavalier felt sluggish after a couple of days devouring rich French food without his usual physical workouts. He cleared the floor in the presidential suite and went through a rigorous exercise routine, including calisthenics and yoga.

Late morning, he received a text message from Smith:

Have intercepted messages from Bangkok. IS branch in Basilan (Philippines) is set for an attack in Malaysia, next 24 hours. Mention of bullion in communications. Making assumption that they may target Express. Possible points Penang, Kuala Lumpur. Would need access to roads in and out if bullion is target.

Cavalier now felt compelled to stay on the train and not join the tour group, which he doubted would be attacked. The train, sitting at a station, would be the likely target. He informed Jacinta, who suggested to Huloton and Azelaporn that the passengers and security guards stay on alert on the train.

'What are they attacking for?' Azelaporn asked. 'If it's to rob the passengers that is one thing. The bullion is another.'

'I would imagine it's the bullion,' Jacinta said. 'My information is that there has been a flurry of exchanges on the IS networks with mention of bullion. Given their cash shortages, I doubt they are mounting an attack for Rolexes.'

'Where did you obtain this?'

'Good contacts,' Jacinta said, 'impeccable.'

'You should share them!' Azelaporn said.

'Not a chance.' She turned to Huloton. 'Alert the Mexicans. And have your guard doubled at that end of the train.'

'Mon Dieu! What about the passengers?'

Jacinta pondered this for a moment. 'On second thoughts, let them go on the tour of Penang. That way they won't be in harm's way should there be an attack on the train itself. But make it a shorter trip. No more than three hours. Have four train guards go with them. See if you can commandeer some local police as well for both the train and the passengers.'

After the meeting, the Express jolted its way into Butterworth station, located on the northwest coast of peninsular Malaysia. The bland, gleaming white, ultra-modern structure had an eerie, almost morgue-like feel about it. No other train was on any track. No passengers were in sight. The Malaysian police had done a thorough job, it seemed, in shutting down the station, if not the surrounding area.

Jacinta knocked on Garriaud's door. He let her in. She noticed five canisters on the bed.

'What are you going to do?'

'If there is a fire fight, opportunities might arise. Chaos can provide good cover.'

'You'd be better staying out of it. You'd be exposed. Azelaporn would have you arrested.'

'By whom? He's not a cop any more. We're not in Thailand.'

'The train *is* Thai territory. Please don't put me in an invidious position.'

'I doubt that the train's status would stand up in a court of law,' Cavalier chuckled. 'The French could claim it's *their* territory.'

'Huloton could inform the Malaysian police.' Jacinta glanced at the canisters. 'You'd have some answering to do over your rifle.'

'You knew about that?'

'When you escaped down the Mekong to Vietnam last year, you shot at my boat with unerring accuracy. My brother monk was your pilot. He saw you assembling it.'

'You know pretty well everything now,' he said with a half-gesture of resignation.

'I don't think so,' she said.

Cavalier showed her to the door, keeping out of sight of passing passengers.

*

Cavalier assembled his rifle and loaded it. He sat by the window watching the passengers file out of the train and into a bus that would take them to Penang's Georgetown. He could hear them complaining about the heat, which was nudging forty-four degrees; many were using fans. He'd seen the sights along the town's cobbled streets before and did not envy them the conditions on a tour.

After the bus left, he saw about twenty police, including a local version of a SWAT team with automatic rifles, arriving. Huloton could be seen waving his arms in the direction of the rear of the train. With him was Rodriguez wearing another immaculate suit, this time a pinstripe, its pure wool unsuited to the weather. They were soon joined on the platform by Jacinta dressed in her all-black uniform of vest, trousers and cap. The only thing missing was the Thai Special Unit of Investigation (SIU) insignia on her cap and the breast pocket of her shirt.

He could see her taking charge, directing Huloton and giving an order to a rattled Azelaporn. She was also in a brief discussion with first Rodriguez, then Cortez. Cavalier gripped his rifle. *One shot*, he thought, his emotions taking control of him for a second. If he opened the window now, he would be almost certain to make a kill from about thirty paces. He put aside the temptation once more, aware it would have been a suicidal move. He looked along the platform for his daughter. She was not in sight. What had he done with her, Cavalier wondered for a depressing moment. He imagined an IS attack in which he could somehow fire off a shot at Cortez. However, he thought that the chances of doing a swab, extracting blood and taking snaps of the body would be next to impossible in such circumstances.

A nervous three hours passed. Cavalier tried reading the biography of Napoleon but could not concentrate. He spent time cleaning the rifle and his handgun once more. He was watchful when four women wearing white Muslim hijabs wandered onto the platform, and seemed confused as to their location. They pointed in every direction. His concern lessened as the women were joined by four Muslim men, then a squad of officious police, who ushered them brusquely off the platform, upstairs and out of sight.

The tour group returned. The train was away swiftly after they arrived and any possible attack had been averted, perhaps by the show of local police strength. Anyone spying on the Express would have reported on up to fifty armed officers, Mexican guards and train security personnel. It would have taken at least that many attackers in a concerted ambush to have any impact.

Huloton made the decision that there would now be no stop in Kuala Lumpur after consulting the Malaysian police, who were worried that there could be an ISIS strike there. They had cornered two trucks driven by suspected terrorists of a convoy of five in the city. The remaining three had slipped away and their whereabouts were unknown.

The Express swept through Kuala Lumpur's beautiful Moorish-style building at the south-east of the National Mosque, with several passengers complaining that they wished to photograph the renaissance-like facade and arched colonnades.

'You can see wonderful pictures of it on the net,' Huloton told them, knowing full well that some would grumble about not receiving full value for the trip as promised.

When a few protested further, he shut the conversation down by telling them, 'I am sorry, it is a security matter, about which I cannot speak.'

Cavalier dismantled his rifle and thought he should make an appearance as Blenkiron in his wheelchair. He rolled into the observation carriage and sat staring at the dense, impenetrable, dark-green Malaysian jungle. He wore his special glasses and hearing aids while others, including for a time Azelaporn and Rodriguez, relaxed. The heat was too much, so he wheeled into the airconditioned observation lounge and kept his lone vigil. He was absorbing the movements of the Mexican carriage as much as possible. There was activity in the region of Cortez's cabin. Cavalier had timed, to the second, how long it would take him to wheel from where he was to that door, open it, and then go through with his mission.

He believed he had to strike in the coming night. It was his last chance.

33

MARTYRS ON THE MOVE

The three-truck terrorist convoy lumbered south out of Kuala Lumpur just after midnight. In the lead truck were the ten members of the Philippines contingent making up one part of the Islamic State offshoot, Servants of Allah. They were all in the twenties and thirties. Most were attending to their weapons—rifles, AK-47s, handguns and swords. Some were singing; one had a banjo; others listened to music on their phones. One or two jokes flew around, perhaps to calm nerves, or just from bravado. Most of them were clean-shaven with short hair. Their dress was Western casual, primarily jeans and T-shirts; anything but traditional Muslim. Most were wearing caps, with various American and Japanese baseball team insignias. Apart from the weapons, they could have been on their way to a ball game or a picnic. This was the way the ISIS leaders had dictated they look. The terrorists had been flown in at different times over the past two weeks from the island of Basilan, the largest in the Philippines' Sulu archipelago. Their leader, known to all as 'Hercules', was a short, muscular man of twenty-eight with a shaven head. He looked as if he spent all day pumping iron—his biceps were too big for shirts and he always wore a collarless white vest.

The second truck held the home-grown and -trained Malaysian contingent of ten in this first-ever joint terrorist attack by extremists from the two countries. It would have been three, had the two captured Indonesian intelligence gatherers Irina and Nani been included. They were now languishing in a Kuala Lumpur jail. The average age of this group was about twenty-one years. They all had hair growth. A couple looked so young that it may have been a struggle to demonstrate this manliness. They wore blood-red martial arts uniforms and navy blue bandanas. Their weapons—all high-powered rifles—were sitting in a crate in the centre of the truck. The Malaysians were quiet and moved on cue into a prayer formation in the cramped area for a solemn session.

Truck three carried the overall commander and planner of the combined force, Syrian Abu Hal Basha, thirty-three years of age. He was roly-poly and cheerful, a condition and disposition that belied his role in the mission. Apart from the twenty warriors, he had to mind four suicide bombers, three of them sitting quietly in the back and one in the front with him as he drove the truck.

One was a thirty-year-old defector from the UK, named Robert George McKenna, who had been born Catholic to a British mother. His American father named Patrick had worked as a co-producer in Hollywood action movies including *Dances with Wolves, Superman II, Batman, Sixty Seconds* and *Death Warrior 11.* Patrick had been disappointed by his outstandingly good-looking son, who had toyed in his teens with becoming an actor, a career decision Patrick could have helped with through his wide film industry contacts.

Robert had looked for an adventurous outlet. He had settled on radical Islam, much to his parent's shock, and had flown in secret to Syria, going by the name Abdulla-al-Englandi ('the Englishman'). His conviction had faltered a month earlier when he learnt his wife was pregnant. With the help of drugs and some well-placed inspiration from the jolly Basha, he had firmed up once more for the mission, knowing that whatever the outcome of today's exercise, he would never see his wife again or meet his child.

The second in the rear was a bespectacled Syrian male, twenty-five-year-old Abu Moanmar, who was single, and regarded by everyone as a humble, deferential scholar with an unfathomable command of the Koran. He needed no substances to inspire him to the act of blowing himself up for the extreme Islamic cause. Moanmar was a true fanatic. He believed that he would control a harem of seventy-two virgins promised in the afterlife, although he wasn't clear what this meant or what he should do with so many of them. He was excited because Basha had been so enthusiastic about how wonderful it would be.

Moanmar claimed in his diary to have found reference to the certainty of his post-death grand sexual fortune in religious scriptures. He referred unselfconsciously, under the current circumstances, to being blessed for two things: he was himself unsullied and not homosexual.

The third suicide bomber was a thirteen-year-old female, known only as 'Amula the Paris Princess'. She was a pretty child with a round face and plump body. Her fourteenth birthday would coincide with the attack on the *Bangkok Express*, and the end of her life. In her drug-controlled state, Amula was convinced she would spend most of her special day in heaven. She had been born in France to Iraqi immigrants and had fallen in with a radical crowd at school in Paris's Arab enclave.

Brainwashed by local radical imams, she had been spirited to Aleppo in Syria to service the Islamic State fighters, along with thousands of other gullible young women, who believed that they were doing honourable and great things for the cause.

Used and abused by scores of young men, she had tried to commit suicide. Amula had been drugged into believing it would be a more admirable departure from earth if she became a martyr. She looked sullen and fiddled with two gold rings on her left hand, despite Basha's attempts to humour her and keep her from backing out of the mission.

'C'mon Amula,' Basha said, twisting in the seat to look at her, 'you've done a wonderful job with the warriors. They have all been lifted by their intimacy with you and will fight all the more in the knowledge that they will have many more like you when they enter the realms above.'

Amula did not respond. She stared at her leather sandals that poked out from under a long black dress. She was either buried in her own thoughts or petrified by what was about to occur.

'It is written that you will marry a prince of Islam,' Basha assured her, 'and that Allah forgives you and smiles upon you for your work and wonderful sacrifice.'

Amula now looked up, her face a changing vista of hope, fear and uncertainty. Basha smiled perfunctorily. In the end he would have no compunction about shooting her, a point he made clear in arguing that it was better to die *honourably* in Allah's name, rather than being executed in a way that would shame her memory and her family.

Bomber number four was the simplest and most malleable, Syrian Abu Qasawarta, just eighteen, who sat next to Basha in the front, begging him to teach him to drive once they reached the jungle outside Kuala Lumpur. Basha relented and let him take over the wheel, which led to a series of jolts before the young man adjusted to this new and challenging task.

'Where is the speedometer?' he asked.

'Are you really worried about speeding at this important time?' Basha asked in a moment of levity that he shared with those in the back. 'You're on your way to martyrdom!'

34

KILLING TIME

At 2 a.m. on the third night of the trip, Cavalier sat in his chair in the observation car minutes before the pre-arranged meeting of Rodriguez, Cortez and Azelaporn, who again were congregated at the end of train.

'I feel like pushing that creep out of the train,' Cortez said, jerking a thumb in Cavalier's direction as they arrived. 'He is here every night, staring out at the blackness.'

The others ignored the remark.

'What did you make of the security alert at Butterworth and the bypassing of KL?' Rodriguez asked, straightening his tie, and glancing around to see the Makanathans settling down and lighting cigarettes. The others shrugged without replying.

'Now *they* are a couple I'd like to push off the train,' Azelaporn said with a nod in the couple's direction. 'She makes me very nervous. Huloton informs me she is officially the most senior Thai on board the train, now we are in Malaysia. While on board we are still in Thai territory.'

'Does she carry a gun?' Cortez asked drily.

'Wouldn't think so,' Azelaporn replied.

'Then I don't think she is the most senior person on board,' Cortez said, tapping his vest, which hid a gun strapped to his side.

'I'd like to know about security in Singapore,' Rodriguez said.

'We will not be involving the Singaporean police,' Cortez said. 'They would be most interested in our steel boxes.' He grinned. The others were not amused.

'I don't think there would be an issue with terrorists,' Azelaporn said with a reassuring shake of his head. 'Apart from your guard, the bank will send its own trucks and guards. I've warned them to be extra vigilant and well armed.'

At that point Cavalier sloped off in his chair, leaving the carriage.

He heard Cortez say, 'Lucky he left when he did. That American prick gets on my nerves.'

'Has he said something to you?' Rodriguez asked.

'No. I just hate all Yankees!'

Cavalier glanced at his watch as he rolled through the observation lounge and into carriage 30. He pulled skin-coloured surgical gloves from his left trouser pocket and put them on. He then removed his all-purpose key from his right trouser pocket. He slipped the key into the lock, snapping open the door to the cabin. He rolled in, jumped from the chair and locked the door. He collapsed the chair and pushed it into the bathroom. Cavalier heard Pon stirring on the top bunk. He removed the KK pack, gun and silencer from the arm of the chair, and climbed up onto the top bunk, where his daughter was asleep, on her side and facing the wall. Pon was snoring lightly with shallow, sharp breaths, made louder in his ears, even though he had turned the ESEPs down low. He judged she was heavily sedated as he eased up next her. Cavalier wished to touch her tenderly and whisper that he was here and that everything would be all right. Yet he dare not. The shock would be too much for Pon.

He opened the kit, just as he heard movement from the observation lounge. He had no time to prepare the kit. Cavalier slipped the silencer onto the handgun. Cavalier could hear his own heart beating through the earpiece. He took the earpiece out just as Cortez fumbled with the lock. He stepped in and locked the door. Hearing Pon make a slight noise, the Mexican hesitated, his hand near the light switch. Cavalier's glasses allowed him to see Cortez clearly. Cortez switched on the light, turned and looked up to see Cavalier pointing the gun at him. Cortez sucked in his breath, his fish-like eye widening to show for a millisecond inside his murderous mind, yet it showed also fear. He had recognised Cavalier.

'She is all right,' Cortez said motioning to Pon, 'I ... I have looked after her. Please ... what good would killing me do?'

'I'm glad you know who I am, Señor,' Cavalier said. 'I'd hate to see you die without realising who your killer was. I will be your last sight.'

Cavalier took a step down the ladder, keeping his gun trained on the Mexican.

'Please, Señor, I mean you no harm ...'

'You tried to kill me on the Mekong River.'

'Please, please, Sir. I have billions in gold on board. You can have a share of it ... anything ...' His voice was trembling. He kept talking, hoping that help would come, or he could reach for his holstered gun under his vest. 'You must know I have billions in gold bullion. You can have as much as you like. I can arrange it. Please take it.'

Cavalier lifted his glasses so that they rested on his head.

'Think of that,' he said, 'what a wonderful last thought! All that gold you'll never be able to use. You'll be dead; like Mendez.'

Pon stirred again.

Cavalier put a finger to his lips and indicated that the Mexican move to the centre of the room.

'Lie on your back on the floor,' Cavalier said.

'What?'

'You heard me. Do it!'

Shaken, Cortez did as ordered. As he dropped to his knees, he reached for his gun. He turned to fire. Cavalier saw the movement. He shot the Mexican in the chest. Cortez crumpled, fell forward and rolled onto his side. The fall jarred the gun out of his hand. The muffled sound of the bullet, louder than Cavalier expected, caused Pon to roll over. Her eyes fluttered. Cavalier waited a few seconds, his gun trained on Cortez, before descending two more steps down the bunk ladder, gun in one hand, KK pack in the other. The Mexican's right hand seemed to reach for his weapon. Cavalier thought at first that it could have been a reflex action. Then he noticed the Mexican's one good eye burning with a flame of shock mingled with hate.

Cavalier reached the floor and stood a metre from his victim's feet. He fired a second shot into the Mexican's chest. The force of the bullet jolted Cortez's false eye from its socket and out from under the tartan patch. In the ensuing silence as Cavalier stepped closer, the white glass eye rolled towards his feet. He kicked it aside and pulled Cortez onto his back. He felt for his neck and wrist pulse. There was none. Blood had already seeped over his shirt vest and the upper part of his trousers. Cavalier glanced at the 'good' eye. It stared back, truly dead now and without the flame that had reflected his careless, soulless attitude to his own victims.

Cavalier pulled a swab from the KK pack and pushed it into the Mexican's mouth. His teeth set tight on it, snapping the swab. Half of it stayed lodged in the Mexican's mouth.

'Bugger you!' Cavalier muttered.

He removed the camera from the pack and took eight photos, four of the face from different angles and the same with the body. He pocketed the camera and noticed that Cortez's mouth was open again. Cavalier used the second swab, more gently this time, and collected mucus. Satisfied he had a good deal of moisture on it, he pushed it into its small cylinder. There was plenty of blood, still oozing from the chest, from which to draw a sample into the syringe. Cavalier kept clear of it, though, knowing that it could be judged as contaminated. He felt for a neck artery and plunged the syringe needle deep into it, drawing a good sample, before placing it too in its cylinder.

Concerned about the first swab in Cortez's throat, Cavalier took a knife and spoon from the bench, wedged open his mouth and tried to fish out the swab. Again, the glasses were helpful as he found it lodged partially in the Mexican's throat. After much dentist-like probing, he was able to retrieve it. He placed it in its cylinder.

Pon stirred on the bunk above. Cavalier waited. She mumbled something and gave a sustained cry but was soon snoring again. Cavalier took off the gloves, put them in the KK pack and wrapped it up. He lifted the wheelchair from the bathroom, took it to the door and placed his gun and the KK pack in the right-arm chair-rest pocket. He put on his hearing aid. He could hear Rodriguez and Azelaporn making their way into carriage 30.

Cavalier heard Rodriguez say:

'I want you to ask him now.'

'He may be in bed,' Azelaporn said.

'I don't care,' Rodriguez said. 'He only left us five minutes ago.'

Rodriguez knocked on the door. There was no response. Cavalier waited, his heart seeming to burst through the earpieces. Rodriguez kept banging. Pon half sat up on the bunk. She groaned a semi-conscious protest, and then fell back on the bunk without looking down at her stricken captor and Cavalier. Rodriguez heard her reaction and banged again.

Doing his best to sound like Cortez, he called, 'Cannot!'

'What's he doing in there?' Rodriguez asked

'Fucking, by the sounds of it,' Azelaporn said.

'See me first thing in the morning,' Rodriguez shouted, 'before breakfast!'

Cavalier grunted a response.

Rodriguez and Azelaporn shuffled off, Rodriguez still complaining. Cavalier was about to leave the cabin when he heard footsteps coming along the corridor from both directions. The Makanathans had finished their short break and were heading back to their cabin. They greeted two other couples who passed them. A minute later there was no one in the corridor near him. Cavalier switched off the light, opened the door, stepped outside and slipped into the wheelchair. He wheeled along the corridor, mindful of the guard outside Garriaud's door. Cavalier could see the guard's legs as he sat on a chair.

Cavalier stopped at his door, opened it and rolled in. He noticed the guard move just as Cavalier shut and locked the door, making as little sound as possible. He slumped in the chair for about thirty seconds, trying to bring himself down. The adrenaline rush he'd been experiencing was not about to subside. He eased out of the chair, removed his glasses and hearing aid, and took his camera from his pocket. He sent the eight photos of Cortez's body to Smith's secure phone and email address. As insurance, he sent the photos to his own secure email address.

Cavalier used the presidential suite bathroom to wash and scrub thoroughly. He had been careful not to allow any blood or mucus on his clothing. He dressed as the Frenchman and lay on his bunk, thinking over every aspect of the last twenty minutes. He felt his mobile vibrating. It was a text from Smith:

'Congrats! Are you? Did you manage the swab or blood sample? My team is already in Singapore, ready. I have reinforcements from a brother agency. We will note the train schedule. If there is a delay, please inform.

Cavalier replied:

Thank you. Yes. Yes. Good. Will do.

He used his 'vanish' app to destroy the communication.

He was now consumed with how to steal Pon off the train safely. Cavalier could not take on the entire Mexican contingent, especially when they discovered Cortez had been assassinated. He had about six hours to work out a plan for his daughter. Thinking ahead first, he sent a text to Smith:

Have ambulance and medico ready at Singapore and arrange immediate flight to BKK. The (late) Cortez had a drugged woman under his control. She will need immediate treatment.

Ambulances, medicos and plane will be on standby. Will the Mexicans resist?

Remains to be seen. Leaderless. May be desperate. Plan for worst case.

35

DOCTOR DEATH TAKES CHARGE

At 4 a.m. the Express ground to a halt. Cavalier pulled the window curtain across to see only thick jungle. He heard shouting, threw up the cabin's window and saw three security guards running along beside the stationary train. The locomotive driver had used high-beam lights and had spotted something large on the line. He had informed the guards. They investigated. Within two minutes, the guards were hastening back onto the train. Cavalier closed the window and opened his cabin door slightly, so he could hear what was going on.

'There's a block on the line!' one of the guards said to Huloton.

'Block? What do you mean?'

'We … we could see something piled up on the line. When we ventured close with our torches, men appeared. We think they had weapons!'

Huloton rushed to gather the rest of the guards and alert Cortez. He knocked on the Mexican's door. When there was no reaction he banged hard. This woke Pon. In her dazed state, she noticed a terrible stench. She struggled down the steps from the top bunk and nearly tripped on Cortez's body. She screamed.

'Open the door, Madame,' Huloton ordered, 'open it!'

With a squeal, Pon slipped on blood that had formed an asymmetrical ring around Cortez's body. She managed to keep upright, and then unlocked the door.

Huloton switched on the light. He stood there, gaping at the body. The Mexican guards took one look at the stricken leader and hurried off to gather the others. Within a minute security guards were struggling to restrain the armed Mexicans, who had filled the carriage corridor; they were shouting and waving their guns. Rodriguez was summonsed. Soon he, Azelaporn, Huloton and Jacinta were in urgent conference.

'You must take charge of the Mexicans,' Huloton said to Rodriguez. 'They are your men, your people!'

'And you must find the killer!' Rodriguez fired back. 'I take it you are in charge?'

'Under the circumstances, this is not my jurisdiction, Monsieur. That falls to Dr Makanathan. She has a senior position in the Department of Justice.'

'Then fetch her!'

Huloton was offended by the young Mexican's aggressive tone. Jacinta volunteered to raise the doctor in carriage 16. She and a security guard helped a very shaky, distressed Pon along the corridors. Jacinta stopped at Makanathan's door and the guard took Pon on to the infirmary in carriage 3.

Makanathan, her colourful hair awry, did not have time to look other than unkempt as she pulled on casual clothes and took a few seconds to dab on her face powder. She filled her green shoulder bag with work items and followed Jacinta along the corridors.

'My role in Justice is effectively an inactive post now,' Makanathan said to her as they hastened along towards the train's rear. 'But this may be an emergency.'

'I'm told that you have the power to investigate the murder. Manager Huloton is washing his hands of the responsibility. But in any case, he is not Thai.'

'Any suspects?'

'Not yet. I would think it would be better to wait until we arrive in Singapore before making a proper investigation.'

'I would prefer that too, but if the killer is on the train, it is better to apprehend her now. You see—' she cut her sentence short, as if avoiding saying something she should not disclose.

'Yes?'

'I am not popular with the police and politicians in Singapore. Or Malaysia, for that matter.'

'Oh?'

'I was asked to investigate the deaths of politicians in those countries.'

'I remember. Azelaporn showed me reports. Their governments were embarrassed by your findings.'

'Not even our own beloved government has been enraptured with me. The junta tolerates me, just.' She emitted a short, cynical laugh. 'That is until I expose a killer they'd rather not know about.'

They arrived to find the Mexicans in a potentially dangerous confrontation with Huloton and train security. Azelaporn and Rodriguez were also in a heated discussion over how to proceed. Makanathan took charge.

'Control your countrymen, sir,' she ordered Rodriguez, 'before there is an international incident.' Then she took Huloton aside and asked him for his assessment. Huloton stammered over what he knew.

'His girlfriend possibly could have done it,' he said. 'We could not find a gun, Madame. Monsieur Cortez has been shot twice.'

'I don't think she was in any state to do anything, let alone shoot someone,' Jacinta said.

'Where is the girl?' Makanathan asked.

'In the train infirmary in carriage number 3,' Jacinta said. 'The train doctor is examining her now, I trust.'

'How did she look when you entered the cabin?' Makanathan asked Huloton.

'Oh, pfft!' he said, flapping his arms. 'She seemed drugged to the eyeballs. She claims she woke up when I knocked on the door. She said she looked down and saw the body.'

'I'll examine her later,' Makanathan said. She ordered everyone out of carriage 30.

'You are all contaminating the crime scene,' she said, speaking loudly. 'Please leave.'

Jacinta watched as Makanathan put on gloves, bent down beside the body and began her examination. She ignored the bullet wounds and paid more attention to the syringe puncture mark in Cortez's neck. She looked in the corpse's mouth.

'Well, blessed be the Buddha,' she muttered, 'there are signs of minor abrasions in his throat.' Makanathan looked up at Jacinta. 'This is looking like a professional killing,' she said softly. 'She knew what she was doing.'

'She?'

'I always say "she",' Makanathan said with a grin. 'Why should men always get the credit for such skilful work?'

Jacinta half-smiled at this macabre remark. 'What makes you say "she" is professional?' she asked.

'Not the actual kill. Two shots from close range could be fired accurately by a boy, even.' She pointed to the neck mark. 'That's been done as well as the shots.'

'A lethal injection?'

'Maybe. Only forensics will discover if that was a cause of death. But the marks in the mouth and throat are very interesting.'

'An attempt to choke him, perhaps?'

'Not really. More in keeping with someone scooping something out rather than putting something in.'

Makanathan probed further. She took tweezers from her bag. After some delicate teasing, she pulled out a wafer-thin splinter of wood about three centimetres in length.

'Exhibit A,' she said with a smile, clearly enjoying her work.

'Any clues?'

'There are a couple of possibilities emerging. First, a doctor or nurse would inject a poison. Or second, she wanted to *extract* blood, and ...' Makanathan paused, pointing at the slither of wood sitting on a white cloth, 'perhaps a mucus sample from the mouth?'

'I am confused.'

'Oh, so am I, my friend, so am I ...'

Jacinta was ahead of her, or at least up with her thinking, but did not want to express her knowledgeable views.

'What do you extract blood for, and mucus?' Makanathan asked.

'Identity.'

'We've both done it many times, haven't we? Taken samples from a body, Ms Cin Lai? I am aware of your excellent work with the SIU.'

'I'm afraid I have lost that post.'

'I'd prefer to say you've been "sidelined". I have been there too after the investigations into those political killings. I have been restored. As you will be, I am sure.'

Jacinta was flattered by these comments from such a prominent Thai.

'I have seen you box, too!' Makanathan added. 'My Buddha! How my husband and I cheered for you when you flattened that massive Russian last year! I also had a five thousand baht bet on you at very good odds.' Jacinta was caught off guard. She blushed. 'Are you going to fight again? I read a report that you were thinking about it after you were … er … stood down?'

'I had no money,' Jacinta said frankly, 'that's why I took this job.'

'I don't know how you could associate again with that pig Azelaporn! Surely the ring, where you are so successful, would be preferable to supporting him?'

'In some ways, yes,' Jacinta said, showing emotion, 'but I have had my time.'

'Sorry, I do understand. Boxing is a very tough profession, especially when you give away so much weight to men when you fight.'

Makanathan went on with her investigation. 'Judging from the wounds,' she mumbled after a while, half to herself, 'he was shot from above—in the bunk, I suspect. You see? The weight of the bullet has pushed in harder from above. The impression is raised at the top when it entered. The two bullets hit dead centre of the heart, exploding it. Normally a professional would aim at the brain from such close range, disabling the victim.' Makanathan stroked her chin and stood erect, just as her husband came in and handed her a cup of coffee. She thanked him and he left as silently as he came in.

'Who was in the top bunk, again?' Makanathan asked.

'His … er … mistress.'

'Oh, yes, that poor, poor woman. Mistress is a bit euphemistic, don't you think? More like his captive, at least from the way he treated her, and she looked.'

'Is there a chance she did it?'

'I can say categorically, no.'

'She had a motive.'

'Oh, yes,' Makanathan agreed, 'but from what I have seen already, unless she is a professional assassin with a very cool head—cool enough to extract blood and mucus for whatever purpose—she could not have perpetrated this rather dreadful crime.'

'So, if someone took those samples, they were wanting to show proof of identity?'

'That is exactly what I am thinking! Jacinta, my dear, you have brains, exceptional beauty and great sporting prowess! The Buddha has been most favourable to you!'

'A well-planned killing,' Jacinta went on, ignoring the extra flattery. 'One where the assassin was compelled to prove he'd carried out the "hit"?'

'Exactly, again! This would narrow down the murderer to someone in the business of killing.'

'There are plenty on board.'

'What do you mean?'

'Well, all the Mexicans.'

'Of course! But then, the motive?'

'Who knows? Anger? Jealousy? A bid to be top dog?'

'Why extract samples? Once a killing had occurred, none of the Mexicans would bother, would they?'

'I guess not.'

'No, we have two strands here. If we can find someone who fits the profile of a professional with a motive, we have our woman!'

Makanathan continued her searching and examining. She took out a tape and measured distances from various positions on the bunk and stairs. After a few minutes of silence, she looked up and smiled cunningly.

'I was just thinking after I joked about a "she" doing the job here. I asked questions about you after the Leonardo Mendez forensics were finished—a case, by the way that your dear boss Azelaporn would not let me near. I learned from a source that you are an expert shot.' Makanathan waited and scrutinised Jacinta's reaction. 'I have to ask you, where were you between 2 a.m. and, say, 3 a.m.?'

'I was asleep in my bunk.'

'Alone?'

'Yes.'

'Okay, don't be offended. We may have to interrogate everyone on the train before it reaches Singapore.' She laughed. 'Even my husband will receive a grilling!' She began to pack away her instruments. 'That reminds me, why has the train stopped?'

'Huloton says there is an obstruction on the line a few hundred metres away. He was distracted by Cortez's murder but is doing something now.'

*

Huloton stood by the side of the front of the train's locomotive.

'Go and see what that obstruction is,' he ordered three train guards. He lit a cigarette and smoked nervously as the guards trudged off down the track. About fifty metres from the obstruction, shots were fired at them and they stopped and ran back to the Express. Huloton dropped his cigarette, climbed inside the train and dialled the Malaysian police, with whom he had liaised over the train not stopping at Kuala Lumpur. Huloton explained the situation.

'We can get a SWAT team to you in an hour or so,' the Malaysian Chief of Police said.

'That is too long, Monsieur,' Huloton said. 'Please make it sooner!'

36

SUSPECTS

Azelaporn and Huloton did their best to have Rodriguez placate the Mexicans, now they had lost their commander. He was their new leader, yet doing everything not to be labelled that way. Huloton told him that he had to bring his men under control.

'If they start a fight with my security people,' Huloton said, showing surprising strength for a persistent ditherer, 'there will a bloodbath—admittedly, with your people winning. They outnumber my men.'

'I have never had direct control over them,' Rodriguez said.

'Sir, the issue for them should be protecting the bullion,' Azelaporn said. 'It is most regrettable that Señor Cortez has been dealt with this way. But now the issue is the fortune in those chests. If you let your men lose control, the KL police will take the bullion over. It won't reach Singapore.'

Rodriguez nodded his reluctant agreement.

'I'll do what I can,' he said with a sigh.

'Why not offer them incentives for behaving themselves? What's a few ingots among thousands, after all?'

'I was thinking of that.'

'Please don't just think, *do* something!' Huloton pleaded.

Rodriguez adjusted his silk tie and strode off to bring his countrymen and indirect employees to heel.

*

One by one in the train's central piano bar carriage, Makanathan questioned possible suspects. By quizzing the Mexicans and security guards, she had an idea of the passengers who had come through carriages 30, 31 and 32 and on to the observation cars.

There was Ben Dempster the Australian grazier, who'd had an altercation with the Mexicans in the Kanchanaburi Cemetery. He would have a vague motive, perhaps, to murder Cortez, and he admitted being handy with rifle and handgun. But his wife swore she had been with him all night. They were in carriage 8 and had not been near carriage 30, except on one occasion in the afternoon. That was backed up by two of the security guards who sat in on the interrogations. They had not seen the Australian near carriage 30 for twenty-four hours.

There was also Bowles, the large American former construction business owner. He had been in the Vietnam War and knew how to use a range of weaponry. He was at first bemused by the questions and later distinctly amused when asked if he had any reason to want to kill the Mexican.

'Depends on what business he was in,' the American said and followed it by a loud guffaw. 'I have operations in Texas. I both love them because they are prepared to work cheaply for my companies, and hate 'em for the goddamn drugs they bring in.' He laughed again. 'But I didn't know the guy. What did he do?'

'Er, this is not the issue,' Makanathan said, unwilling to mention Cortez's background. She dismissed the American and, just as she called for the next couple, was surprised to see Hinkley and Cowboy walk into the bar.

'Sorry to jump the queue,' Hinkley said in her forthright manner, 'but Cowboy thinks he knows who did the killing.'

'Oh, really?' Makanathan said, glancing at her watch, which said 5 a.m. 'Who?'

'He thinks it's either the nice Frenchman or the American in the wheelchair. He is not sure which one.'

'It can't be the Frenchman,' Makanathan said. 'This guard here was outside his door all night.' The guard in question acknowledged her comment with a firm nod. 'Monsieur Garriaud did not venture out. In fact, as far as we know he has not been out since the late afternoon. But please reassure Cowboy I shall be speaking with him very soon.'

Cowboy stomped his foot twice.

'What about the American in the wheelchair?' Hinkley asked, responding to Cowboy's second choice.

'You don't think he is just relating to someone in a similar situation to himself? Someone … er … *different*?'

'Cowboy notices everything.'

'Is there anything specific about the American's behaviour that has caught Cowboy's attention?'

'He noticed him crying. He also noted the Frenchman crying.'

'Crying?'

'That's what he observed,' Hinkley said confidently, despite the paucity of the evidence. 'He's also suspicious that the American never came to the set lunches and dinners.'

'This American,' Makanathan glanced at her passenger list, 'Mr Blenkiron, has a disability. He is eighty. Does Cowboy realise that this makes it very difficult for him to carry out this heinous crime, physically?'

'He notices anomalies. They stay with him. He sees many different things we don't.'

'It's true that Mr Blenkiron was in the observation car area at the time. But there were fifteen people in that category.'

'Cowboy notices patterns in behaviour that others miss.'

'Are you saying he is a savant?'

'No, but his intelligence is very different. He observed and thought about these two individuals because they were alone, they cried, and he had been in contact with both. I think he sees them as similar kinds of people.'

'Meaning?'

'Not sure. It has to do with character. He likes them both, despite him thinking that the Frenchman was coming on to me.'

'Did he?'

'No,' Hinkley said, blushing, 'if anything, I was interested in him. He was a touch aloof.'

Makanathan looked at her watch again.

'We really must move on,' she said with a hint of impatience, while glancing at others waiting at the other end of the piano bar, 'but I promise you and Cowboy that I will chat with Mr Blenkiron.'

37

SIEGE PREPARATION

Cavalier was torn between visiting the infirmary to see his daughter and tidying up his two sleeping quarters.

He decided on the latter, aware that she was at least receiving care from the train medico and nurses. Anticipating trouble, he cleared and cleaned the suite. Then Cavalier pulled on surgical gloves and placed all Blenkiron's belongings in two light-green plastic bags. He hurled them out the window as far as he could, gambling that the train would leave before darkness and none of the items, including toiletries, would be detected. To be certain, he dressed as the Frenchman, left the train and took the bags forty metres into the jungle to the Muar River and dropped them into the water. He watched them floating downstream at a speed he judged would take them several hundred metres away from the train.

Cavalier hastened back to the train and slipped unseen into Garriaud's carriage and then Blenkiron's. He kept the handgun, which was the main item that could incriminate him, and the glasses. He also retained the American's wallet,

263

credit cards and passport, all documents that may have him traced back to Chiang Mai.

Cavalier left the empty suitcase on one of the beds. Finally, after a quick survey of the suite, he shifted to the adjoining cabin and made sure the door between them was closed.

He began locating his exact position using Google Maps and a phone app. He found the Muar River is sixty-five kilometres south of a town called Gemas, which in turn is about a hundred and fifty kilometres south-east of Kuala Lumpur. Cavalier remembered there had been an important battle in the area for the 8th Division of the Australian Army in World War II. He thought it was at a bridge over a creek called 'Gemencheh'. He pinpointed it on the map and reckoned he was within half a kilometre of it. This caused him to shove his two pairs of glasses in his pocket and hurry the length of the train to see where the Express's front was situated. He shuffled through the piano bar past Hinkley and Cowboy as they were leaving, and the other 'suspects' yet to be interviewed.

'Monsieur!' Makanathan called after him, 'we wish to …'

'Je connais, Madame,' Cavalier said with a respectful nod. 'I will be back.'

He passed the infirmary where his daughter was and reached the locomotive. A guard blocked his entrance. Cavalier found an exit door and stepped outside the Express. He ducked down beside the carriages and made his way to the front. He put on the glasses and scanned the area. Just beyond the train there was a rice field of about three hundred square metres. Adjusting the glasses, he could make out a wooden bridge beyond the field. Cavalier saw three stationary trucks on the bridge or near it. He scanned the train track ahead.

At about three or four hundred metres, he could see what looked like steel poles piled high across the line.

Cavalier was startled by his phone vibrating in his pocket. Gregory was on the line from Australia.

'We got wind of an ISIS attack somewhere in Malaysia,' he said. 'The police there say they have arrested six suspects in Kuala Lumpur. Guess who was with them? Our two Indonesian students. The police say they had supplied all the data about the ??????. There could be an attack on it planned, judging from what the police said they found: maps, drawings of the train carriages and photos. We let our American cousins know.'

'I know,' Cavalier said stepping back onto the train. 'Smith informed me.'

'Could there be another terrorist attack imminent?'

'Possibly. I'm on the *Bangkok Express* and we're ...'

'Jeez, mate! Thanks for letting us know!'

'Sorry ...'

'Where exactly is the train now?'

'It's stopped. I'll send you the location.'

'The KL police say the guys they've arrested had hired trucks but no one knows why. Some sort of "action" was expected in KL, but may have been nipped in the bud.'

'Not sure about that. There are three trucks parked on a bridge about four hundred metres away.'

'Be bloody careful! Sounds dodgy from this distance.'

'There is gold bullion on board.'

Gregory was silent for a moment before he exclaimed: 'Bullion? That explains something! The communications flying around the ISIS networks have been alluding to a plan to grab gold somewhere in South East Asia.'

'Must be it.'

'Can you leave the train?'

'Maybe, but Pon is on board,' Cavalier said, moving back to the train and climbing aboard the second carriage.

'Pon, your daughter …? I thought she was …'

'She's alive! It's a long story …'

Cavalier rang off, walked back to the train's third carriage. He knocked on the door to the infirmary.

A Thai nurse opened it. 'Can I help you, sir?'

'I'm enquiring about a young woman, Pon.'

'Who are you?'

'A friend. I heard she was ill.'

'She is heavily sedated.'

'Is she okay?'

'We think so, Sir,' she said reassuringly as she glanced at the surgery door. 'The doctor is running tests.'

Cavalier desperately wanted to see her, but instead thanked the nurse and hurried on down the train past Makanathan again. She sent a steward after him. Cavalier had only been inside his cabin a few seconds before the steward knocked.

'Sorry to disturb, Monsieur Garriaud,' the steward said, bowing low, 'but Dr Makanathan wants to meet you in the piano bar.' Cavalier could see two security guards standing behind the steward. 'She is interviewing everyone. It is her duty.'

'Of course, it is,' Cavalier said casually. 'Let her know I'll be there in a few minutes.'

'Sorry, Sir; she wants you there now.'

'She'll have to wait ten minutes, *merci*.' Cavalier shut the door.

A text from Smith put Cavalier further on edge.

ISIS group affiliate set to attack train.

There was a gap of twenty seconds before Smith phoned him. 'Our intelligence is picking up that they are set to move on a target designated as quote "now stationary near Gemas".'

'That's the Express.'

'Logistically tough for us to do anything. Good luck and God bless.'

Cavalier put on a jacket and shoved his gun into the inside pocket. He sent a text to Jacinta, urging her to prepare the train for an attack. She rang him.

'No time to discuss it,' Cavalier said. 'Organise the Mexicans to guard the bullion. They won't budge anyway. Have Azelaporn do it with Rodriguez's help. Spread the rest of the security guards along the train. You and I should be there in the locomotive.'

'Why the front?'

'The attackers will want to either immobilise the train or move it closer to their trucks.'

'The passengers?'

'They should stay locked in the carriages. Do you have an armoury?'

'If you call twenty rifles an armoury, yes.'

'Take three rifles and ammunition to the locomotive.'

'Three?'

'One for you, me and a third person, who can shoot. I believe they will attack any time now ...'

Jacinta hurried to Huloton, Azelaporn and Rodriguez.

*

In the piano bar in the middle of the train, Makanathan continued interviewing her list of suspects, but was interrupted by Huloton and a steward.

'We are under siege, Madame!' a distressed Huloton shouted. 'My beautiful train may be destroyed!' He turned, waved his arms at other passengers and yelled: 'Go to your cabins! Lock yourself in and stay away from the windows!'

He rushed Makanathan and her husband to their cabin and placed a security guard outside the door. As he did so, other guards, rifles in hand, trotted past to take up positions along the train corridors.

*

In carriages 31 and 32, the twelve Mexicans had been bribed with promises of a share of the booty they were protecting. There were four in each carriage at entrances and windows, while another four were in the observation car, staring out into the thick, dark and uncompromising jungle. They were armed with rifles, handguns, grenades, knives and machetes. All wore boots; most wore Stetsons; two had other headgear that looked like modified bike helmets. Half of them were smoking cigarettes; the others, cigars.

All had been in vicious internecine drug wars in Mexico, and were battle-hardened. To qualify to be in Mendez's bodyguard each man had had to prove their toughness by carrying out two beheadings. Cortez had been no less brutal. He wanted killers. Like Mendez, he paid them well and promised women and booze wherever they went.

In Mexico, they had fought for their cartel's supremacy over territory and criminal trade in drugs, prostitution and people trafficking. Here on the Express they were more than eager to defend the ten chests of booty stowed in the cabins. In keeping with tradition, most were drinking tequila, in this case Talia Tequila, the brand that had been funded by their slain boss, now lying in a large refrigerator in one of the Express's three kitchens. They were handing bottles around for liberal swigs.

Rodriguez had placed one of them, Alberto Bruno, in charge of the defence with an offer of a bigger bonus than the rest. He was tall, thin, bearded, and with a ponytail under his hat. He took his role seriously and ordered two of the Mexicans to stop singing. He wanted silence to hear the attackers' approach. Bruno also ordered all cigars and cigarettes extinguished.

'I promise you each six dozen very experienced, sexy Latina women here on earth once this is over,' he said to them. They all laughed. He hushed them again. The Mexicans readied themselves for the kind combat they thrived on.

Rodriguez locked himself and his wife in their suite with his two bodyguards posted outside his door and under orders to shoot any attackers.

*

Cavalier, his two pairs of eyeglasses in his pocket, jumped from the train and bending low hurried along beside it for seven hundred metres until he reached the locomotive. He phoned Jacinta and she opened its door for him.

38

MEXICAN STAND-OFF

A bu Hal Basha waddled away from the railway line, satisfied that his forward scouts had done a useful job in piling eighty steel poles and ten thick wooden sleepers on the railway line. Basha kept up a confident facade, although he was nervous. The original plan had been to hold up the train, rob the passengers and take hostages. Then his two spies in Bangkok had discovered that the Mexicans were loading steel crates onto the train's rear. The weight of the crates caused ISIS to believe they were smuggling a fair-sized amount of bullion out of Thailand. Knowing of the assassination of the cartel leader Mendez, it seemed logical that they would be moving their assets elsewhere, possibly back to Mexico.

This had led to ISIS changing its plans in what Basha complained was a rushed, logistically difficult operation. But he was himself under threat of death if he did not comply with his commanders' wishes. He had to organise the hijack of the Express and the stealing of the bullion. He had asked for another twenty ISIS-trained extremists, but had been refused. Two dozen under his command were enough, he was told.

Hoping and praying he was not undermanned, he sent the Filipino warriors through the jungle to attack and disable the rear of the train. His plan was to capture the passengers and force them to carry the bullion to the trucks at the Gemencheh Bridge. The passengers would then be machine-gunned to death. The four suicide bombers would be directed to blow up the locomotive at the front to totally disable the Express. Five of the second contingent of Malaysians would come in behind the bombers, while the remaining five would stay with the trucks to protect the bombers and Basha himself.

The England-born Robert McKenna was trembling as the minutes counted down to the attack. He had begged Basha to let him ring his wife in England; he longed to hear her voice for the last time and to remind her he loved her. He just wanted to know how the baby was. Basha had refused, worried that McKenna would have another crisis of confidence and refuse to go through with his mission. To put his mind back on the job, Basha had demanded he recite the drills, which the bomber had done so many times that he woke up some nights mumbling the instructions.

'When I reach within forty metres of the target,' he said, voice steady, 'I pull the first safety cord. When I am at the train I pull the second safety cord.'

'And shout what, brother?'

'Allah is good! Allah is great!!'

Basha shook his hand. He winked and nodded at the second bomber, Abu Moanmar, who played self-consciously with his glasses. He looked studious, as if he were just going to another university lecture. He needed no bolstering. Moanmar was ready.

By contrast, Abu Qasawarta was in good, even jovial, spirits as Basha went through the drill a final time with him. 'What happens if I pull the second cord first?'

'That would not allow you to reach heaven, Abu,' Basha said in a kindly tone.

'I thought that would be the case,' he said with a grin.

Basha stood next to Amula.

'How are you feeling, my little sister?' he asked.

She looked up at him, her head shaking slightly and her top lip trembling as she fidgeted with the rings on her hand.

Basha leaned close and whispered: 'You know what you must do, for the Islamic State. Remember it is Allah's will.'

She shook her head more vigorously.

Basha drew his gun from a hip holster and hissed in her ear, 'You will do it with honour, or die in disgrace!'

*

Jacinta had the locomotive cabin evacuated of the two drivers and engineer and placed herself, Cavalier and the Australian grazier Ben Dempster at open windows facing the track. They all carried rifles. The lights were off and the three could hardly see each other in the blackness.

'You sure you're okay with this?' Jacinta said to Dempster.

'I think so. But why choose me?'

'The way you handled yourself at Kanchanaburi when you stopped the Mexicans from brutalising that poor woman. And we know you how to use a rifle.'

Cavalier moved close to Jacinta and handed her a pair of the glasses.

'Here,' he said, 'these will help.'

She examined them in the poor light.

'They look like …'

Cavalier put his fingers to his lips.

Jacinta tried them on.

'Oh, my Buddha!'

'Good?'

'Amazing!' she whispered.

Cavalier moved back to his position, put on his glasses and scanned the paddy field in front of him. It was still dark. He could not see any movement.

'If they strike, it will be before dawn,' he said. 'They have less than half an hour.'

He glanced at Dempster and could sense his unease.

'You seem very calm, mate,' Dempster remarked.

'I'm not. I have a person dear to me on board,' Cavalier said, keeping to his French accent. 'I'll do anything to protect her.'

'My wife is here …'

'It boils down to this; we must defend our loved ones. We have no choice.'

'Do you think we can? How many of them do you expect?'

'Don't know.'

'All you have to do is to fire when we do,' Jacinta said.

*

Basha took the four suicide bombers to the edge of the rice field and embraced them, being careful not to squeeze them in case he triggered the bombs in their backpacks. He wished them Godspeed.

One by one they moved off towards the train. Amula hesitated. She began running away. Basha pointed his gun at her, causing her to change direction and head for the train. McKenna tried to fill his mind with images of heaven, but

273

could not rid himself of thoughts of his wife. He too started crying, but he kept moving. There was no turning back now.

*

Cavalier was alerted to movement. His glasses picked up shapes.

'Wait,' he whispered. He could see a person running across the paddy field towards the train. He scanned along the railway track. Another person was striding forward along it. He detected a third figure, with no obvious weapon, also running in the field.

Cavalier concentrated on the person about seventy metres away in the paddy field. He fired at what appeared to be a backpack. The resultant explosion sent a fireball up a tree close to the field's edge. The train shook.

'Jesus!' Dempster said. 'What was that?'

'Suicide bomber.'

'How did you know?'

'Didn't. I aimed at a backpack.'

'I see one on the track,' Jacinta said. She took aim and fired, felling the target. He struggled to his feet and stumbled into the field. Jacinta and Cavalier fired again. There was a second explosion, smaller than the first, but enough to blow the bomber to pieces.

'I can't see a thing,' Dempster complained.

'Don't worry, just follow our lead,' Jacinta repeated. 'When we fire, you follow.'

Cavalier lined up the third assailant he had spotted, who was a smaller figure. He heard a high-pitched, continuous scream. He paused a precious ten seconds, believing the oncoming figure could be a child. Jacinta glanced at Cavalier.

Seeing his hesitation, she took aim and fired. The second explosion, closer than the others, was bigger than the first two. It shook the carriage again and lit up the track. Cavalier scanned the area. Jacinta's target was nowhere to be seen and he assumed had been eliminated.

The several seconds of sustained light from the bomb was enough for Jacinta to take aim and fire at a fourth attacker, who went down. There was no explosion. Cavalier fired a few seconds later, aiming at the fourth bomber's backpack. He hit it, but still the bomb remained intact. An eerie silence followed for about twenty seconds before the noise of a concerted attack at the other end of the train filled the air.

*

Hercules, hidden in the undergrowth with his ten Filipino charges near the rear of the Express, checked his backpack of explosives. He intended to set them off once the gold was secured. The terrorists hoped to immobilise the train and cause maximum chaos to the railway system running through Malaysia. Hercules had five of his men one side of the observation car and the other five with him. He prepared a flare, which would be the signal for the terrorists to attack. Before that he and his men all swallowed strong-dose, fast-acting methamphetamine pills and waited several minutes.

'Remember, martyrs,' he whispered to those close to him, 'if you die, you see the face of Allah! If you live, we wait for another chance to be in his great presence!'

He then ordered them to drink from hip flasks of rum meant to fortify them in the initial burst. Hercules then lit the flare, which shot high and burst well clear of the train.

He then lifted his assault rifle, the signal to attack. He burst out of the darkness, screaming, 'Allah! Allah! Allan is great!'

All Mexican eyes lifted skyward as the flare lit up the night sky and the area around for several hundred metres in every direction. Moments later they were startled when the terrorists' screams from both sides of the car cut the still, humid air. Instinctively two Mexicans stood and aimed the weapons at the noise. They were cut down, one falling from the rear of the train, the other slumping forward in the carriage.

Hercules reached the railing at the train's rear. Two Mexicans fired from the other end of the carriage and missed, but hit two Filipinos close behind him. One was killed; the other slumped back and crawled along the track away from the train. Alberto charged at Hercules with his machete, bringing it down hard on his left hand that gripped the railing. Hercules screamed, but it did not stop him. With his hand dangling by a few tendons, he straddled the railing. Alberto swung his machete again, this time into Hercules' mighty torso. Hercules fell to the track. A Mexican fired, missed Hercules and hit his pack. It exploded, killing Hercules and three of the Mexicans, who had advanced to help Alberto. He was brought down but not killed by the blast.

The observation car roof and walls caught fire. Seeing their leader struck down, the Filipino attackers fell back. Alberto was on his side in the observation car, stunned and badly injured. One of the Mexicans rushed to stem the flow of blood from his shoulder and chest as the fire threatened to engulf the entire carriage and spread.

'Wait!' Alberto yelled to his men, who were firing blindly at the retreating Filipinos. 'They will … come … again …'

Three Mexicans dragged him clear of the observation car and into the next carriage just before the fire took hold. Moments later Alberto was dead.

*

Emboldened by the sight of the car on fire, the Filipinos rallied for a second assault, but without the fearless Hercules, the effort was not as organised or fulsome. One managed to climb into the burning car, but was shot in the leg. He fell forward into the fire. He was soon burning and suffocating. Two of his compatriots fired at the next car and attempted to climb the steps leading to the observation lounge into which the Mexicans had hastily moved. The invaders were met and sprayed with bullets from AK-15 assault rifles at only a few metres. They were both killed but not before a stray shot from one of them hit a Mexican in the throat and killed him. Two Filipinos rushed to drag one of their squad who had been shot in the abdomen when he was hit just behind Hercules. They were spotted.

'There! Near the track!' one Mexican called. This led to a continuous volley of shots from them, which killed the three Filipinos. One of the two remaining attackers received a call to his mobile. It was Basha.

'Fidel, are you in?' he demanded. 'Have you secured the gold?'

'No,' the Filipino said, voice trembling, as he and the other surviving Filipinos hurried off in retreat.

'What do you mean, no?'

'We were outnumbered! We are coming back to the bridge ...'

'How many down?'

'I think only me and Ejercito are left.'

Basha cursed and used binoculars to look along the track at the train. He had heard explosions but the locomotive was intact. He was concerned now also with the train's rear, where weapons' fire had abated.

'You!' he yelled to two of the Malaysians. 'Go to the locomotive and see what has happened! Use your grenades to destroy it!'

The two terrorists hesitated.

Basha fired his handgun over their heads, causing them to hurry off down the track.

*

The train's two firemen and several Mexicans struggled to bring the fire in the observation car under control. Huloton, who had stayed clear of the fighting, now took charge again.

'Form a bucket chain!' he directed six stewards. 'Use all basins and anything that will carry water! Hurry!'

*

In contrast to the torrent of shouting now at the bullion end of the Express, all was still quiet at the front. Cavalier, much to the protests of Jacinta and Dempster, had slipped out of the train and into the jungle near the paddy field. The first fingers of dawn were beginning to creep over the area, but he still needed the glasses to see his way through the undergrowth and alert him to further attacks. He had moved fifty metres clear of the train when two moving human shapes appeared on the railway track. Both carried rifles.

Cavalier propped and fired, wounding one of them. Dempster and Jacinta could see them in the quarter-light, still some distance from the train and equidistant from the poles blocking the track. Then one moving figure fired down the track at the Express, causing Dempster and Jacinta to duck under the window frame. The figure hustled forward, enough for Cavalier to fix him in his sights. He fired twice, bringing him down. Cavalier then hastened to the track. The wounded Malaysian was lying on his side. He managed to train his AK-47 on the advancing Cavalier, who ducked behind a tree. When the AK-47 stopped spitting bullets, Cavalier moved in front of the tree. He propped and fired almost simultaneously with Jacinta and Dempster. The Malaysian terrorist was hit by at least three bullets. He fell on the track.

Making sure there were no attackers on the move, Cavalier edged along beside the track and then into the open in the paddy field.

'What the hell is he doing?' Dempster asked.

'I don't know,' Jacinta said quietly.

Cavalier trained his glasses on the ground and could make out what appeared to be the remains of the smaller assailant. A rainbow of colours, dominated by red, almost made viewing impossible. He adjusted the glasses and kept searching. He accidentally touched the scorched tree, which was still burning, and it caused him to jump.

Cavalier stopped and bent down. He could see a tiny severed hand of a female, judging from the gold rings on two fingers. He felt ill. The motto 'kill or be killed' always steeled him to be proactive, but there were limits. Seeing the scattered remains verified what he feared in those few seconds when he hesitated before Jacinta fired at the smaller assailant: the suicide bomber was a child or young person. Cavalier pocketed his glasses and moved briskly back to the locomotive, his heart thumping as he thought of his own daughter so near, but not yet secure from danger.

'What were you looking for?' Dempster asked.

'Evidence,' Cavalier said.

'Of what?'

'Just evidence,' Cavalier said without elaboration. After a pause, he wondered aloud, 'How many more?'

He was answered by a prolonged silence at both ends of the train, except for some urgent yelling from those putting out the fire in the observation car. With no one running interference, the fire set off by the bomb explosion at the bullion end was extinguished in twenty minutes, leaving the carriage a burnt-out shell, yet still mobile.

*

Basha retreated to the truck convoy with the eight remaining Malaysian terrorists. They were soon joined by the two Filipino survivors from the fiasco at the train's rear, bringing further bad news about the failed attack.

'Get in the front truck!' he screamed in a panic. 'Everyone!'

He realised now that the mission was a complete disaster. He feared the reaction from his Syrian masters. Just as he planned to evacuate the area, squads of Malaysian police cars descended on the Gemencheh Bridge from three directions.

39

THE DISAPPEARANCE

Cavalier and Dempster left the rifles they had used in the locomotive and walked back along the corridors the half-kilometre to his cabin. On the way they were confronted by Cowboy coming out of his suite with his mother.

'Is it over?' Hinkley asked them. 'We heard shooting! The back of the train was on fire!'

'I don't know,' Dempster said, attempting to move on, 'I was at the front of the train ...'

'Excuse me, Madame,' Cavalier said and brushed past her, moving quicker now to his cabin, ten carriages away. Once inside, he calmed himself.

*

Dawn had opened up a clear vista to the bridge, where another battle had broken out. Smoke from the suicide- bomber explosions and the weapon fire filtered across the paddy field and down the track to the train. The odour of cordite lingered with it. Malaysian police vehicles pulled up around the trucks. Police fired into the vehicles and the odd retaliatory rifle shot could be heard. Soon afterwards, the fight ended and the police moved in close on the trucks. Terrorists including Basha filed out of the trucks, hands behind their heads, and into waiting police wagons.

With the fighting stopped, Huloton, who had been in touch with the Malaysian police a second time, and Makanathan, guarded by Jacinta and three of the train's security men, wandered along the track. They noted the burnt-out tree trunk created by the explosion of the first suicide bomber. They could see the dismembered pieces of the bombers and their attire scattered over a wide area. The strong stench caused Makanathan to place a green handkerchief over her face. Vultures were in the fields and on the track picking at burnt flesh and cawing in appreciation. Makanathan, following her professional instincts, moved off the track and approached the prone figure of the bomber whose detonator had not gone off.

'No, Doctor!' Jacinta yelled. 'Don't examine him! His pack didn't explode. It could be on a hair trigger right now.'

'I'll see that Malaysian police send a disposal squad.' Makanathan tried to sound in command, but looked rattled as she backed off. 'Who killed these terrorists?' she asked.

'I did,' Jacinta said.

Minutes later Makanathan had regained control and was reporting to the chief of the Malaysian police operation, a lean, mustachioed man of about forty. She told him that she was in charge of investigating everything that occurred on the train. He was only too happy to agree to this. The police had apprehended at least nine terrorists at the bridge and on the surface now seemed to have completed a successful mission to stop their deadly acts. The chief did not want the responsibility of probing into events on the Express. Any damage to the train or any passengers would only make it appear as if the Malaysian police efforts had been less than efficient. He was keen for the Express to move on to Singapore, if it could.

He was less impressed when he was informed of the eight dead Filipinos, two Malaysians and four suicide bombers lying dead by the track. But that could be covered up and the media would not be informed. And even if the extra killings were ever made public, he would have the option of claiming his police squad had been responsible for the further fourteen terrorists' deaths.

Huloton spoke politely to him. 'I hope, Monsieur that we can keep the Express side of it away from the media?'

'Of course,' the chief replied with a pleasant grin.

Shortly afterwards, forty Gemas townspeople were helping train staff to clear the tracks of poles and sleepers.

*

While Makanathan was in touch with the Malaysian police, her husband began sweating profusely in their cabin. He checked his own pulse. It was erratic. He informed a guard, who helped him along the carriages to the infirmary, where a doctor attended to him.

'I believe I've had a heart attack,' the former surgeon said as calmly as if he was announcing he had a cold. The Thai doctor moved fast.

'Lie down,' he said, pointing to a single bed. He began hooking his new patient up to an electrocardiogram. 'We'll see if you have diagnosed yourself correctly ...'

A Thai nurse assisted.

'He has gone grey,' she commented urgently to the Thai doctor. 'He is going to pass out.'

Cavalier heard the train whistle blow just on 7 a.m. Much to his relief the long snake of the Express, with its injured tail, began to limp on its way, slowly building speed for the last few hours ride into Singapore. He looked out the window at the palm plantations that dominated the early morning and imagined that the two green bags carrying Blenkiron's now deceased identity were now some distance down the river.

*

In the frantic defence of the Express, the search for Cortez's assassin had been forgotten by everyone except Cowboy, who nagged his mother with his own sign language gestures, grunts, banging of his fist and stomping of his foot.

Makanathan's priorities changed. She was upset to learn of her husband's illness and was informed he had suffered a mild heart attack. The train doctor had treated him and his condition had been stabilised. It did not stop her carrying out her duties. Stoically, and assuming her role as coroner, which in effect she was in this event, she had to assess the scene of not one killing on the Express, but six. The five Mexicans killed were laid out next to Cortez in the refrigerator, all with name tags attached to their right big toes.

'I understand why she is known as Doctor Death in Thailand,' Huloton remarked in French to Cavalier when he knocked to collect his passport for the final ride over the Johor Causeway between Malaysia and Singapore. 'She has positively revelled in the whole experience, despite her husband's illness. I heard her humming a tune, not too loudly of course, when she examined the bodies. It was French. I believe it was "La vie en rose".'

'A woman of unremarkable taste in clothes and hairstyle,' Cavalier responded in French, 'brave and with remarkable taste in ancient face powder and wonderful forensic skills.'

'Nevertheless, she did not find the murderer of that horror of a person, Cortez. Were you aware, Monsieur that you were under suspicion for it?'

'No.'

''Owever, as you did not leave your cabin during the fatal period, you are in the clear.'

'As I should be, Monsieur,' Cavalier said with a suitably Gallic shrug of indignation.

'Of course, Sir, I told the good doctor of my certainty of your innocence. Would you believe, your next-door neighbour in the wheelchair was suspected also? Absurd, no?'

'Suspected by whom?'

'That Australian imbecile.'

'Cowboy? He is no imbecile, I can assure you, Monsieur Huloton.'

'Granted, Monsieur. I "mis-spoke".'

'What?'

'It is a word the Americans use when they make an error. I've been watching the presidential election on TV.'

'Cowboy's views should be taken seriously. He has perfect recall, although, it should be said, perhaps not in perfect sequence, or of any consequence. His mind could well be quite brilliant and useful, like satellite junk in space: valuable if it could be captured, yet useless when floating to nowhere.'

'Exactly.'

Cavalier handed over his passport.

'By the way, have you *seen* our American friend?' Huloton asked. 'I have just knocked on his door and there was no answer.'

'No.'

'Have you ever spoken to him?'

'I can honestly say I have not.'

'That is most odd, Monsieur, seeing he has been next door to you.'

'Bit reclusive, isn't he?'

'Yes, a recluse; that is the best description.' Huloton gave a tight laugh and pouted. 'One wonders why he bothered to take the trip in the first place. If you do see him, remind him we need his passport to enter Singapore. It is urgent.'

'I promise to look out for him,' Cavalier said.

'Many of the passengers are failing to answer the knock at their doors. We've had to slip notes to assure them that all is back to normal. What with the disturbance, and before that the murder, they are naturally worried.'

'They know about the murder?'

'*Mais, bien sur*! Rumours of anything out of the ordinary spreads like wildfire on a train.'

'You've had murders before?'

'Mon Dieu, no! But we have had deaths.'

*

Despite his sudden and unexpected proximity to the murderers employed by the cartel operations in Asia, Marco Rodriguez could not bring himself to associate with them beyond the absolute necessity to do so. He'd left that to Cortez and wished to distance himself from the cartel's more nefarious activities in South East Asia. But now Cortez was dead, along with five other Mexican cut-throats, and Rodriguez was responsible for the remainder of the gang.

As the train nosed towards it destination, he and his wife Maria finished packing. 'I don't want to associate with my compatriots,' he told his wife as she painted her nails. 'They are a link to my uncle's past. I want nothing to do with them.'

'But darling, they saved the bullion. You have to help them.'

'That's all I care about. I must claim it on behalf of my company. Don't you see? My direct association with them will get questions from everyone about how it was acquired. The Singapore banks will not accept it if they think it's hot or somehow ill-gotten.'

'Don't be silly,' Maria said, standing to adjust her bra as if it and her breasts had to be aligned and displayed in a centimetre-perfect manner. 'Gold is gold. Your company has control of it. You have receipts from all those trading shops you bought it from, for a start.'

'Someone is going to challenge our ownership,' he said with a frown, 'perhaps the Thai government. Its junta likes such booty. Or even the Singaporeans or Malaysians.'

'I'd be more concerned about the Americans.'

'I can only hope that the lawyers I've already lined up will be able to allow it to be taken to the banks.'

*

Azelaporn ordered Jacinta to join him and his Chinese courtesans in his suite for breakfast.

'I don't think I can pay you the rest of your money,' he said, hoping that his two women would stop Jacinta from reacting.

'Tell me why,' she said, stirring her coffee and staring. 'We are ensuring safe passage of the bullion, aren't we?'

'You don't understand,' he said, opening his hands to her plaintively. 'I did the deal with Cortez. There was only a hand-shake agreement; nothing was written down.'

'Not even an email?'

'Any communication was deleted long ago.'

Jacinta gave him a withering look.

'Oh, but you've been paid, haven't you?'

'No.'

'You are a liar!'

'I was to be paid once the bullion was delivered to Singapore.'

'Doesn't Rodriguez realise you have not been protecting him and the gold for nothing?'

Azelaporn feigned helplessness.

'Ask him about it,' she said, glancing at the Chinese, 'or I will.'

*

After breakfast was served in the last hour of the trip, the steward could not raise Blenkiron. He sent another staff member to find Huloton, who was in the infirmary with Makanathan. Seeing that her husband was asleep and being monitored, she accompanied Huloton to Blenkiron's presidential suite. Huloton used his master key to open the door. He walked in, followed by the steward and Makanathan. A distinct odour of cleaning fluid pervaded the suite. The first thing they saw was the empty wheelchair with a pair of crutches resting on it. It faced a window, which had been raised.

'Mon Dieu!' Huloton said. 'He has committed suicide!'

'Not necessarily,' Makanathan said, taking out a camera and examining the room, the bathroom and the cupboards. 'He has left a suitcase. It is empty.'

'Do we have his passport?' Huloton said to the steward.

'No, Sir, he never surrendered it for the final border.'

'You have photocopies?' Makanathan asked.

'We do.'

'Hmm,' Makanathan mumbled, 'I will do a DNA sweep of the room, although it seems someone has done a thorough job in cleaning up, and perhaps destroying evidence.'

'No one has been in the room, except the American, since the journey began,' Huloton informed her.

Makanathan began examining the door-sized partition to the adjoining cabin.

'It is sealed and can't be opened,' Huloton said dismissively as he watched her. 'All the carriages' main suites have them. They were never used, at least since my company took control of the train.'

Makanathan pulled a face and nodded.

'What are your thoughts, Doctor?' Huloton asked.

'I can see two possibilities. One was of course, that he jumped, or in his case fell, from the train. How long has it been since he was seen?'

'About 2.15 a.m. this morning, just before the murder …'

'Or two, someone has made it *seem* that he jumped.' She ruffled her spiky hair and muttered, almost to herself, 'There is a chance that Cowboy was right, after all.'

'What do you mean?'

'The American is the only passenger to have left the train after the murder of Cortez. He must be top of the list of suspects.'

40

CHANGE OF TUNE

Makanathan had been distracted from her tireless work through the night by her husband's heart attack. She was preoccupied with supervising by phone his emergency transportation to hospital as soon as the Express reached Singapore. She then wasted no time in reporting the events of the night by email to the local police, who would rely entirely on her confidential findings.

'This night provided enough work for a dozen coroners and investigators,' she complained to Huloton at the door to the infirmary, 'but I did not even have time to take sufficient notes. It has been the most dreadful and intense time in my entire career!'

'With respect, Madame,' he said, 'you should look after your husband first. The dead are dead. There is no hope for them.'

'You are right, and I am. I have run out of time.' The train stuttered as it began to slow down ten kilometres from Singapore station. 'I tell you confidentially, I have a sense of failure for the first time in my career. I have been thwarted before, yes, by governments. But I have always solved the crime.' She began to light a cigarette. Huloton stopped her.

'Only in the observation car,' he said. 'Sorry, Madame.'

Makanathan began to weep. Huloton put his arm around her shoulder.

'There, there,' he said, 'it is not a failure. You will have time later ...'

'No, no. I cannot reconstruct events. Ninety per cent of the passengers will have disappeared in a day or two.'

'May I say, Madame,' Huloton said, 'you could look at the whole affair from a different perspective.' He paused to glance both ways along the corridor. 'Someone has done the world a great service.'

'What?'

Huloton tilted his head and pouted. 'I am told the deceased Jose Cortez has killed many people,' he said, dropping his voice. 'He was an extraordinary assassin working for a drug cartel.'

'Who told you that?'

'It was in total confidence, Madame.'

'You must tell me more.'

'With respect, I cannot. But there is public knowledge about him. The Americans have been wanting to eliminate him for some time.'

'The Americans? Does that mean our lost wheelchair passenger could have had a motive?'

Huloton raised his eyebrows and nodded slightly.

'Food for thought,' he said, 'and worth investigating perhaps, when you have a clear head and time?'

*

Melody Smith, forewarned by Cavalier of the bullion, had already put in an official US Government claim for the gold, which she branded 'contraband' from the proceeds of drugs, prostitution and people trafficking. Smith also wanted the Mexican bodyguards arrested and extradited to the US.

Rodriguez planned to put in a demand for the gold, claiming that the proceeds were the legitimate result of business by his newly acquired company, Golden Eagle Constructions. He also would say he did not have control of when or how the bullion was generated. In the end, the Singapore courts, and even an international court after that, were expected to decide the gold's ownership and the fate of the Mexicans, who in the meantime were expected to be sent to a local detention centre.

Rodriguez had a lingering dilemma over the remainder of his inherited squad of killers. He decided, with some reluctance, to fund the legal effort to stop the remaining Mexicans being extradited to the US.

Huloton had successfully pleaded with all parties that the happenings on the *Bangkok Express* be kept secret from the press and public. Every passenger signed a legal agreement not to mention the events in exchange for a complete trip refund and a further payout of a hundred thousand US dollars per person. The press, however, were bound to hear rumours.

'How long do you think the bribe to passengers will last?' Cavalier asked Huloton as he eased from his cabin, his backpack over his shoulder.

'You will not think of blackmail, I trust, Monsieur, as one Frenchman to another?'

'Never!'

'My hope, my prayer, for my company's sake is that our story will last until the whole affair appears like a rumour,' he replied. 'We will even put out photographs of the burnt-out observation car for the media, along with a plausible explanation of the fire to cover for the more dramatic events.'

'And the deceased Mexicans?'

'What Mexicans, Monsieur? The press will not learn of our kitchen morgue. At least, I pray to God not.'

'But Dr Makanathan will not hide her investigation, will she?'

'She will submit any report to a senior government official, which we and the Thai junta will not want made public. You see, it would all be very bad for tourism.'

'I see.'

'We are taking the high ground, like a good battle commander.'

'Hmm,' Cavalier said, 'I do hope so. Of course many of the passengers would have heard the gunfire.'

'Muffled, Monsieur, muffled.'

'The bomb explosions?'

'Some passengers thought that it was thunder. At least that is what they hoped it was. They were locked in their cabins, in darkness. Only that Australian who was with Jacinta Cin Lai at the locomotive front witnessed anything.'

Cavalier was pleased that Huloton did not seem to know that he (Cavalier) had been in the locomotive.

'I have offered him a hundred thousand dollars on top of the hundred thousand to keep quiet. He refused the extra gratuity, even at first denying that he had been firing from the locomotive. He told me he did not wish to be exposed for his activity at the front.'

The injured *Bangkok Express* nosed into Singapore's art deco station at noon on the morning of 27 April. At the end of the train, a sixty-strong contingent of Singapore police, all in riot gear, surrounded the Mexicans and Azelaporn as they emerged from carriages 30 and 31. An intense discussion ensued between, on the one side, Huloton, Azelaporn and suited lawyers on behalf of the Mexicans; and on the other side, the local police chief, Melody Smith and twenty DEA agents, all in telltale suits and dark glasses. Makanathan was not among them. She was busy making sure her husband would be taken to hospital.

Eight hundred metres away, two ambulances were waiting near the exit barrier where at least a hundred passengers were lined up, eager to enter Singapore. Very few were speaking. Some were dishevelled; others were fatigued. Most had not slept much. The shock of the attacks on the train during the night had left them dispirited and confused, although none expressed anger. They were thankful they had survived, with the promise of good recompense. Huloton had his staff and security people spread the rumour that 'criminals had been active in a village near where the train had stopped in a siding to let other trains through'. The further claim was that this 'gang of armed thugs had tried to board the train to escape police, but had been forced away'.

*

Janet Hinkley was in the line, comforting Cowboy, who was distressed. He had learnt that the American in the wheelchair had disappeared and was possibly dead. Cowboy flapped his arms and kicked the ground.

'It's okay, Cowboy,' Hinkley said, attempting to comfort him, 'he may be in heaven. Or perhaps he escaped. You know darling, that nice Dr Makanathan thinks you may have been right. The American could have committed the murder. She thinks there is a possibility he may have been pretending to be disabled.'

Cowboy was not appeased. He opened his mouth wide, made a strange clicking noise with his tongue and rolled his eyes. Then he shook his head.

'You don't think the American did it?' Hinkley asked.

Cowboy shook his head in such a vigorous fashion that Hinkley was confused. Was he agreeing or disagreeing with her question?

At that moment Cavalier walked by alongside Pon as she was stretchered to an ambulance. Cowboy jumped and banged his foot on the ground in further agitation.

'Monsieur,' Hinkley said to Cavalier, 'thank you for whatever you did on the train.'

He stopped. 'It is Jacinta you should thank.'

Cowboy made some strange noises, which registered further disquiet.

'He is concerned about the American,' Hinkley said.

'We all are,' Cavalier said, wishing to catch up with Pon. He looked at Cowboy. 'Don't worry, he probably escaped the train during the ... er ... incidents. I am sure he will be okay.'

Cowboy smiled briefly and looked away.

'Thank you,' Hinkley said, 'he will feel better now.'

Cavalier nodded and hurried off to join Pon, who was heavily sedated.

'Do you know her?' Hinkley called, pointing to Pon on the stretcher. Cavalier pretended not to hear and merely waved, just as Melody Smith hurried forward, phone to her ear. She directed DEA agents to escort Cavalier, Pon and Jacinta to an ambulance.

Meanwhile, Makanathan was by her husband's side at one of the ambulances about thirty metres from the first. He was on another mobile stretcher that was about to be slid into the vehicle. She was suddenly alert to him clutching his chest and complaining of further pain. She helped paramedics ease him into the vehicle without looking up to see the first ambulance speeding away, sirens blaring. Her husband was short of breath. He was having a second attack. The paramedics gave him oxygen.

*

Cavalier, a semi-conscious Pon and Jacinta drove a few kilometres to Tengah airfield in Singapore's south-west with a convoy of DEA vehicles, led by Smith. She had arranged a chartered 16-seater plane to fly to Bangkok. Pon, on her stretcher, lay in the aisle. Cavalier was in the cockpit with the pilot.

Smith sat in the cabin next to Jacinta and attempted to quiz her.

'What's his relationship with the woman?' she asked, indicating Pon, who had fallen asleep.

'She's his daughter.'

'Oh, that explains a few things,' Smith said, eyebrows raised. 'And you? How do you know Vic?'

Jacinta considered Smith for a few seconds before answering evasively, 'I wish to help his daughter receive proper medical attention.'

'You are acquaintances?'

Jacinta didn't respond.

'Can you tell me what happened on the train?'

'I think you should ask him.'

'Did he have an accomplice?' Smith asked, in almost a whisper.

'What?'

'In the elimination of Cortez.'

'I have no idea. And I have no idea who dealt with the Mexican.'

Once in Bangkok, Jacinta organised that Pon be taken to the drug rehabilitation unit at Bumrungrad International Hospital—reputedly the best in South East Asia for this work. Pon was expected to remain there for at least a week before being flown to Chiang Rai in Thailand's north. There she would be under the care of her mother, subject to Pin's agreement, at the drug rehabilitation facility in that city.

Cavalier rang Pin to tell her the news that her long-lost daughter was alive.

At first Pin did not believe him. She gripped the phone and cried. After several minutes, and Cavalier's continual reassurance, she managed to speak. 'Serena was right, but you never believed her.'

'Who?'

'My third daughter.'

The name came rushing back down a darker tunnel of his memory. *That bloody doll!*

'Oh, yes, Serena,' he said, without cynicism. 'I'd forgotten about her. Forgive me.'

'I remember we both agreed that Pon had died. Serena never believed that.'

Cavalier vaguely recalled Pin speaking of Serena's 'beliefs'. It seemed like more irrational doll 'commentary' that he had put out of his mind.

'She sits with me right now,' Pin said. 'She is smiling. She always said Pon was alive. Serena is my good luck charm!'

'Have you spoken to your—our—other *real* daughter, Far?'

'Oh, her! She never calls. Occasionally says something on Facebook.'

'I keep in touch. Why not ask her to come home and nurse her sister?' Cavalier said.

Pin began to cry again.

'I am … so happy …' she managed to say, 'please tell me this is true … I am not dreaming. My beautiful Pon is alive!'

*

He booked in at Bangkok's Phachara Suites, a hotel on Soi 6 off Sukhumvit, using his Laurent Blanc French passport. As far as he was concerned, the document in the name of Claude Garriaud had to be retired, forever. On the night of 29 April and not having to assume a false identity, he was met in his room by Smith. He handed over the KK pack. They sauntered down to Hemingway's restaurant, in a garden setting on Soi 14. The evening was warm and humid after a very hot forty-six degrees during the day.

'I have never experienced heat like this,' Smith said to Cavalier, who was always more laconic than normal in her presence. 'By midafternoon, it was so bad that Bangkok's streets seemed almost empty.'

'I don't know,' Cavalier said, 'I saw several Englishman taking their mad dogs for a walk.'

'Really? You're kidding, aren't you?'

Cavalier smiled faintly.

'I can't function when it's like this,' Smith went on. 'It makes me feel, you know ...'

'Inelegant?'

'What?'

'The English novelist Jane Austen once wrote to a friend saying the heat kept her in a constant state of inelegance.'

'That's cute! It makes me feel lethargic.'

'Oscar Wilde once said, "Conversation about the weather is the last refuge of the unimaginative". In your case, I am sure it is to open chat about climate change, no?'

Smith smiled, uncertain of what he meant or if he was being cynical, a trait that was beyond her realm of serious endeavour. They were distracted by two women on a motorcycle roaring along Sukhumvit. The young driver was on the phone. Her mini-skirted female passenger was riding side-saddle and putting on make-up.

'Jeez!' Smith observed. 'That is an accident waiting to happen!'

'Nothing out of the ordinary here,' Cavalier said.

'We are a hundred per cent satisfied the corpse was Cortez,' she told him over dinner. 'We did our own verification once we viewed the body. But thank you for the extra confirmation you provided. You have no idea how many agency people are celebrating over his demise. More so even than Bin Laden. It's personal for quite a few of his victims' friends and family. We are most grateful.' She smiled properly at him for the first time since they had initially met in Chiang Mai. 'So much so that you will find a nice surprise in your bank account tomorrow morning.'

'Much appreciated, thank you.'

'No, thank *you*! Tell me, Dr Makanathan claims that the most likely killer was an American named …' she paused to find her electronic phone notes, 'Edward Blenkiron.

'I don't know anyone by that name. I certainly did not meet him. As you know, I do not work with accomplices.'

'We have already run a check. There is someone of that name, age and description from his passport photo, who is recorded as living somewhere in Asia. Apart from that, nothing.'

'What a coincidence.'

'He was wheelchair-bound,' Smith said with an enigmatic smile.

'Poor fellow.'

'Makanathan believes it's possible that this Blenkiron guy faked his disability, murdered Cortez and jumped the train.'

'Perhaps we should applaud him.'

'She also mentioned some autistic passenger with a sort of sixth sense, who also reckoned Blenkiron may have done it.'

'That's the most credible comment yet. I wouldn't call it a sixth sense. More like a capacity that is real and needs to be explored.'

'The good DNA doctor did not mention you as a passenger.'

'I hope you didn't say anything about me?'

'No, of course not. I gave her nothing. She was confused and disheartened. I don't think she has failed to nail a killer yet; or at least *know* who the assailant was and how she did it.'

'She?'

'Makanathan referred to the murderer that way. I'd be careful with her. She's not only brilliant, she's determined; more dangerous than a hungry raptor.' Smith paused and let Cavalier pour her a beer. 'Her husband had a relapse. She thinks he'll recover. I know she cares very much for him, yet his illness frustrated her investigation. I had the impression from our brief conversation that she was more concerned about identifying Cortez's killer.'

'That's her job.'

'Are you going to give me even a clue how you did it?'

'Does it matter?'

'No, I guess not. I've been mulling over it myself. Just suppose you were masquerading as this Blenkiron guy. We know you left your Chiang Mai condo with his wheelchair. You carry out your mission, and make it look as if he has jumped the train, and then pose as someone else.'

Cavalier did not respond.

'What I can't figure is the logistics on the train,' Smith said, frowning. 'I can only suggest you somehow moved on the outside or top of the train—'

'I don't want to discuss it further,' Cavalier butted in. 'I can tell you one thing: I'm not Spiderman.'

Smith gave him a knowing look, and then beamed. 'I want to let you know that the DEA wants to give you a citation.'

'For what?'

Smith did not answer at first. Her attitude had changed. She seemed almost schoolgirlish in her admiration for Cavalier. 'We want to arrange something for your intrepid journalism,' she said.

'I am most honoured and grateful, but no. It would draw attention to me and I wish to remain in the background.'

'I know you have refused our brother agency's overtures,' she said, scrutinising him, 'but would you be open to other assignments?'

'I can always say "no".'

*

Gregory phoned Cavalier and congratulated him on his successful mission.

'Lovely Melody has changed her tune about you,' he said. 'She was gushing about your "achievement". Did you … er … with her?'

'I promised not to tell,' Cavalier said, 'but the answer is no, I didn't.'

'Perhaps you should have. Her kudos within the DEA has been given an enormous lift by Cortez's liquidation. There is talk in Washington of her becoming the first female director of the DEA, or even the CIA.'

'She's efficient and smart. She'd be very good.'

'I concur. I want to hear detail about your sightseeing trip on the Express.'

'When we meet for those beers we owe each other.'

'You know, Vic, after your train escapade you remind me of John Le Carre's description of his wonderful fictional character, George Smiley: "He travels without labels in the guard's van of life's social express".' 'What now for you?'

'I have some personal matters to clear up,' Cavalier replied without elaboration.

'By the way, the Malaysian police have those two Indonesians. We have asked for extradition. Not sure they'll agree.'

'I can guess why.'

'And you'd be correct. The Malaysians want to make examples of them. They and the other terrorists are likely to be executed.'

41

REUNION

Cavalier, again without disguise, stood at the entrance to Pon's hospital room, which was dominated by a bright, cheerful yellow on walls and ceiling, and a strong whiff of antiseptic. He stared at her as she read a magazine, unaware that he was standing there. Her fair hair was unkempt, and her eyes had dark rims. She looked a decade older than she was. Pon's exceptional beauty had left her, perhaps forever. The hospital's report was not hopeful. Rehabilitation, it advised, could take years and there was no guarantee of a good outcome. It depended much on Pon's will to recover.

Cavalier gripped a big bunch of flowers that he wanted so much to hand her. He had not been able to do this for nearly a decade. He knocked. She looked up. It took her a few moments to register her father. But when she did, she tried to leave her bed. He threw the flowers on the floor and rushed forward to prevent her from collapsing. A nurse bustled in to help.

Pon began with a torrent of words in Thai, English and a Mexican dialect as Cavalier held her.

'He said he would kill you if I didn't do what he wanted!' she blubbered. 'He held that over me for so long. He drugged me ... he raped me! He beat me up! He ... said ... you were a murderer, a professional killer like him ... say it isn't true, Daddy! Please tell me that!'

Cavalier shook his head and held her tight. She cried for so long that he thought he should leave. The nurse motioned that he should go, but Pon clung onto him.

'No, I want you here! I never want you to leave me again! Please! I'm afraid he'll come back ... oh, please!'

Pon gripped his blue shirt so tight that she ripped off a button.

'I'll stay,' Cavalier said to her and the nurse.'

Pon recovered some composure.

'I can't get rid that image of him, dead on the floor, staring up at me ...' She fought tears again, before adding, 'You know, the train manager thought I'd done it.' She managed a laugh. 'Me, a killer!' Pon's face clouded. 'Of course, I would have killed him, if I could.' She looked hard at her father. 'Dr Makanathan said she believed an American on board did it. Do you know anything about that?'

'Not really.'

'I vaguely recall a wheelchair. If the American did do it, I want to meet him and kiss him and thank him!'

'I'm sure he would appreciate that, especially from someone as beautiful as you. The most important thing now is your health. I've arranged for you to be with your mother ...'

'Does she still have that awful doll, Serena?'

Cavalier could not help laughing.

'I believe she does.'

'Oh, no! It freaked me out; it's so old and looks so scary!'

They laughed together. Cavalier felt, but did not say, that this moment could have been the first spark of a recovery.

*

Cavalier only left the hotel to visit the hospital to see Pon each day before her flight to Chiang Rai. She begged him to go with her and he agreed to do so. The day before they left, he ignored several calls from the tenacious Makanathan. He had no desire any more to play the Frenchman in front of her, knowing that she would have had time to reflect on events on the train. He did however, send a text:

> How is your husband? I pray he has recovered.

She replied:

> He is on the mend. We have both given up smoking, as all good doctors should!

In frustration Makanathan left a phone message:

'I just wish to talk about that wheelchair-bound American. I wanted your thoughts about him before I close this case.'

Cavalier sent another text:

> I have no thoughts on him. I never made his acquaintance. Sorry I can't be of more assistance. I wish you and your husband well.

*

The call worried Cavalier. Makanathan had authority and police connections. She was dogmatic and, from the attempt to see him, he guessed she may have suspected him. Perhaps she had learned about the partition between the two cabins on the train. Or had she been told of his fighting off the suicide bombers with Jacinta and Dempster? That would expose him as someone handy with a gun, which would have added to Makanathan's suspicions. Cavalier decided to put his meagre belongings in a backpack and check out for the last night. He still had his Glock 17, and the disassembled rifle in its five canisters.

Jacinta wanted to meet Cavalier for morning coffee. He was reluctant to step out of the hotel before dusk, and would only agree to meet Jacinta if she knew of a discreet place.

'I have a close friend, she is a French archaeologist, who lives in a chateau across the river,' she said. 'Why don't we have a coffee near your hotel and then we can breakfast at the chateau? It's isolated.'

They met at his favourite cafe, Viva in Soi 8. Jacinta wore a black cap jammed on her head, dark glasses, a sloppy jumper, grey slacks and sneakers. Her last public Muay Thai bout had been approaching a year earlier, but she was still a big star in Thailand. The last thing she wanted was autograph hunters tapping her arm and phone cameras flashing.

It was hot for 9 a.m. Four roof fans were humming, augmented by jets of cool air on the open roof area. Two television sets on a wall were showing the Fashion Channel and sport without sound. There was a sprinkling of customers. The women in the parlour across the alley were stirring and listlessly preparing for another day of crying 'massage' and 'where you go, handsome man?'. Farang and locals were in no hurry as they strolled by in the sluggish heat.

Cavalier, carrying his backpack, was on edge when he recognised a middle-aged American woman, who read the papers and then scrutinised a computer tablet so intently that she seemed unaware of others. He recalled speaking to her once, a year ago. The American woman glanced for a second at Jacinta, then Cavalier, before her breakfast was served.

When their coffee arrived, he took off his glasses and glared at an overweight European at the next table whose overpowering cheap cigar smoke was blowing in their direction. He kept looking over at Cavalier as if he knew him. He whispered something to a Thai companion, who glanced at Jacinta and replied. Lip reading, Cavalier saw the Thai say, 'Isn't that Jacinta Cin Lai?'

'My Buddha! I think you are right!' his companion said. The European stubbed his cigar and nodded an apology to Jacinta.

It was enough for Cavalier. He paid the bill and they took a taxi to a private jetty on the Chao Phraya River next to the smart Shangri-La Hotel, where a small wooden boat and its pilot were waiting.

They chugged along on the water. Two tour boats bumped by, creating waves as they headed past two other tour vessels that were anchored mid-river.

'Have you looked at your bank account?' he asked Jacinta.

'Not today, why?'

Jacinta took out her phone, lifted her glasses, and looked up her account. Her eyes widened and she smiled, squeezing Cavalier's arm at the same time.

'Five million baht!' she said under her breath, pulling a face. 'That's too much!'

'I couldn't have achieved a successful assignment had you not been there.'

Jacinta kissed him on the cheek. The boat pilot cheered and caused both of them to laugh. He had recognised Jacinta.

'Now do you have to fight again?' Cavalier asked.

'Not for some time,' she laughed. 'You know that Azelaporn is prevaricating over his promised payment to me?'

'Tell me something that's surprising.'

'You don't want another assignment, do you?' Jacinta said, lowering her voice to a mock conspiratorial tone. 'I could pay you about five million baht to liquidate him.'

They both laughed.

'Where was he during the attack on the train?' Cavalier asked.

'Locked in his cabin protecting his Chinese women.'

'Gutless wonder!'

'All bullies are. You should be pleased. If he'd seen us side by side fending off the attack on the locomotive, he would have been suspicious.'

'Seriously,' Cavalier said, 'you should not fight again, unless you really crave it. Don't do it for the money, please.'

'Not for some time, thank you. Thank you very much!'

'I am sure the DEA and CIA would love to employ you.'

Jacinta did not react.

'I am certain that Tommy Gregory would find work for you,' Cavalier said, thinking aloud. 'I'll have a word to them all if you wish.'

'I need to be in Thailand. I have family who depend on me.'

'Perhaps the work could have you based here. And what about the Thai Government? It talks up a storm about stopping drug and people trafficking. There is no one better placed to tackle that.'

'I don't know if the junta would agree. I am tainted by association with Azelaporn and his corruption.'

'The junta will not be in power forever. A new government might see you differently.'

'Taint sticks,' she said, wrinkling her nose.

'Well I, for one, would love to work with you again.'

'I certainly hope so.'

She pulled a small bag from her pocket. 'Thought you might like these,' she said, showing him the contents. It was the pair of special glasses he had given her on the train.

'Oh, yeah,' he replied, 'there's always something I forget on these missions.'

She handed them to him.

'No,' he said, 'you keep them. I'll say they were destroyed. They may come in handy in your old age.'

Jacinta smiled and thanked him. Then she dropped her voice to an almost inaudible whisper.

'I was wondering about one thing. When those suicide bombers rushed the train, you hesitated and I shot one of them. Afterwards you seemed to be looking for something.'

Cavalier swallowed and considered her for so long that she apologised for querying his actions.

The boat reached the opposite bank and meandered down the Thonburi district's canal Mon. Its shanty houses gave way to some grand homes and colonial-style mansions, then a few chateaux.

'I did the wrong thing,' he said finally. 'I could have endangered everybody.'

'Why?'

'I thought one of the bombers may have been a child. Instead of shooting, I faltered. It could have been a case of "he who hesitates is lost".'

'If you'll permit me another English saying, "to err is human".'

'You could say "humane" too. It is also fatal in our business. If that child …'

'It *was* a child?' Jacinta interjected.

'Yes, a girl, judging from the two gold rings on her fingers. If she had reached the train, you and I and that brave fellow Dempster, and perhaps everyone in the first few carriages, including Pon, would have been killed.'

It was Jacinta's turn to stare.

'What are you thinking?' she asked.

'I have never hesitated before. Never had a dilemma. When I was in my twenties I nearly lost my nerve on an assignment. This was different. I've had nightmares over this … this "lapse".'

Jacinta waited.

'I'm becoming soft and too old for this caper,' he said with a rueful smile.

'Well you can be gentle and at peace in this place and with my friends,' she said, pointing to Chateau William. 'It is like another world and nothing like Bangkok.'

42

CHATEAU OF SURPRISE

Cavalier stood to take a phone picture of the stunning chateaux looming at a bend in the canal about a hundred and thirty metres away as they chugged slowly towards them. Cavalier zoomed as close as he could with the limited range. He stopped, lowered his phone, stepped to the front of the boat and stood on a seat for greater elevation. He turned to Jacinta.

'Could I have those glasses I gave you, please?' he asked.

Jacinta frowned and handed them to him.

Cavalier put them on. He picked up movement in the wooded, sloping garden that ran from Chateau William's lawn about forty metres to a small, wooden jetty.

'Anything the matter?' Jacinta asked.

'Does your French archaeologist friend normally play hide and seek behind trees when guests are arriving?'

'What?'

He handed her the glasses. He watched her reaction. She turned to him.

'I swear, I don't know ...'

Cavalier slipped the Glock 17 from a side pocket in his backpack.

'How many of them …' Cavalier asked nervously, 'police? Did Makanathan put you up to this?'

'You said you trusted me!' Jacinta said, a slash of fear mingled with anger in her expression. 'I tell you, I had nothing to do with this.'

'Sit over there,' Cavalier ordered, motioning to the seat next to the pilot, who had slowed the boat to a near standstill from the shock of seeing the weapon. Cavalier searched the garden again, and then lifted his sights to see the first level of the chateau. He adjusted the vision. He could make out Makanathan at a balcony with another woman.

'Makanathan is there,' he said. He turned to the pilot, pointed to wooden staircase leading to a house on stilts, and in Thai said tersely, 'Pull in there.'

'She must have monitored my call to you this morning,' Jacinta said. 'She could have tapped my phone. My secure cell is not working. I used an old one to speak to you. She must have monitored it.'

'It doesn't matter,' Cavalier said. 'You two get off here.'

'Victor, I swear on my father's grave,' she said in Thai, 'I had nothing to do with any police trap!'

Cavalier motioned for her and the pilot to jump off the boat. When they were on the staircase, he manoeuvred the boat back along the canal. He used the glasses to scour the chateau again. Figures were darting from the garden.

In a few minutes he was out of the canal and on the river, unsure where he should attempt to make land. The boat was very slow. He eased into the river's centre, close to four anchored pleasure boats, about a hundred metres apart, where he could see people congregated on the decks. Bunting, balloons and ribbons festooned the deck areas of the first boat, indicating some sort of celebration was in progress. A large sign hung over the side proclaimed: 'We Stand UNITED. Ten Year at the Top of the Valley.'

As he drew closer, he could hear a band playing. He put away his gun, drove to the forty-five-metre-long boat. He could hear the band playing a dirgy version of *The Godfather* movie theme. He called in Thai to one of the crew members in a smart navy and white suit and bow tie, who was near the railing. The crew member looked down.

'Sorry, I'm late,' Cavalier called, 'could you throw me a rope ladder?'

The man looked shocked and waved him away. One of the tourists was leaning on the railing, a glass in one hand and a cigarette in the other. He bent forward and yelled to Cavalier in an American accent: 'Hey, Buddy! You with the group?'

'Which group are you?'

'United Tech.'

Cavalier nodded, pulled his wallet from his pocket and waved a piece of paper from it.

The man looked momentarily perplexed but told another crewman to throw him a rope ladder. Cavalier grabbed the ladder and pushed the little outboard boat off with its motor running. It drifted down the river towards the second tourist boat.

Cavalier climbed aboard. The American handed him a drink and guided him to about a hundred guests on the deck, who were sipping cocktails and eating pre-lunch snacks.

Judging from the noise, the conviviality had been going on for some time. The American introduced himself just as two police helicopters flew over the ship and distracted them. Cavalier was about to introduce himself as Claude Garriaud, but checked himself, and said, 'I am Laurent'.

'Are you with the French franchise?' the American asked after picking his French accent.

Cavalier nodded, apologised for being late and used the traffic as an excuse.

'Jeez, Laurent!' the American said with a laugh, 'you gotta allow for an extra hour in Bangkok!' He looked over-refreshed as he took a glass of red wine from a passing waiter's tray. The ship rocked a little and began to move.

'We're away!' the American said.

'It's a four-hour trip, isn't it?'

'One goddam way, Buddy! It'll be at least eight hours before we dock back at the hotel.' He downed his drink and looked for a waiter to take another glass.

'Where you staying?' the American asked, slurring his words.

'The Shangri-La.'

'We all are! When did you arrive?' The American looked at his backpack and laughed. 'Travelling light?'

'Got in only an hour ago, from Paris. Knew I was late. Hired the boat and here I am.'

'Like your initiative! The French director is here some-where,' the American said, tiptoeing to look around the crowd. 'I'll find him for you.'

'Can I use the bathroom?'

'Of course. It's below.' The American pointed to a staircase leading to a lower deck. 'Throw your pack down in any of the cabins. It's perfectly safe here.' He winked at Cavalier. 'If you get lucky you can take a gal down there. All the Thais on board are hookers!'

'Thank you, Monsieur,' Cavalier said. He excused himself and descended the stairs. He found a cabin, locked the door and removed the backpack. He looked out a porthole and could see police helicopters flying low over the line of the four tourist ships, which were all pulling up anchor and sailing off.

After Cavalier's boat had been moving a few minutes, he noticed a police launch powering along near the riverbank. It stopped near the little outboard Cavalier had been on. He watched until they were out of sight and then lay back on a bunk bed. He was too uptight to sleep. After an hour, in which his nerves subsided, not even the sound of dancing feet and the clunky band playing old rock numbers could stop him from slumbering off.

*

Jacinta's host Pia laid out breakfast and coffee for her and Makanathan in the beautifully groomed Chateau William gardens. Waiters hovered. One police car was parked near a garage. Two cops were outside their car, waiting for instructions from Makanathan.

'Police choppers are searching for him on the river,' she reported, 'and two cars are driving back to the Shangri-La.' She paused to stare at Jacinta. 'Your friend will be apprehended by the evening. It would be advisable for you to disclose what you know about him.'

Jacinta's expression remained enigmatic.

'Had you known Monsieur Garriaud before the trip?' Makanathan asked.

'Monsieur Garriaud, no.'

'Azelaporn said you slept with him.'

'That's not true, although he ordered me to.'

'Why did he do that?'

'Oh, he suspected him.'

'Of what?'

'Better ask him.' Jacinta shrugged.

Makanathan paused again. She ruffled her spiked hair and sighed. 'Did you suspect Monsieur Garriaud of being an assassin?'

'No. Azelaporn is paranoid.'

'I hate the man. He was very rude to me, as was that horrible Cortez fellow. I can't understand why someone with your talents would work for Azelaporn. He always made it difficult when we had to liaise over a crime.'

Jacinta showed no reaction. Makanathan sipped her coffee.

'That Australian fellow Dempster helped you fight off the terrorists, did he not?' she asked.

'He assisted me, that's true.'

'Was he a good shot?'

'I don't know.'

'But you killed the attackers.'

'You should be thankful he was on board,' Jacinta said, with a measure of indignation. 'He helped stop those suicide bombers from destroying the train, and everyone in it.'

'Of course, I am grateful to you—'

'You and your husband were the most senior Thais on the Express,' Jacinta interrupted. 'We all know how ISIS operates. You would have been killed first. The Filipino offshoot always decapitates the most important victims first.'

Makanathan swallowed involuntarily.

'Do you think the American Blenkiron could have murdered Cortez?' she asked, trying to sound unperturbed.

'I don't see how it could be possible.'

Makanathan pulled a face of agreement.

'Why did you contact Monsieur Claude Garriaud after the train trip was over?'

'I like him. I like him very much. I wanted to see him as a friend.'

'If he is innocent, as I believe you are, why did he escape just now?'

'I have no idea.'

'Hmm,' Makanathan said. Her phone rang. She stood up, mouthed 'excuse me' to Jacinta and wandered a few metres away in the garden. Jacinta heard one end of the conversation.

'Where was it? ... Disappeared! ... You're not saying he went into the water? ... I'll be there in half an hour.'

She rang off and signalled to the policemen at the car.

'I may need to chat with you again,' she said shaking hands with Jacinta. She nodded a farewell and walked up to the police car. She was soon driven off at speed and Jacinta could see her in the backseat on the phone again.

43

LAST NIGHT IN BANGKOK

Cavalier woke at dusk and ventured from the cabin cautiously. The guests were scattered about the deck at bars, on sofas and on the dance floor. The American who had helped him aboard was lying asleep on his back on a sofa, an upturned glass resting on his chest. Cavalier took some sandwiches and water back down to the cabin. After consuming them, he considered his options if, in the worst-case scenario, the police boarded the ship or waited for its guest to disembark. They would be looking for a Frenchman, and someone fitting his general description. It chilled him to consider what Jacinta may have told them. Yet he was sticking to the belief, however shaky now, that she had genuinely not known about the ambush.

He thought of shaving his scalp, yet it was too late and he didn't wish to do a botched job himself. But he would use the 'Bert Trumper' Australian passport. He removed his wig and clothes, placed them in a locker and dressed in the only other outfit left, smart casual blue jeans, shirt and navy blue cap. He wondered what to do about the handgun. The rifle in the detection-free canisters would be put in a small case and checked into the plane's storage hold. They would pass through airport detectors, but he had no such container for the Glock 17, although thirty years ago, it had been designated as undetectable because of its plastic construction. Cavalier could not risk it with modern technology. He thought about tossing it in the river, but on reflection believed it was better to hang onto it until the next morning before he left for the flight to Chiang Rai.

A half-hour before docking he moved to the crew's quarters. Speaking in Thai, he offered a waiter a thousand baht to take his pack off the boat.

'Leave it at the Shangri-La's front desk with a porter,' he said. 'I'll pick it up later.' He showed him his Australian passport in the name of Bert Trumper. The waiter did not even glance at it. He nodded and was only too happy to oblige. Cavalier moved amongst scores of guests who looked tired yet happy. He found two Thai women who looked as if they'd enjoyed the trip to the full. They were both tipsy. One carried a bottle of Champagne. The other held her very tall shoes and was barefoot.

'Where is the party after this?' he said in Thai with a smile, and ordered them drinks.

'Wherever you want,' one said, eyeing him off, 'as long as you're paying!'

'Oh, I can, I assure you.'

He drank and flirted with them, keeping one eye on the wharf. His heart sank. He could see two police cars, lights flashing, on the road at the top of the wide staircase that led up from the wharf. Cavalier ordered more drinks.

'Let's go to Sukhumvit,' he said. 'I know a really smart bar on Soi 11.'

He took two five-hundred-baht notes from his wallet and in the honoured tradition tucked them into the women's bras. This brought a joyful reaction from both. The passengers began to file off the boat down a gangway to the wharf. Cavalier put his arms around the two women and they tottered down the gangway and up the steps close to half a dozen others, who were rowdy and laughing. A crew member pushed up an incline next to the steps with a trolley of bags. At the top, they were placed on another trolley.

Cavalier looked up once to see four policemen watching everyone as they reached the top of the stairs. He pulled his hat well down and clutched both girls close. They staggered in a group past the police and down the cobblestoned *soi* leading to the hotel. He heard footsteps behind him.

'Sir,' a voice said. Cavalier turned to see two police. 'Could we see your identity papers?'

'Yeah, mate, sure,' he said and, after fumbling in his pocket, handed his passport over. The cops examined it, a couple of times looking at him and the document's photo. One mumbled to the other in Thai, 'It's Australian, not French.' The cop's phone rang. He seemed to receive a command from someone. Still with the phone to his ear, he handed back the passport and hurried off with the other cop to where the remaining passengers were coming off the boat.

Cavalier wandered on down the street with the women, sighing at this narrow escape. Just as they neared the entrance to the Shangri-La, a third police car roared by. Cavalier spotted Makanathan, who was on the phone. He asked the women to wait as he entered the hotel. He found a porter, who indicated that bags and other items from the ship were in a corner. Cavalier handed him two hundred baht, winked, walked over to a pile and found his pack. The porter asked to see his passport. Noting it was Australian, he smiled and let Cavalier take the pack.

'Is there another exit?' Cavalier said, handing the porter a hundred baht. 'I'd like to give my girlfriends the slip.' The porter glanced at the two waiting women outside. They were on their phones and smoking. He led Cavalier down a hallway to a revolving door. Cavalier bustled outside, found a waiting taxi and took off. He looked back to see Makanathan flanked by four cops, hurrying past the two Thai women Cavalier had picked up and into the Shangri-La. Cavalier slid down in his seat.

'*Rao-rao, krap!*' he said to the driver, who put his foot down and slipped through the heavy traffic.

*

Cavalier got out near the Bumrungrad Hospital at the beginning of Sukhumvit, which was choked with vehicles and fumes. He thought of visiting Pon, but was nervous about making contact, just in case Makanathan had learned of their relationship. She would be taken by hospital staff to the plane in the morning and he had said he would meet her there. He walked to Soi 23. He stood outside the barber shop below the offices of the beautiful physiotherapist Waew Ing, who had worked on his Achilles on his previous visit. He could see the light was on in the barber shop at ground level and the surgery above it. Mustering courage, he stepped into the barber shop. He would be making an internal flight with his daughter to

Chiang Rai in Thailand's north the next day. But he would still have to show proof of identity and it would be better to look like the passport photo of 'Bert Trumper'.

A corpulent woman with a walleye greeted him.

'I want you to shave my head completely,' he said in Thai. She was at first not sure if he were serious.

'But you have such wonderful, thick hair,' she said with a frown.

'It's what I want,' he said.

A half-hour later, he left the barber shop, his scalp shaven, wearing brown contact lenses. He now had to find somewhere to stay for the night, and preferably not a hotel where he would be registered. He hesitated and then on a whim stepped up the creaking stairs in the hope of seeing Waew Ing. He knew it was a risk. Waew had been interrogated about him (as Cavalier) over the assassination of Leonardo Mendez just after Cavalier had fled Bangkok in the previous year. He had not made contact with her in almost a year since their last night together.

He had no idea how she would react or if she'd even recognise him with his nude dome. As he described it in his diary, he had 'fallen heavily in like with her' in their brief encounters. She had hardly been a distraction then because he was on a mission, and then an escape plan. Yet he had been taken by her character and looks, and was sorry that he could not have done much about it at the time, or since. Cavalier had fantasised over her and, when faced with the chance to see her again, could not resist the temptation. Ideally, he could spend the last night in Bangkok at her apartment and go undetected if Makanathan had instigated a dragnet of Bangkok.

An elegant, bespectacled woman of about fifty met him at the door to the physiotherapist's surgery. She ushered him in. A large framed photographic head-and-shoulder portrait of Waew hung on the wall behind a desk. It featured her striking looks of large, wide eyes set well apart, sensual mouth, perfect jawline and long neck. So much like, but even more attractive than, a young Jackie Kennedy, he mused, rekindling a feeling for the Thai.

'Is Waew Ing here?' Cavalier asked.

'No, she is away. Do you want an appointment?'

'Do you know where she is?'

'Paris.'

'With a boyfriend?'

The woman nodded.

'Any idea when she'll return?'

'In a week.'

Cavalier thanked her, hiding his disappointment.

'Should I say who called?' she asked. 'I am her mother.'

'No, thank you,' he said, trying not to show his surprise, and suppressing a flirtatious line such as 'now I know where she gets her beauty, grace, and femininity from'.

'You're not ...?' she asked, a tension in her voice and expression as she recalled her daughter mentioning the farang who had seen her interrogated by the police.

'No, I'm not.'

She frowned and looked at him quizzically. Cavalier held her gaze, bowed slightly and left. He walked dejectedly down into the muggy night that was settling on the crowded, sometimes dangerous, always exciting Bangkok. His phone was ringing. He didn't recognise the number.

'It's me,' Jacinta said. 'I am ringing on a new phone. I'm really sorry ...'

'Don't say any more, please.'

'I just want to say, do not use your Claude Garriaud passport, even on internal flights.'

'I won't. I'm worried about what will happen to you.'

'Makanathan has interrogated me. I gave her nothing. She wanted to know if I'd been involved in Cortez's demise.'

'What did you tell her?

'I denied it. There is no proof of any collaboration with you.'

'Did she accept that?'

'Not sure. Before she could say something, I pointed out that if I hadn't been at the front of the train, she and her husband would probably be dead. That gave her something to think about.'

'How'd you explain that you were on the boat with me?'

'She thought I'd slept with you. Blabbermouth Azelaporn lied to her. I said we were acquaintances and had made contact after the train trip.' Jacinta paused. 'Now do you understand I did not lead you into a second trap?'

'On the boat, I had to think about flight, not accusations or analysis. I have no doubt you did not.'

'Thank you,' she said, her relief palpable.

'Good luck, my beautiful Jacinta,' Cavalier said, 'and thanks for all your support, a second time.'

'Please be extra careful. Makanathan is not a brutal type, but she is persistent.'

'And without ruth.'

'Pardon?'

'Go on.'

324

'She really hates the idea of not solving the Cortez case,' Jacinta said.

'No evidence means no case against anyone, even for the legendary Dr Makanathan.'

'Will we see each other again?'

'Not in Bangkok for some time. But you know where to find me. And I'll be speaking to Gregory and Smith about some position for you.'

'Thank you, Victor,' Jacinta said, 'but only in Thailand. Are you going to stay?'

'It depends on how hot it becomes,' he said. 'I'm getting too old for the heat.'

THE END

www.ingramcontent.com/pod-product-compliance
Lightning Source LLC
Chambersburg PA
CBHW071200100726
47908CB00002B/448